UNRAVISHED

D1052461

CALGARY PUBLIC LIBRARY

DEC   2014

UNRAVISHED

STORIES

Hester Kaplan

PUBLISHING
Brooklyn, New York

Copyright © 2014 by Hester Kaplan.
All rights reserved.

Grateful acknowledgement is made to the National Endowment for the Arts and the Rhode Island Council on the Arts.

Some of the stories in this collection first appeared in the following publications:

"Unravished" in *Copper Nickel*
"The School of Politics" in *Indiana Review*
"The Aerialist" in *Salamander*
"Companion Animal" in *Ploughshares*
"Natural Wonder" in *Ploughshares*
"Lovesick" in *Night Train*
"This is Your Last Swim" in *Mt. Hope*

Library of Congress Cataloging-in-Publication Data

Kaplan, Hester, 1959-
  [Short stories. Selections]
  Unravished / Hester Kaplan.
    pages cm
  ISBN 978-1-935439-90-5 (paperback)
  I. Title.
  PS3561.A5577A6 2014
  813'.54--dc23

                          2014012327

For Michael, Tobias, Alexander, and for love

CONTENTS

UNRAVISHED

They pursued me down the jetty one day, through the white cedars and into the pond the next, those bitches, to talk to me about the women in Tillman's famous paintings, women who gazed out windows, leaned on counters or sat on beds with their knees pulled up. Not beautiful—none of us are beautiful anymore, Alice, they said—but lonely and soulful, don't you think? What they meant was that I must have been lonely and soulful like those women because I was married to August Weiner, the devil.

"Please, leave me alone," I told them.

And now another of those pursuers had me cornered in the drugstore, my back against the toothbrushes. The thunderous July afternoon had driven people from the beaches, and the parking lot thrummed with the efficient disappointment of errands. She touched my arm and said she knew how hard it was to be married to a certain kind of man. Those boastful, proud bullies, she meant, know-it-alls, non-apologizers. Her laugh was light and unromantic. I couldn't remember her name, though I'd known her for years. Aug's prescriptions were rattling in my bag, and he was waiting in the car, diminished by his failing heart and a long morning with Boston's doctors, his rosacea rioting in the humidity. Talk to him, the woman urged. Just talk to him about art and beauty and Tillman's legacy. Get him to change his mind about building that ruinous house of his.

Art and beauty and legacy? What amazing, pompous

bullshit these people spouted. I didn't know how could they stand themselves. "Please, leave me alone," I told her.

In the car, Aug had slid down in his seat, either from fatigue or persecution, though he'd deny both. He was, at sixty-six, a proud, boastful, know-it-all, sometimes a bully. We'd been married for ten years. He was the most entitled man I'd ever loved and been loved by. He'd saved me from a small life of compromise and disappointments.

"Oh, sweetheart, there you are. I've been watching this rain the whole time," he said, full of awe at its power to make people scatter. "When I was a kid, the water used to come pouring in under the windowsills. The walls would swell for days." The neck of his white shirt was damp with sweat and uncharacteristic nostalgia. My blouse was soaked, too, and I started to shiver. Aug didn't talk about his past often, but he'd described his child-hood in Worcester as screechingly poor, beyond dirt and into dust. Mine had been not so different, but with some slugging and slapping, and the front door slamming so often it came off its hinges.

Was I lonely married to Aug? Only sometimes, but you hear enough terrible things said about the one you love, as I'd been hearing that summer, and you're not persuaded, but a kind of puzzlement creeps in. The mind reconsiders even what it first dismissed. It is a wife's anguish to one day allow herself to see her husband the way others see him—and I was terrified of that day. The woman from the drugstore passed in front of our car and hesitated as she considered haranguing us even there in the downpour, but something made her tug at her slicker and go on. Aug was disappointed. A fight might revive him; it was his best mode then, and what kept his heat pumping juicily. He would never accept that it was his defenseless pallor, that yeasty hue of coronary decline, that made her keep going. He would rather be reviled than have people know he was sick and mortal.

A year and a half earlier, Aug, rich for over a decade by then, had overnight scooped up the piece of land that now so inflamed people, thirteen untouched acres that rested between two hills swaying with beach grass, from a man who'd hit a fatally bad patch of business. At one end, the property slid into Block Island Sound, the other end narrowing into locust trees, rugosa, and an unpaved stretch leading out towards New Town Road. If you stood on the beach with the water at your back, as Aug and I had done from time to time admiring what we owned, you could see the famous Tillman house to the right of our property—small, modest, dusty white like a bone, set back for the widest vista. This was the landscape that had inspired Tillman to paint those bereft, gazing women, and sometimes the soulful water, and it was this landscape and view Aug was accused of destroying with the house he planned to build. What he was doing was immoral, his enemies said, like hitting a child. They called themselves the Shoreline Citizens, and they would fight him and contest his plans at every step. That Aug owned textile mills like some wicked master out of a darker time made perfect sense to those who opposed him. He was the rich industrialist, they were on the side of angels.

August was determined to go to the selectmen's meeting about the building permit for the house that evening even though he hadn't been feeling well or energetic since the medical visit in Boston two weeks before. I told him I didn't want him to go, but he was adamant, and eyed me warily, prepared for a challenge. He called me into the bathroom where he'd dumped my make-up into the sink.

"What the hell am I looking for?"

The new medication sometimes swamped his mind with

irritation. His jaw line had become pronounced, the slack of health almost used up. He wanted to paint away the dark swags under his eyes because he couldn't have people think this house trouble was getting to him, keeping him up at night or making him sick. I smeared on some foundation, but he wanted more color, though he was already too cakey, like an old drag queen. I asked him again not to go; I couldn't stand the thought of those people seeing him like this. In the mirror, we were alarmingly mismatched; I was taller, twenty years younger, still vigorous. I looked away first.

"The picture of health," he announced, but who knew which one of us he'd meant.

In the town hall, the windows were open in the second floor hearing room. The night was a thick blue-black, bugs tapping out their code against the screens, and in that airless space, we were all floating above the contested ground, those selectmen and the so-called Shoreline Citizens, my husband and me. Someone had enlisted an expert from New York to talk about Tillman's place in American art, and the man spoke deliberately, as if everyone—but especially Aug—was an idiot. When the lights were turned off, he showed slides of Tillman's work. It was hard not to be moved, but who hadn't seen those paintings of women a million times on calendars and kitchen towels and mouse pads? People anonymously dropped off books of the art on our doorstep, like turds in a brown paper bag. They sent us postcards of Tillman's work. One, unsigned, read, "I was in the National Gallery, saw this and thought of you." Tillman's view, the one that would be disturbed by our house if it was built, was a national treasure, and if left unravished—that was the expert's word that tried to untangle itself in my head—would continue to inspire others. Aug grunted and pulled at his last tuft of gray hair; inspire how, exactly? He didn't deal in abstractions or potentials, just hard work and endurance and final decisions. The house, with its sight of the water from every room, was what he'd wanted since he was a kid tossing on a filthy mattress. It was his due now, and why not?

"Let people find their own fucking inspiration," he said, loud enough for others to hear.

"Let's be civil," one of the selectmen said. The art expert adopted a vacant look.

When the lights went on, Diana, a former friend of ours, spoke about environmental concerns—the broom crowberry, the eastern spade-footed toad, the north harrier hawk, as if those things existed on Aug's piece of land and no where else on earth. He yawned ostentatiously. Finally, the uneasy, middle-aged son of the dead painter's dead friend spoke to the room. He owned the Tillman place—it had been left to him to see to its preservation—but he didn't live there. No one had since Tillman himself. He had an uneasy manner and a sunburned nose he kept touching. A few times his ambivalent eye fell on me. He never said which side of the fight he was on, and it was this aftertaste of uncertainty he left when he sped away from the meeting that re-energized the crowd.

But this was only a hearing, there wouldn't be a decision tonight, or likely for a long while, maybe a year or more, which meant our plans were on hold indefinitely. The room buzzed with victorious whispers, while Aug's cool pose only further hardened people against him. The whole thing had begun to seem like a race of biblical concerns; which would come first, the kingdom or the king's death?

Aug stayed to talk to one of the selectmen, while I went downstairs and outside to wait for him. Just beyond the town hall steps, a woman called my name and waved me over to her group.

"We're wondering how you feel about all this, Alice," she said. The others looked at me expectantly. "You've been notably quiet on the subject. You're his wife, but that doesn't mean you're not allowed to have an opinion of your own." The men laughed moronically.

These people had known August and me from the days when we were still invited to their parties, before all this grief about a house that didn't even exist yet. Aug had watched their sacred sunsets dip behind the horizon and he'd swirled his drink covetously; he didn't hide the fact that this was exactly what he wanted for himself. I suspected that they disliked him even then because they thought he was crude and avaricious. But to me, their faded clothes, old station wagons, frayed sneakers, damp summer houses, long, academic vacations—their hidden affluence in a world of desperation—was the crudest and falsest of all. They already had what they wanted.

"Yes, tell us how you feel about this," another woman urged.

As a second, younger wife, I knew they'd always suspected me of marrying Aug for his money. I was blond, strong shouldered, a mystery they thought they understood, and they'd assumed that I could be their instrument of persuasion. These women, these almost but never friends of mine, these pursuers.

"How do I feel?" I asked, smiling and pressing a hand to my chest where my heart stomped with rage at them. "I'm really looking forward to our new house. It's going to be beautiful, the sight of water from every window."

Their heads tilted like dogs; was I fucking with them? I lifted the hair from my neck and let it fall again as though nothing bothered me except a little summer night's heat. The men kicked at the dirt. I was not like their wives; I knew I was still beautiful. I turned to see Aug making his way down from the second floor, his hand grasping the railing. Maybe these Shoreline Citizens thought they would beat him down eventually, believed that no man could withstand public opinion that shunned him and called him a heartless, selfish prick, but they didn't know Aug and didn't understand that if you're hated and you're facing the end of your life, none of that mattered. Or that it only produced the opposite effect. He would fight forever.

His depth perception was newly shaky from the Aldactone, and his sneakered foot hovered over each riser. His reading glasses, perched on the top of his head, reflected the moonlight. Every step, compromised as it was, seemed to say screw you to the others, I'll build my big house and outlive all of you. I was frozen with worry for him and the way his wide mouth was open as if a breath of health might blow in and cure him. Near the bottom, he gazed out and something like dread crossed his face and clouded his eyes. I like to think it was that he knew what was about to happen, and not about the way the people looked at him with such contempt. His legs folded, his head dropped in resignation, and he rolled over himself and down the last seven wooden stairs. His forehead hit the bottom granite stoop, his glasses went flying into the thick groundcover, and he curled into their tiny leaves, and then into himself.

There was a sickening inhale of the crowd as I rushed to Aug. No one else moved. He blinked like a baby while the two-inch gash on his forehead filled with blood, flooded his eyes and mixed with the pasty make-up. I tried to shield him and hold his twitching hands in mine. When he looked up at me, I knew he could see that I was alone with him, that behind me were not people to help, but just the white, indifferent clapboards of the town hall, and beyond that, the starless sky. I was a mourning bride without a train of concern. Aug began to shake and so did I. His head fell heavy in my hands. I was by myself, the ground soft under me, the cold heat of other bodies at a distance. Was this the end? Blood twined through his hair and my fingers.

"Will someone help me?" I yelled. "Please?"

Some of these Shoreline Citizens might be falling down stairs themselves soon, or clutching their heart on a benign summer evening, and now they were caught in their own dilemma of helping a man they'd sworn not to help. But they weren't terrible people, and they finally began to stir and move towards us. Someone grabbed a blanket from a car, someone put a hand on my back. If they didn't know Aug was sick before, they knew it now. But they were unsure of the outcome, like a group of kids that suspects it has gone too far.

Diana bent down and said something to me, but I blocked her self-righteous gawking. The EMTs came, and at the hospital, August's head was scanned and stitched, and I explained his condition and medications so many times, I wondered if the doctors were trying to break me down like a criminal. I drove us home just as it was getting light out, and Aug kept his hand on my leg not only out of affection, I thought, but out of a need to hold on to something that wouldn't escape his grasp. He was humiliated and silent. I told him he looked like a hero in a war photo, his face bruised and puffy and a startling white bandage around his head at a jaunty angle, but he didn't react. I was ridiculously jocular and scared. I stopped at the town hall to dig around for Aug's glasses, but couldn't find them. My hands came up wet and empty. Back at the small house Aug had lived in for only one summer with his first wife and their daughter, and now me, he went up to bed. I pulled the shades down against the promised heat and unfolded a cool sheet over his legs. During that long day, I was captive in the house, surrounded by a forest of scrub pines brushing against each other and the watery feeling of having been spared something terrible.

Years before we were married, I had tutored Aug's eight-year-old daughter, Molly, in reading. Her school might have given her the help she needed, but I saw that her father wanted to protect his only child from whatever label might be pinned on her—slow or dumb or worse. I wondered what had been pinned on him as a kid—Jew, shrimp, kike (all that and shit poor too, it turned out). Molly had eczema on the inside of her arms, and a thin, nervous mother. There was clearly little money; the house was flaking and bruised, the stove spattered, the wife wide-eyed. Once I heard August battling with her in another room while Molly pretended not to notice and raked her skin. The child was distracted and dense as sludge. We took the summer off, and when we started again in September, August had moved out and a divorce was in the works. The wife was oddly solicitous of me then, but she was more than I wanted to take on, and I ended the tutoring. I couldn't take their money anymore, and couldn't stomach the unhappiness that hung in the air like the smell of a bad meal. From time to time, I thought about that family and what might have happened to them, and how I'd come into and out of their lives like a painting brought in to distract from a room with crumbling walls.

I saw August a couple of years later in a diner where I was having breakfast with my boyfriend. He and Molly sat at the counter. Her legs had grown long and improbably smooth in the way of pubescent girls and she was wearing pink shorts even in October. She swiveled on her stool and chattered on while August was silent, elbows ground into the formica, his back hunched, hands around a cup of coffee. An asshole, I decided. After breakfast, my boyfriend and I went apple picking at a place just beyond the diner. We were forcing a last good time on each other until we could end what we had going, and then, there was August and his daughter again at another line of trees, and I thought, what are the chances of this happening? Not for years, and then twice in a morning? August stayed in one place and held a bag open while Molly ran around collecting fruit and dropping it in. But he wasn't disengaged or bored as I'd thought he'd been back at the diner, but rather some emotion he had no idea how to express had overcome and frozen him.

He turned to me and waved me over—he would not come to me, that wasn't the way it worked with him—and we talked. My boyfriend had wandered off and Molly flitted between the trees. When August looked at me, I could tell he was trying to remember something, maybe his earlier impressions and if they matched up with what he saw now. I was vibrant and talkative, my cheeks rouged with the morning and his attention. It was the only time I'd ever felt more powerful than August. I looked over my shoulder at Molly who we'd been talking about.

"Is she having any more reading issues?" I asked.

"Issues?" he laughed. "Jesus, is that how you people really talk?" He glanced at my boyfriend and measured his own want against the other man's. "I'd like to go out with you sometime. Give me your number." It was only after we were married that he told me he'd followed me to the orchard that morning.

Now the fall down the town hall steps had set him back— or forward—and he rarely got out of bed anymore. One late afternoon, Molly, who'd moved to Houston with her mother soon after I'd seen her apple picking thirteen years earlier, finally phoned her father. This was after I'd emailed too many times to tell her how sick he was, and how she should think about coming to see him, and to remind her that she hadn't responded, not even once. She'd grown brooding and unforgiving of Aug after the divorce, and they rarely saw each other or spoke. She was Aug's deepest regret, one he kept to himself, as if to let it run in the open space might kill him. He'd asked me to shut the door when she called, and when it was over, he began to not so much cry as bleat. It was a shocking, hollow sound—an animal on the edge of a cliff. When I went in, he was sitting on the edge of the bed in his boxers, his sunken stomach pulsing in and out, his hands behind his neck.

"What did she say?" I asked. I had to look away from his glass of water that had grown too cloudy on the nightstand. There was nothing benign to focus on anymore. The television was on to a baseball game without the sound. "Tell me, Aug."

He shook his head; he wouldn't talk about it. Tears pooled in his defeated cheeks and he touched my face. "Why aren't I feeling better? It was just a fall, a missed step," he said. "This isn't right. It's not supposed to be like this."

"No, it isn't," I said.

But I wanted to say, it's because you're dying, Aug, and because you're never going to feel better than this, and because it wasn't just a fall or a single step; it was a plummet. I wanted to say how awful it was that his only child had deserted him, that she could make him cry when nothing else could, and how we should have had a child of our own when we'd had the chance. Our union was simple math; what he loved about me was that I loved him back. Neither of us had had much of that in our lives, and we knew its worth. I saw him again as that dust-poor child, the picked-on, the neglected. His daughter's grabbed-up love had been the deepest deprivation of all.

"They're doing this to me, Alice," he said, after a few minutes. "They're going to kill me with this."

I rested my head on his rocky knee and smelled his body in foul decline. For the first time, I didn't want to breathe him in; I was afraid now it would kill me, too, and I sat back, ashamed. I replayed his fall down the town hall stairs, but this time I pictured myself going back there a hundred times in the dark, kneeling in the spot where he'd curled up, looking for a dead man's glasses. No one was there to help me, and no one would come, but they'd watch from a distance, or stay hidden in the trees. I was my own cautionary tale.

I didn't want to live like that. I might have a house on the water, a victory of sorts, but Aug would be gone by then and I'd be alone in the place, with all that scorn burning at my back. If he and I had shared during our marriage, a notion that it was us against them, I couldn't sustain that alone. I'd seen that fearsome isolation the night he'd fallen and didn't want to see it again. It was my life I was protecting now.

"This fight is poisonous," I said, and sat back on my heels. "Let's not build the house. We'll stay right here, in this one. This is perfect, it always has been. This is where we live. I don't want another house."

His mouth moved as if he were working at a hard candy. "I wasn't talking about the house," he said, with strange calm. "I was talking about the doctors." He lay down on the bed and pulled the sheet up. "But now I see. I understand."

"I only want you. I don't care where we live."

"There's no 'we,' sweetheart, don't you see? I'm doing this for you so you'll have it later on. So I can picture you someplace when I'm dead. But it's okay, Alice, it really is. It's okay." He closed his eyes as if I'd left the room already. "It's okay," he said again, this time soothing himself. "We'll stop."

If desire was life, then I'd just killed his.

I watched the sheet rise and fall on his fading form. I asked him to open his eyes, but he wasn't stirred when I undressed, or when I lay next to him, careful to keep my weight off him. He was pale bones, and while the scar on his forehead reddened like a traitor, his penis remained motionless, a betrayed, lilac curl, even when I put my mouth to it. He sighed and pushed me away.

Aug slept most days until midday, then woke restless and uncomfortable, trying to stretch his joints back into place. In the afternoons, he often trawled the house in his sagging boxers as though he'd lost something—which he had in giving up the fight. And if he came upon me, he'd ask what I was doing, or what I'd done earlier, what I'd eaten, who I'd seen, as if I'd gone away and seen the sights. But I hadn't gone anywhere, and was captive everywhere, pursued by him if I stayed home, pursued by neighbors if I left. Women approached me at the pond and the post office. They said Aug hadn't been seen around town; had he finally changed his mind? They forced me to hold my breath too long in the water to avoid them, until I saw the mulchy bottom and the white blooms of underwater flowers, and in the post office until my hand went numb clutching the inconsequential mail.

One afternoon, a man Aug used to play backgammon with on summer afternoons, wept as he talked to me about how Aug was going to destroy his favorite place on earth. What about me? I stood there, unmoving, but stirred to the core, until he was too embarrassed to go on. I got some absurd satisfaction out of not telling him that we were giving up the fight. I understood that for him, what remained untouched remained ageless. Everyone was just trying to hold on forever, including Aug, including me.

When I got home, Aug was waiting for me in the front room. I told him about running into his former friend.

"Old crybaby," Aug said, fondly.

I sat next to him and put my head on his shoulder. "Forgive me," I said.

"Forgive you for what? There's nothing to forgive, Alice." He pushed my head off. "You were honest. I can't be angry at that, but I can be sad that you don't want what I'm giving you, what I've worked a lifetime for." With effort, he rose from the couch and went upstairs.

The next morning, I called his doctor and got something to help Aug sleep through those dismal hours of each dwindling day when he wandered or ambushed. Not his dismal hours, but mine. The house of a dying man is a museum of intentions, and I couldn't bear to be in it. By 5:00, he was out for the night, his breathing raspy, the cat sleeping loyally between his skinny legs.

Some evenings, when Aug was in his narcotized sleep, I drove up and down Route 6, not sure what I was looking for. I wondered if I wasn't waiting to see an accident, a sharp disaster that would define the day. One airless evening, I found myself turning off New Town Road and driving towards our property. I parked at the end of the dirt road and trudged through the beach grass and the rugosa and the dip between the hills and onto the dunes. I didn't know if it was the view or the walk or the smell of salt and roses that left me breathless. There was a party down on the beach, and a bonfire that was pale against the sky. I knew nothing about it, but I missed being part of it anyway. The tide had pulled out and water skimmed the sandbars. Behind me, the Tillman house was yellowing in the lowering sun, and I walked over to it. I peered in the waterside windows and saw a day bed covered with a faded Indian print bedspread, a couple of canvas chairs, a table bleached by the relentless light, a closed door. Empty of people, but full of the suggestion that you could live there and feel something every day. Maybe this was the house I was meant to live in. I lay down on the splintery deck, my hands over my chest. I was content, even, thrilled to be illicit and undetected, to have found this place where no one would find me. They'd never look for me there. The bugs tuned up, testing their wings. Then there were footsteps inside the house, a light went on, a door opened, and a man came out, stretched his arms up and let out a long, low fart.

"Holy shit," he said, looking at me. He was Ray, the owner of the place who'd spoken at the selectmen's meeting. He backed towards the door. It was absurd to think I could scare anyone, and I laughed, first from my own fear and embarrassment, and then because I didn't know what else to do. He looked at me on his porch like I was an animal or a drunk.

"I am so sorry," I said. "Obviously, I didn't know anyone was here. I'm mortified."

"I know you. You're the wife of the guy who wants to build the house. You were at the town hall meeting." He was clearly amused and still puzzled.

"I'm Alice and I don't know what I was thinking." Ray had the soft, sleepy look of someone who's fallen headfirst into relaxation. "Actually, I was thinking no one was here or I wouldn't have come. Didn't you say the house was empty?"

"Was empty." He turned his face at a slight angle. "Then you're not here to get me on your side?"

"Of course not."

"You'd be amazed. People do this all the time, just walk up here and stand on the deck like the place is open to the public. Then they try to talk to me." He made a gesture like he was swatting at a fly. "And I don't want to talk to them."

"It is the famous Tillman view, after all, a national treasure. The source of all inspiration."

"So people keep reminding me," he said, shrugging.

The fire at the beach party flared. "I should go. I'm sorry again."

"It's okay. Stay—I mean now that you're here, you might as well. I know it happens every night, but at least watch the sunset."

I smiled, a public joke that felt almost private. Ray seemed as glad for the company as I was to have found it. We sat on the deck drinking beer, our legs over the side. He said that he hadn't planned on staying after the selectmen's meeting, but had changed his mind after his first night in the house, which he'd found compelling but confusing. He wasn't used to the light, the colors, or the absence of urban noise, the smell of moonlight cooling the water. He'd visited a few times as a kid when his father was there with Tillman and while his mother, not his father's wife anymore, waited out on the road in the car doing a crossword puzzle. There was more to the story, it practically pounded to be let out, but he stopped there. He had a kind of halting manner about him that felt in part like resignation, in part sadness. He averted his eyes too often, ran one hand over the other, and occasionally looked at the place on his wrist where his watch usually was.

"How's your husband?" he asked. "Actually, forget it, you don't have to tell me. It's just I heard—people have told me—that he fell after the meeting."

"Do you see? They'll say anything. He's fine. Going ahead with the plans."

"Pissing people off."

I told him how I was pursued during the day, and how I'd started only going out evenings because of it. I did not tell him about how I blacked Aug out until morning with something strong—for my own good.

"Same with me," he said. "I can't go anywhere without being ambushed, cornered, followed. What a funny town this is. Looks nice from the outside, but inside, it's all this grinding self-righteousness and privilege. Personally, I don't give a shit one way or the other about how this works out." He nodded towards Aug's land. "But I can definitely see why you'd want to put a house there. For the view. If you like that sort of thing."

He seemed pleased that he could make me laugh. But a view was nothing you could hold or take to bed with you or trace the borders of. A view wasn't what you saw, but what you felt when you saw it—and what could I feel when it was about the end of my husband? I pictured him, lips caught on dry teeth, drugged for the night. Who knew what Ray felt? I said I had to go, but it was fully dark, and I couldn't see my way back. He found a flashlight and stood on the deck with it, providing me with a beam of light to follow through the grass until it became too faint to see, but by then, I'd found my way back to the road.

The late July air sucked up the last drops of moisture, and when I came back from a walk one morning, I was covered with dust and Aug was downstairs looking over a set of architect's plans FedEx had just delivered. He'd spread them across the table and in the hazy morning sun, his body was as shocking as his strange new energy. His hair was a wild frizz, and he was all dip and slack tendon, his limbs held together by loose string. It was alarming enough to stop me in the doorway. He waved me over to the drawings, and traced the geometry of windows, doors, roof peaks, corners. He was punishing me with every lovely detail, reminding me of what I'd said I didn't want, but to me, these plans were stamped with his absence. I tried to leave, but he caught me by the wrist.

"And this," he said, pressing two fingers against the violet paper, "is the bedroom and here's the window facing the water." He swept a hand over where the water would be. "What do you think?" He smiled patiently, but I could see the anger behind it. He brushed the dust off my face.

"Are you really going ahead with this?" I asked. "I thought we were done with this."

"No, dear, *you* were done with it. Did you really expect I

would stop fighting now?"

I retreated to the kitchen. "What would you like for lunch?" I called out. My chest ached, my hands were freezing. I thought about sitting on the floor for a few hundred days.

"I want," he said. "I want. What I want is," but he was unable to finish the sentence. He'd exhausted himself. I heard in his want all the disappointments in his life, which included me now, but I didn't help him finish his thought or make his way back to bed as I once might have. I rolled up the plans and put them behind the couch.

What I wanted, for an instant, was for him to be dead already, for all this to be over. I could leave then and never come back.

At the end of the week, Diana, defender of endangered species at the selectmen's meeting, showed up at our house. She carried a clear plastic cage the size of a small purse. There was something she wanted to show August, she said.

"He's sleeping," I told her. "This isn't a good time."

Aug must have heard her car pull up because he stood at the top of the stairs. "Sure it's a good time. What do you have there, old girl?" he boomed.

"Two Eastern Spadefoot Toads," she called up. "Found on your land, actually."

"My land? So you were trespassing." He started down the stairs, the cat bounding past him and out the door. "Maybe I should call the police and report you. Have you arrested."

Diana gave his smirk a disapproving look, then noted his bare chest with its wisps of hair, the ways his bones protruded, his nose arcing out from his face like a challenge. Aug peered into the container she'd put on the table. Two toads in a corner stared at twigs and moss.

"I used to like these things when I was a kid," Aug said, tapping the side. "You could pick them up by the dozens in the alleys. Come on boys, let's see a little action in there. Hop to it." "Don't do that," Diana said. "You'll scare them." "Alice, come look at these things." Aug waved me over, but I stayed in the kitchen doorway. He was playing with Diana, his disgust in that single finger which continued to bang on the plastic.

"They're on the watch list, you know," she said. "If you build that house you're planning, you'll destroy their habitat. I just wanted to make sure you understand that."

Aug began to take off the top of the cage. Diana said she'd prefer he didn't do that. "Keeping them in this Tupperware thing doesn't seem so environmentally friendly. Shouldn't we let them go?" he asked, all false benevolence. "Let them be free-range toads again?"

He picked up the container and went to the door. It looked like he was going to fling the toads in their plastic UFO to their death, and I thought, he's capable of anything now, even acts of cruelty. But then he kneeled and let the toads out with the gentlest push. They were like tourists, unsure which way to go, but he coaxed and assured them it was okay to move forward.

Diana squeezed my arm too hard and I yanked away. "Can't you do something?" she pleaded. "He's your husband."

"Go away," I whispered. "Please, just go away. Leave us alone."

The three of us spotted the cat lurking under the day lilies, waiting for gifts—birds, mice—to kill and bring to Aug, her lover. Diana's toads would be next. She handed me Aug's lost glasses and left.

"I don't think," Aug said as he went back upstairs, "that woman knows I'm on the watch list, too." He looked down at me with a blank expression. "I woke up the other night and you weren't here. Where were you, Alice?"

"Here. I'm always here," I said. "It was a dream."

"Maybe I dreamed that when I called for you, you didn't answer, and when I came downstairs and looked for you, you were gone, the car was gone."

"You were asleep all night."

"Possible, but I don't think so." His accusatory tone was corrupted by a sudden bout of coughing. He waved me away, but said, "Don't leave me, Alice. I get scared when you're not here. I think I'm already dead then. Do you know what that feels like? Please don't leave me."

"I won't leave you," I said. "I promise."

The night I'd come back from the Tillman house and slipped into bed next to Aug, he hadn't moved. I wondered what he'd detected on me even in his sleep—the beer, the bug spray, the scratches on my legs from the blackberry thorns. When Aug was back upstairs, I called Molly and left another message. Come see your father, I said. She didn't call back.

Aug's cat killed one of Diana's toads, and its battered body lay by the door, untouched for two weeks, a kind of desiccating trophy I stepped over. One evening, I went again to the Tillman house. I was sure Ray had gone back to Chicago by then, but he stormed out of the house when I pulled up.

"Go away. This is private property," he yelled even before I'd gotten out of the car. He was furious and looked ready to grab something menacing. "You're trespassing."

I hesitated. Did he know it was me? I leaned out of the window, but it took him too long to consider who I was. "Okay, going," I yelled back.

"Jesus. Alice? Is that you?" he said. "Sorry, I don't have my glasses on, and these assholes keep showing up. I'm going crazy."

He asked me inside and showed me a jar of beach plum jelly one of the Shoreline Citizens had dropped off that morning. Yesterday, there'd been a van full of German tourists stopping to see the site before heading into Boston for the weekend. Someone else had brought him steamers that he'd made for dinner and which I'd clearly interrupted. Bribes, he called the booty, offering me a seat and a clam. Ray seemed different, more comfortable in the house, as though he'd finally realized he had something others wanted.

"The trouble is that these people still don't get that it doesn't matter what I think," he said. "I have no power, no say over what happens. It's your land, not mine."

"Not mine, either," I said. "My husband's." The steamer was sweet and messy and left the scent of the ocean on my upper lip.

"Isn't it that the same thing though? Yours and his?" he asked. When I gave a pained shrug, Ray consoled me by dabbing a drop of butter off my chin.

"I want to explain," I said.

"Please, don't. No need. Eat up. There's fudge next."

Ray struck me as a man who was alone a lot, though not by choice. I knew almost nothing about him, but you cannot put a man and a woman in a room—not with a bowl of steamers, not with the bay looking on and slapping the sand—and not have it occur to the woman, at least, that sex might be possible. The calculation is primal, essential. Attraction has almost nothing to do with it; sometimes it's about survival and possibility. Ray dangled a steamer above his mouth.

"Why do you hate this place?" I asked.

"You know, I'm supposed to be back in Chicago by now. I have work." He stroked his upper lip in evasion and looked down at an evening shadow playing on the table. "My father and Tillman used to sit on the deck and drink gin and send me down to the beach to swim. I was scared to swim alone. They were lovers and they wanted their time together. I didn't figure it out until I was about fourteen," he said, shaking his head at how dense he'd been. It was a sad story.

"And all those paintings of women," I said. "Maybe not making love to them was what it took for Tillman to get them right."

"That's a scary thought. I'd like to get a woman right one of these days." Ray smirked.

"You must have been surprised when your father left you the house."

"Yes, surprised. It would have been nice to know why, when we were about as distant as a father and son can be, but it's hard to make a corpse explain itself." He sat back in his chair and wiped his hands on his shorts. "If you know what I mean."

"I know what you mean." We laughed. "I came by because I thought I'd take you to a pond for a swim, if you're interested. It's the only time I can go without being hassled—and it's beautiful at this hour."

We left the house, the steamers and the shells still scattered across the table, and when we got to the pond, the last car was just pulling out. It slowed to get a look at us gathering our towels from the trunk. The water was brassy, the surface broken by dipping dragonflies. Ray was a slow and graceless swimmer, breathing too hard and following me too far out. I turned around, worried about him getting back to shore.

When the water was at his waist, and he'd caught his breath, he said, "They tell me your husband's not doing so well. They say he's going to die before anything's decided."

The trees ringing the pond were still. A current wound around my ankles. Diana must have reported back about Aug's bones, his dry lips, his vigilant shuffle, the stink of illness in the house.

"They think you'll never go ahead with the house," Ray said. "That you don't have the stomach for it, that you're not like him."

There is a kind of anger that turns you cold and rigid, and as soon as I dove away from Ray, I knew I was in trouble. The water was too heavy, my fingers were sieves, and my heart had no rhythm. So this is drowning, I thought, as I saw roots tangled like nerve endings. My feet touched the bottom and pushed me up.

Ray handed me a towel when I got out. "Why didn't you tell me, Alice? Why did you tell me he's fine if he isn't?"

"He's dying," I said, my throat straining. "He almost never gets out of bed. He's lost so much weight I can see his skull under his skin. He can't sit on a chair because it's too hard on his tailbone. I drug him in the afternoon so he sleeps until the morning, just so I can get a break. He's building the house for me to live in when he's dead and I don't want it. How's that? Is that what I should have told you?"

Ray didn't know what to say, and I plodded back through the woods to the car. Ray followed and we didn't speak again until I'd pulled up to his house. I turned off the engine and stared ahead.

"There's really no place for you to go, is there," he said.

I nodded. "Anywhere I am, I've made the wrong decision."

Ray put his arm around my shoulder, an awkward move in the car, both of us still damp and mostly strangers to each other. But the way he rested his face against mine, I thought we'd found in the other, for just a moment, some familiar and tender ache.

When I got home, August was downstairs on the couch, wrapped in a blanket, despite the unrelenting heat. He looked at me in my suit, my clothes in one hand, my wet towel. "Nice swim?" he asked. "See anyone?"

"I had the pond to myself. Why are you down here? Are you okay?"

"Did you swim alone?" His voice was weak, but sharply edged.

"I told you—I had the place to myself. I want to get out of my suit." I turned to leave the room.

"No, don't go. Take it off here," he said. "Let me see you."

"No," I said, and went upstairs to the bedroom where I knew he couldn't reach me. My fingers were stiff and inept pulling at my suit, which stuck to my skin. Nausea pressed under my tongue. I smelled steamers and pond water. But August had managed the stairs and stood in the doorway. He stared at my body. I was all health and exertion, while his chest rose too quickly. I saw how illness was scooping him out. He sat on the bed and motioned for me to come close so he could press his face against my belly. He told me I was beautiful. I thought I would cry when he reached for my breast.

"You smell like sex." He pushed me away. I looked down at his pale, babyish head. "I didn't take my pill before, Alice. I don't want to sleep anymore. Why should I be asleep for the rest of my life and see nothing more? I want to see everything." He looked up at me. "No man will ever love you again," he said. "I'm your last. You know that, don't you?"

"How can you say that to me?"

"How can I not?"

I saw that when he'd gotten out of bed earlier, he'd pulled up his side of the sheets to show me that he was not coming back, that I'd sleep alone. He went downstairs again where he would stay until he died, getting more horizontal on the couch every day. I lay down, but couldn't sleep. Around midnight, I went downstairs for a glass of water.

"I know you've left me already," August said, out of the dark. "I've made everyone hate me, even you. A bad habit of mine—to get them before they get me. Not a way to live, but not a bad way to die."

I was a room apart but I could have already been talking to Aug's ghost when I asked, "Did you know you were sick when you bought the land? Did you know I'd always be alone there?" He didn't answer. "Was that your plan?"

I went to see Ray the next evening, walking past Aug who was still on the couch, but now sunken into it, a fossil in the making. He hadn't eaten all day and he didn't ask me where I was going. When I got to the Tillman house, Ray's car was there, but he wasn't. I went around to the deck and saw him down on the beach, walking the sandbars. As I waited for him, what I wished for was a hurricane to flatten the Tillman house and Aug's land, uproot the dunes until they slid into the water and disappeared. Or a fire. But the air was motionless, and the sky a beautiful, late summer boast.

"I'm going home tomorrow," Ray said, stepping onto the deck. It was amazing how quickly I'd gotten used to his awkward delivery. One cheek was covered with sand, as though he'd been sleeping on beach.

"Do you think you'll come back?"

"Not for a long time, probably not unless I have to." He sat next to me. "One time when I was here as a kid, when my father and Tillman sent me down to the beach to swim, I nearly drowned. When I looked up for my father to help me, he and Tillman had gone inside. They were fucking when I came in, scared and wet." He let out a thin, unhappy laugh. "Funny now—not so funny then."

Is that the memory his father had wanted to leave him

with when he'd left him the house? That while one is drowning, another is making love? That life is full of such fateful contrasts? When I leaned over to kiss Ray, he pulled away and looked alarmed, but I tilted at him, pressed my lips against his closed, resistant mouth. I put his hand on my breast, but he was inert, and his hand dropped.

"Sorry," Ray said. "It's nothing personal, Alice. I just have to leave this place. I'm sorry." He stood and walked to another part of the deck.

I wasn't humiliated by what had just happened, but instead felt as though I'd emerged from a perfect swim, my body celebrating its vitality. Aug was dying, but I wasn't, and it seemed to me then in that singular moment of solitude, this was what he'd been trying to do with the house. He'd wanted me to hear this last yell of his, see his last desire spread out in front of me, so I'd know the difference every day between living and concession. I hadn't wanted the house before because I thought it would kill me—with grief and loneliness—but now I did. I wanted the house. I don't know how long I sat there, or how long Ray was inside packing up his things, but at some point, I watched head-lights sweep over the beach grass on Aug's property. A car had come down the road as far as it could and parked.

"An inspiration seeker," I called to Ray. "Even in the dark, they're looking for something."

The driver's side opened and a woman got out. She took a few steps towards the water and lit a cigarette. Soon, someone else got out of the car, a hunched figure with movement that was only a memory of movement. It was August. I didn't understand what I was seeing, what he was doing, who he was with. He rested a hand on the woman's shoulders and turned on a flash-light. Its beam roamed over the grass, then the Tillman house, then my frozen face.

"It's my husband," I told Ray who'd come outside. Aug had come looking for me, and he had always known where I was.

Aug drew a path to him with the flashlight and I left the deck and Ray. I was anxious to explain everything now. Closer, I saw that the woman was Molly. Even in the poor light, I could see that she had a bitter mouth and that it was set against me.

"Look who showed up," Aug said to me. "Isn't it wonderful? My darling Molly, my daughter."

She said hello with the same cold tenor I'd heard over the phone in the early summer. It seemed impossible that I'd once sat at a table with her while she'd sounded out consonants, or that I'd watched her pick apples. She'd driven from Boston, she explained, in a rental car. She and Aug had been making plans for weeks.

"You didn't tell me," I said to Aug.

"This is a surprise then, isn't it?" He shined his beam on Ray on the deck, and in the slow lowering of the light, Aug dismissed him. "I was showing Molly the land. I wanted to show her where her bedroom is going to be, where the window is, the deck onto the water. At night, she can walk out and see the stars. I showed her the plans. You like them, don't you, sweetheart?"

"Sure. I mean, who wouldn't?"

"Alice doesn't, but it doesn't matter. I've done this for you," he said, clutching her elbow in an ancient way. "All my life I've worked for you, Molly." He said her name, but he was looking at me. I hadn't wanted what he was determined to give me and this was my punishment and his retribution.

"This is your house," he told Molly again.

He'd gotten his daughter back; whether she loved him or not didn't matter. He could pretend, and he could picture her here when he was dead. She was not looking for inspiration, but maybe what she felt was owed her. I looked back at Ray's, but he'd gone inside. In the morning, he'd lock the windows and pull the shades, and the Tillman place would be empty again, and anyone who wanted to sit on the deck and search the view for something they'd never find was welcome to come. I'd do it a couple of time myself most likely, but now August was ready to go home, and he said his daughter would take him.

THE SCHOOL OF POLITICS

Not everyone could say they had slept with a felon. Not that the Mayor was a felon back then—or even convicted yet—but still, he'd always been a criminal in Francine's mind. Since his trial began, she'd taken to watching it every morning before work on the tiny television on the kitchen counter. The June sun fell singular and admiringly on the Mayor who trotted up the courtroom steps, and she noted how porcine he'd gotten in the eighteen years since they'd known each other. Back then in his apartment on Pratt Street, he had preened, sleek and invincible, and she'd been a little awed by him. Now each day she catalogued the sad evidence of age and corruption on his body; the excess of double chin, the money-stuffed bags under his dark and cautious gaze, the infantile white of his scalp where the hair had thinned.

"He'll walk," Sanford announced, moving from the counter where he'd also been watching the morning procession of defendants. "Criminal, thug, intimidator. Dag's always gotten away with it, and he always will. This is his city, after all."

Her husband's certainty irked Francine. It wasn't that Sanford was wrong about the Mayor—she preferred Mayor to the dopey nickname Dag, short for Albert—but his pronouncement provoked in her an unsettling feeling of protectiveness for the man. Somewhere in the grand courthouse, there was a ninety-seven count indictment with the Mayor's name written all over it. She thought of the document, the history of a public man converted to twenty-five pounds of damning heft, as just slightly more than the combined birth weights of her three children, slightly less than the dog who spent her winding-down days twitching under the deck. The Mayor was charged with running a criminal enterprise out of City Hall. The accusation was like a game, as though he'd been caught cheating at Monopoly, siphoning pastel-colored money from the bank to buy Park Place, juggling hotels in his pocket. He could shrug it off yet.

She wished she could tell Sanford that she'd seen fear and contrition in the Mayor's expression when he looked out of the television and directly at her, but it would have been a lie on several counts. She'd really only seen the usual arrogance there, a curl of the almost girlish lips, and the knowledge that he could still get a good seat in any restaurant no matter what happened. And, of course, the Mayor hadn't looked at her at all, as Sanford might have pointed out unnecessarily, but only at his own fearsome reflection in the television cameras. Instead, she was the one trying to penetrate the impossible distance, hoping to find what had once drawn her to the man.

"I'll give you a lift to work," Sanford called from the deck where he'd been filling the dog's water bowl. The Mayor disappeared into the courthouse, and Francine turned off the television.

They lived in a medium-size city, and though it often seemed much smaller, it had taken until last year to actually come face to face again with the Mayor. She'd been in the same room with him before, of course, along with hundreds of other people in ballroom fundraisers for cancer or the shrinking wetlands, and even at the opening of the municipal skating rink where she'd watched as her son nearly had his hand yanked off by the Mayor's vigorous shaking of it. But this time it had been at the Mayor's elegant house during a May fundraiser for the gay men's health center on whose board Sanford, a shrink, sat.

The party was set up in the garden, but she and Sanford had gone inside to snoop. They hadn't voted for the Mayor and so felt fine about what they were about to do; political dis-alliance justified such an honorable American tradition. Sanford goaded Francine's curiosity about the Mayor because he assumed it was the same as his and all good citizens; simply, *who the hell is this person?* In her sudden surge of nerves, being so close again to the man she'd slept with a long time ago, she twisted the silk scarf around her neck, strangled what was left of her better will, and moved forward.

The richly lit public rooms were crowded with leather furniture, brass lamps, spiky plants, and glass decanters of various golden liquors. To Francine the place looked like a set. Shelves displayed an array of cheap tokens given to the Mayor by anyone hoping to do business with him. There were miniature beer steins, origami boxes, the key to another metropolis, a baseball cap preserved in a Plexiglas coffin. Nothing you couldn't buy yourself in a souvenir shop.

In a minute, they'd found what they weren't supposed to—the Mayor's private living room. It was down several steps, relegated to basement status. The lighting was dim and would cast no blame, but still revealed a filthy beige carpet underfoot, a thousand shoes wiped dismissively on it. A distressed couch faced a television, and a signed poster of the Super Bowl champs of a decade earlier hung over the fireplace which held a listing pile of magazines. The room was so reminiscent of the Mayor's old apartment, so discouragingly the same after all these powerful, commanding years that it made Francine sigh with disappointment—for him and for her. Sanford grinned, nodded, and misunderstood her. *Wow*, he mouthed as though he'd come across something blinding, *yes*.

What, she wondered, had they stupidly thought they might discover here? Still, she played along with her husband and sniggered about the secret life of the emperor—open cans of Diet Coke and full ashtrays—realizing with a kind of terrifying amusement that she could have been Mrs. Mayor. Not really, not fucking likely actually, but still within the widest realm of possibility. It could have been her instead of the real Mrs. Mayor who was now the ex and mostly forgotten, living in another state with the lone kid who had a substance abuse problem. The Mayor was a bachelor again, always seen in the company of a drink, a woman, and the rumor that he'd even screwed the six-foot ostrich-necked wife of the college president. He liked them tall. Francine had been part of that pattern, albeit before it was firmly established; she had three inches on the Mayor. He'd measured once in bed, leveling his head with hers while his feet came to her anklebones.

Francine crossed the floor towards where she assumed the bedroom was, the layout of her city's historic homes being her thing. Behind her, Sanford suggested they'd gone far enough, that their wandering was wandering into something else, and shouldn't they get something to eat before it was all gone? Two glasses of wine swirled in her chest beneath the silk and perfume, giving her the confidence to be nosing around, and she ignored him. After all, she'd had the Mayor in her mouth more than once, and if that didn't give her the right to witness now his restless blankets, his pillow indented by his scheming head, the sour bathrobe balled on the floor, then nothing did. She recalled how the Mayor had liked to look at her naked and touch his erection which rose so ambitiously, how they'd both been turned on by their own part in the ritual. It wasn't thinking about Dag's hard-on now that made her shiver in discomfort, but a sudden understanding of the humbling nature of longing and that human instant that could make even the most powerful man fall to his knees.

"Francine," Sanford hissed. "Come on. Even he deserves some privacy."

But the Mayor's life was public, though how bereft of contentment and consolation he was in private, she saw. Francine's pulse beat wildly. She considered telling Sanford that she'd slept with the Mayor way back when, had a thing with him, but then she would have to explain why she'd never told him before. To say that it was a different time in her life was pious and inadequate. Sanford would be speechless, wounded. Disgust might pass over his hearty, intelligent face, he'd be stunned that he and Dag had in common that they'd touched the same woman's heart, but most of all, he'd be curious. *Really?* He'd ask, sensible and tolerant after he forced himself to get over it, *what was he like? What were you like?* And would he really mean, *who are you, Francine, after all these years?* And how could she answer that when she didn't know herself? This, then, was hers, and wasn't it okay to hoard a single piece of experience and shame?

"Oh, no, you can't be back here," the Mayor commanded, suddenly emerging to claim his ground from her. "This space is off-limits."

Francine turned quickly; she felt her feet might trip her. "I'm sorry. I thought these were public rooms, for everyone," she said mindlessly, sensing his weighty presence close at her back.

He gave an obvious laugh. "Nope. The party's in the garden. This way."

As he ushered them back through the house, Francine detected the Listerine breath of a man who's just stolen some time away to check himself in the mirror and wonder, *what do I think when I'm alone?* And then, in the dim of the front hall where they stopped before stepping outside, Francine thought he might have recognized her, but his gaze was already gone when he asked, "How are you folks tonight?"

"We're terrific," Sanford told him, glancing at Francine who'd gone silent and bloodless. "Good party."

"Well, those men have done a nice job," the Mayor said, and then, because he'd never expected there would be quite so many queers in his garden, he gave Sanford a virile pat on the shoulder before moving into the crowd.

"He was pretty gracious—considering." Sanford touched Francine's arm; he was ready to go. "Considering he's a thug."

How are you? The Mayor said that to everyone—this had become the "How are you" city. A different context (clothed now), another haircut, but wasn't Francine's face essentially the same? Pale, gray-eyed, an imbalance or two just short of classic, a look people sometimes read as cool. The Mayor had once told her she looked like something out of a Bonicello painting. *You mean Boticelli?* she'd asked (she was far from it, she knew, with tiny breasts and hips). Bonicello, he insisted to her, the art history major. Now her face hadn't appeared to spark anything in him and she was saddened by this lack of ignition, this extinguished place in his memory.

But she was angry, too, at her smug husband and at the Mayor. Hey Dag, you fucked me once upon a time, remember? How *should* I be? Talk of his likely indictment was floating around even then, wafting through the early lilacs and the men in their blazers, the tonic water going flat and the ice dripping onto the bluestone, and the truth was, Francine knew well enough, the man was a politician; he'd fucked everyone at some point or other.

*   *   *

Ambition is a muscle; the more you work it, the stronger it gets. That was the kind of knowledge the Mayor had spooned out to her years before. Pretty pretentious stuff, she thought then, even if she now knew it was mostly true. Because here she was, another day in her enviable perch of an office, because she'd worked that muscle pretty damn hard—head, heart, and hand of it—to get to this second-floor parlor of the Hunt-Paring House. It was a dream job in many respects, something solid to aspire to. A private family endowment paid for the preservation and her dutiful running of the 1786 Georgian mansion, a museum open three days a week. It paid to call her Executive Director, and have the toilets scrubbed with silk threads if she decided that's what should be done. There was priceless furniture and art throughout the enormous, meandering house, cupboards of silver, booty from the China trade, five exquisite Millerton landscapes, two Sargeants and, most remarkably, a La Pense. In her own office, off-limits to museum visitors, there was a luminous painting—*The Stream* by Grosvenor—a Robintrough bronze, a da Concci vase, a Davida-Lowell highboy, a green velvet chaise. She had a board which generally agreed with her, the freedom to roam the halls, explore the vast storerooms, and curate small, jewel-like exhibits. Snuff boxes, flora in the art of Angus Lentin, children's toys—and soon, a show of fine embroidery. During her search for pieces to include, she'd discovered, the week before, a tiny, porcelain rooster hidden in the back of one of the Longe armoires. It was a funny object, stashed away for a century by one of the Hunt-Paring children, she guessed—a single, small treasured thing among the thousands, and she'd brought it to her office.

As she admired the rooster this morning, her neglect in cataloguing it—of declaring its existence at all—nagged dully at

her. The fact was, she told herself as she put it down, her ambition had once been flexed, but now it was atrophied, and on
many days, her career felt like being the farmer of ten-thou-
sand plastic cows. What could ever sway their permanent and
dopey pose? What was ever urgent here, and what would ever be
missed? Voices rose outside and she rolled her chair to the window where she saw the head gardener Lewis berating his men
for idling in the skirts of pachysandra. He was a sour, sinewy
guy, descended from a long line of Hunt-Paring employees, who
thought Francine's compliance with certain laws—such as pay-
ing disability when Virgilio lost the tip of a finger in the weed
whacker—went against the spirit of the Hunt-Parings. Which
she was absolutely sure it did, though she wouldn't ever say that
to Lewis. Did any visitor, eyes blinded by the ridiculous gluttony
of this family, ever wonder about how the wealth was gotten or
about the more than nine-hundred slaving voyages sponsored
by merchants like Mr. Hunt-Paring? She very much doubted it.
Wealth was blameless.

Beyond Lewis, Francine could make out the courthouse
downtown and the phalanx of radio vans and television trucks
following the Mayor's trial, now in its sixth week. Gleaming
mobile antennae rose in the sky like giant drinking straws; the
city might be sucked dry by this disgrace. For days, Sanford had
left the house at six o'clock, toothpaste foam rabid in the corners
of his mouth, to stand on line for a seat at the proceedings, only
to discover he'd been beaten out by people who were even more
obsessed than he was. At dinner with her husband, it was Dag
on linguine, Dag on the grille, Dag in the ice cube in her second
or third glass of wine. Their interest in the man looked enough
alike, but Francine's played with her mind in a way Sanford
could never imagine. Talking with him about Dag, she felt like
the criminal who makes a clumsy attempt at innocence when

he tells the detective to go ahead, search my closets, dig up my basement floor, I have nothing to hide.

Search my city, the mayor had taunted his accusers, ransack my administration and you'll find nothing amiss. It wasn't a bad town, after all, at least from the outside, but the place was rotten at heart; corruption and deceit ran through it like its river—deep, sludgy, and diverted so many times over the years no one could remember how it had originally flowed. There'd been too many years of people looking away, of not calling the mayor on anything while living off his largesse, and in this silence, Francine knew, was their complicity, and her own, now in her marriage.

*   *   *

She had met Dag at a barbeque on Ives Street the summer after college. She found his stride obnoxious but hard to ignore, because who strode when everyone else worked so hard to be smooth and steady? His voice was too loud in the jammed backyard, his accent too local, his haircut and clothes not quite right, he was a decade older than anyone there. *Ugh*, she'd said to a woman next to her, *who is that guy?*

Dag had appeared at first to know everyone at the party but have no one to talk to. She watched him move endlessly, offering *hi-how-are-ya's* and eyeing the imported beers and the cold crowd. When he tugged at his collar, she saw a heartbeat of self-consciousness in a single gesture.

"Tough crowd," he said when he caught her staring. Later, she understood he'd meant just the opposite; these were Ivy League pussies, not city lions. The men she knew expected to ease into the spots reserved for them, while she sensed Dag would soon sit atop the hill he had pushed together with his own hands. The people at the party might have disdain for him, but that didn't bother Dag. Already he accepted the realities of a public life; it wasn't a bad thing to be disliked, it was only a bad thing to be ignored. Already, he understood the division of his city, and here it was in the clearest form, even in the July night: him and her.

She shrugged. "So who do you know here?"

"No one yet." He smiled, swiped two beers off the steps she was sitting on, and slipped them into his pockets. "I try never to miss a good party though."

Of all his purposeful choreography that evening, it was the stealing of the beers, and no one challenging him—though he seemed almost to invite it—that she found so appealing. Because how could a person simply do that, take what he wanted and what wasn't his? It was near beautiful in its riskiness, as though this was an entirely different way to live and operate. She was excited by her sudden, illogical attraction to him and the way he was looking at her. No one would approve of what she might do with him or how she might slip into this other world, if only briefly. Already she felt the summer stretching too thin, her pose of independence and the prospect of graduate school losing a little more of its charm.

"I'm not sure how good a party this is," she'd told him. "There are probably better ones we could find."

He seemed surprised that she said anything more to him, and Francine saw that when it came to maneuvering through the uncertain corridors of the female heart, he was not nearly so sure of himself. She felt her own particular power slice through the air.

*   *   *

Below Francine, Lewis worked on his single topiary, a bear with stumpy, outstretched arms that looked to be begging for quarters. The blades of his shears sent cooling slivers of sound through the open window.

Dee leaned into the room. "There's a call," Francine's assistant said. "About booking an event." This wasn't Francine's department, and she gave the girl a look to show that she'd been in the middle of something very important. "It's about the Mayor," Dee added. "I thought you'd want this one."

I've been caught, Francine thought—but at what? And she hadn't been asked for by name, had she? "Yes, how can I help you?" she said officiously into the phone.

Friends of the Mayor, that infamous cabal, wanted to book the Hunt-Paring House for a private party.

"I thought maybe you were calling me to be a character witness." Francine laughed nervously, tipping too far back in her chair. "How original of me," she said when she'd righted herself. "Everyone must say that."

The woman on the other end was chilly. "I wouldn't know, I really don't have anything to do with that sort of thing."

It was pointless to explain that she'd been joking, when really she hadn't been entirely. And the woman hadn't questioned who Francine was to even know the Mayor enough to be a character witness, because everyone claimed to know the man, whether they thought he was a crook or not. Even Sanford recently referred to the time he'd personally met Dag.

"I'm surprised the Mayor's in the mood to celebrate right now," Francine said. She'd seen it that morning on the television again; the Mayor shrinking like an old lady, disgrace beginning to collect at his ankles like slipping stockings. She couldn't imagine that her fellow citizens would be too happy to look up the hill and see him dancing it up and smashing around in the flowerbeds.

"Before we go any further, I should tell you that during our busy season we require a 100% non-refundable deposit," Francine lied. "In other words, this policy applies to everyone."

"You understand I'm calling from Friends of the Mayor."

"I understand perfectly, and I'm sure the Mayor appreciates a democratic policy when he sees one. But tell me this: Why here?" She glanced at the porcelain rooster again, understanding finally at that moment its strange and strong appeal to her; the animal's essential ugliness had been made to look proud. "After all, it doesn't seem like his kind of place."

"The Mayor's always liked the house," the woman told her. "He's very interested in antiques and art, you know. It's one of his hobbies."

The Mayor's only hobby was politics and arm-twisting, and as far as Francine knew, he had never set foot in the Hunt-Paring House. Probably because there were no Bonicello's. The real answer to her question, Francine supposed, was much simpler; nowhere else would have him.

When the woman put her on hold, she thought about the time her sublet apartment had been broken into a month after she and the Mayor had started sleeping together. The police had told her it was junkies because it had all the earmarks of a smash and grab job. She'd been in the shower when it happened. Though she didn't have much worth stealing besides her radio and her electric typewriter, the break-in left her edgy and doubtful about staying. The Mayor had been calming, chummy with the cops. He stayed with her when she didn't want to stay alone, he brought over another typewriter and radio and she didn't ask him where they'd come from. At night, he made calls and parted the curtains to look outside. While she felt safer for it, she also knew that such protectiveness was frightening in its own way—because what did it say about what might happen without it? As she watched him one night surveying the dark street, Francine understood what she and Dag weren't to each other and never would be; they were too different for that to ever change. But most surprisingly, the same understanding had also felt like longing—to be known when it appeared impossible.

It would have been simple to lie then and say to the Mayor's organizer, the Panikolopolos-Chu wedding is on that evening you want, or the golden anniversary party of Mr. and Mrs. Walter Crestman is booked for the following week. Sorry, all full, she'd explain, and never have to see Dag in her world. Shut him out like she'd begun to shut off the television every morning, despite Sanford's protests. But oddly, it was that longing, unearthed after so many years as something still beating that kept her from turning the Mayor away.

She knew she'd have to inform the board and assuage the last Hunt-Paring who was hotly anti-Mayor and wouldn't want him fouling the family home. You may not like him, she'd explain with a degree of level-headedness that had always garnered respect—and to Sanford as well, though here she might have to look away—but the man hasn't been found guilty of anything yet, and isn't this still America, after all?

*   *   *

"If anyone tries to solicit a bribe from you, I'll cut their dick off," the Mayor had allegedly said. This was according to the latest reports from the trial she heard on Lewis's radio which he carried around with him as he pruned his way through the verdant grounds.

The Mayor would have said tits had he been threatening a woman. One night, Dag had taken her to Doubles, a popular waterfront restaurant wedged between the shipyards. The sign on the door said, "No Muscle Shirts Allowed." On a hot August night the parking lot was bright with tail lights and cigarettes and mobbed with people waiting to get in. Dag worked the crowd—now here were his people—like an elected official. He had a way in which his right hand would simply flip out, like a turning signal, to shake someone else's hand while still moving ahead. Francine knew she was out of place in her white pants and simple sandals, her hair pulled back. The Mayor wore a long-sleeved shirt and blue blazer, as though he'd come out of an important meeting and was on his way to another after dinner with his girl, when really, they'd just come from fucking in her overheated bedroom. He slipped the maitre d' some money and something whispered, and they were shown to a table by the window.

"All those people were here before us," she'd said, "and we just waltzed in front of them. And no one said anything." The cool power of what Dag had done left her both admiring and slightly ashamed. "I mean, is that fair?"

"Oh, I see. You want to get back in line," Dag said, a palm flat on the table. "I thought you were hungry, but if you'd rather wait for a couple of hours, fine."

It was breezy by the window, and the waitress smiled patiently. Dag nodded and then ordered what he always had— two chops, a second scotch. He made a face when she ordered bluefish. They'd had plenty of sex, and he always clung to her at the height of it, revealing himself to be terrified of those seconds out of control, but what did they really know about each other, including their tastes? During dinner, they discovered that while she'd been attending arty camps during the summers, he'd been working at his uncle's industrial laundry delivering clean linens to hotels and picking up dirty ones. Once he'd found an afterbirth wrapped in a pillow case.

"Must have been while you were playing the flute," he said, his tone and face suddenly hard. "From happy camp to happy college, and now what is it, happy graduate school? Art history? There's something useful. Jesus, you've had it easy, had it handed to you, and you never even wonder how it all happens. No wonder you're such a good girl." A bite of meat was suspended in front of his mouth as he cast a narrowed eye at her clothes, her unpainted nails, her spartan fish, and she saw that he had a deep, cellular disdain for her he didn't even realize.

His comment stung. "Well, who are you?" she demanded.

"Apparently I'm just the asshole who gets you the best table, who doesn't play fair according to you."

It was pointless for her to be defensive; she'd only played at being someone who was secure. Their differences began to spread like a spill on the white tablecloth. He might marry a woman like me, she thought, and I might marry a man like him, because we'd mistakenly think it is brave and good to colonize foreign soil. But she didn't know who he was anymore than he knew who she was or how privilege wasn't the same as certainty or power, neither of which she felt she possessed. The tide went out during the rest of their wordless, unraveling dinner, revealing the abandoned bones of an old dock.

Later that night, Dag took her to the armory at the top of Lincoln Hill, a deserted brick building with vast high-ceilinged rooms. The place had a disheartened, pissed-in smell, and was dark except for the moonlight that came in through panes etched with dirt. Chalkboards and chairs were pushed against the walls, the general and colonels having abandoned their fortress seemingly in a great hurry. She felt the need to hold on to Dag's arm, to salvage the evening, and though he had appeared at first to be on proprietary terms with the place, brandishing his gleaming key at the front door, he didn't seem to know where the staircase up to the view was.

"You haven't been here before, have you?" she asked.

"Of course I have," he told her, and then with the kind of logic she'd see later in his years in City Hall, he explained, "How else do you think I got a key?"

Eventually they found the stairs to the turret. It was a beautiful night by the open view, heat tempered with a breath of approaching September, and the trees mixed it up wildly. Dag pointed out various sites, named the neighborhoods that spread out before them—*Kike Hill, Darktown, Spicville.* He told her about shifting routes and planned development and what used to be where.

"From this very site, in fact," he said, "our men fought the British. Not a great battle by any means, so you might not know of it, but it was significant—The Battle of Lincoln."

Francine heard stray noises below, rats possibly, but more likely the city's soul in a disgusted sigh at such a perversion, because she knew that what Dag had just told her was a complete lie. She'd done some research on the site once for an architecture project and knew that nothing more interesting than a four-minute visit from Lyndon Johnson had ever occurred in it. He turned in the moonlight to kiss her.

"That's not true," she said, pulling away from him, "about the battle. It didn't happen here. Nothing did."

"Shhh." He grasped her arm, touched her lips. His fingers smelled of dinner. "Don't be such a know-it-all. It's not attractive. I want to kiss you now."

There was a fluttering and a crash, as though a blackboard downstairs had fallen over. It's the wind, Dag assured as his grip on her tightened, the westerly summer gusts—had she ever spent a summer in his city? He ran his hands over her breasts and pinched her nipples meanly. She slapped his hands away.

"Why do you make things up?" Francine demanded. "Why do you pretend that you know everything? That's not attractive." They heard voices then, the tangled sounds of another man and woman in an argument. "We left the door open," she said breathlessly, fearful of being trapped on the turret, but also scared of Dag whose look was unreadable. "Maybe they'll go away."

He shook his head at her like a disappointed parent, and moved to the stairs. She followed, and by the time they reached the ground floor, the man and woman were engaged in a screaming match and wouldn't have noticed if she and Dag had just slipped out. They clutched at each other, off balance, sloppy and drugged-up.

"Get the fuck out of here," Dag barked, his spit silvering in the air. The two stopped, shocked straight for a minute. The woman, all teased hair and bones, moved away. Dag stood over the man whose eyes shifted unevenly.

"Piece of shit junkies," Dag said.

"Fuck you, fat asshole college boy," the man returned.

Junkies; Francine's spine burned with hate. They took her radio and typewriter and security, and if not them precisely, then one of their friends; the city was full of them, Dag had often told her. She watched Dag's body tense as he delivered a punch to the man's stomach. Like his woman, the junkie was unsteady and folded like wet paper. For Francine, the episode could have ended there—a measured, if imprecise retribution—with the man wheezing on his knees in the armory dust. But Dag took a jump and leveled an unnecessary, toppling kick to his kidneys. Twin jolts of shock and shame collided at the base of Francine's skull, a sensation that was tonal like the man's moan, so that many years later, a certain pitch could make her feel as though she were suspended at the top of a cliff, her fall imminent.

"Those people make me sick," the Mayor said when they

were out on the street. He took a greedy drag of his cigarette. "Fucking bloodsuckers."

"Why did you do that?" A cold fist had lodged in Francine's throat. "Why did you have to go so far?"

"So far?" Dag stopped and looked at her.

"You already hit him once. That was enough."

"Didn't you see that they were going to mug us? That he was going to rape you maybe, Francine?"

"He could hardly stand. You could have left them alone." She shook her head; how would she ever know what might have happened? "That wasn't right."

"Right," he repeated, and flicked his cigarette into the street. "Did I hear you trying to stop me? No, I didn't think so. One hit is okay, but two isn't? You want it both ways. Jesus, you're so fucking naïve."

For a week after, Francine's phone rang but she wouldn't answer it. A police cruiser crawled up and down her street and then disappeared. One night, Dag got inside the apartment building and called her name from the other side of the door. His tone was unfamiliar; locked out, fearful of his need for her, exposed. She thought of how he clutched her when he came. Through her misery, she understood that in their time together, he'd never hidden himself from her. He'd shown her exactly who he was, even that night in the armory. That much was honest in its own way, more so than she'd ever been with him. How could she admit that what she'd admired in him was also what she hated him for, and that maybe they were not so different? Much sooner than she'd imagined, he was silent, and then she heard him leave. Less than two months together, and it was over, a clean, if ugly cut; still it stunned her to have been moved past so easily, to have left him so untouched.

There never was anything in the paper about a dead junkie,

Francine had gone to grad school as planned, gotten married, had kids, and become Executive Director. She knew exactly how her life had happened, step by step, though on some days it still surprised her. Occasionally when she drove down Manton Avenue, she'd look for the pair from the armory, and every time she was waylaid by an addict in the supermarket parking lot, she'd give him a few dollars. A number of times since that night in the armory, she and Sanford had seen the Mayor eating alone in a restaurant—alone despite his popularity—and it never failed to recall for her his plaintive voice outside her door, and how she might have opened it again if he'd waited a little longer.

*   *   *

By August, no one could say if the Mayor would go to prison if convicted, but his opponents pawed at the air, anxious to get into the ring and take the title from him. On Thursday, Sanford brought home two "Langstrom for Mayor" placards and stuck them in the front yard.

"The guy talks about how the people want clean government as though this is some brilliant insight," she told Sanford. "But we're too far past that. This isn't kindergarten, for chrissake. I really don't want those signs up."

"Langstrom's not perfect," Sanford argued, "but this says we're ready for something else. The reign of Dag is over." Her husband's enthusiasm had a hard edge to it. "You think all this deception and intimidation doesn't ever reach down to where you are? Think again. You're scared of it just like everyone else," he told Francine, as though she were to blame, and the Mayor's upcoming party was only more evidence of her corruptibility. "And that's pretty fucking sad."

A few nights later, she vandalized the signs which were

already softened by the sprinkler that had gone on at midnight. They'd been too much like For Sale signs, she realized, suggesting flight. The next morning Sanford was distressed, but not really surprised, when he looked out at the pieces of paper which littered the lawn.

In the city's last summer weeks, Lewis's lilies bent under their own weight, and the kids got on the camp bus like prisoners. Sometimes in the slow hours in her office, in the days before the Mayor's party, Francine sensed the Hunt-Paring House inching closer to death, not from inattention or dwindling funds, but from a lack of urgency. If it was change and progress that reaffirmed purpose, what was there left to do here? The rooster still sat on her desk—a defiant, tiny crime with a blue eye—as she fiddled with the final copy for the embroidery show. There was some beautiful, illuminating work, but the captivity of the women who made the pieces was overwhelming to her.

By mid-day of the Mayor's party, an affable breeze had wrapped itself around the house, showing up like the caterers to set things in motion, and at just after seven, Francine watched from her office window as the Mayor stepped out of his Lincoln. For the second he stood directly below her, his head was a landing pad for a drop of rain or spit. The tanned skin of women in backless dresses punctuated a grove of dark suits. Beyond the party and down the hill, the city was beginning to light up while her office darkened. She felt the arrhythmic pulse of a car stereo down the block.

"So? Tell me everything that's happened," Sanford urged when she called later, but she had only a single detail to give him; she'd been the Mayor's lover once.

"I don't have anything to tell," she said.

He hesitated. "Are you okay then?"

"I should go," she said, risk fading fast in her.

There were people arguing in the bathroom down the hall when no one was supposed to be upstairs. Months ago, Francine had taken her first of many baths there on a late Sunday afternoon when the house was empty and she was lured by the prospect of a soak in these aristocratic waters. It was a luxurious basin with silken sides and such a rushing sound of water it was like standing by the cataract of a waterfall loud enough to drown out any sense that she shouldn't be there. This too had become her private room, a strand of her pubic hair teasing at the drain, the ghost of her wet footprints on the floor.

As she stood outside the bathroom, she heard that it was the Mayor doing the belittling of whoever was in there with him. In a minute, the door opened, and a man fled down the stairs. When she looked in, Francine would have liked to see the Mayor gazing achingly from the window at the town he'd screwed, his shoulders falling in resignation that he'd made a mess of things. What the city wanted, what it really needed, she knew, was not just his apology, but his admission. But what she saw instead was the Mayor about to take a piss without lifting the toilet seat.

"Oh, no," she said, alarmed, "you can't do that here. You have to go downstairs."

He laughed without looking at her and zipped up. "It's been a while since anyone told me where I could take a leak."

Get used to it, she was tempted to say. "This is not a public bathroom."

He held his hands up in an exaggerated defense. "Okay, okay, I didn't do it, I promise." There was still an aggressive charm to his tone.

"These rooms are private, off-limits."

"So I gather." He straightened his tie and turned to stare down the faceless, dark space where she knew he couldn't see her. "My mistake then, obviously. I thought these were public rooms. You know—for everyone."

These were Francine's words, spoken as though she were trespassing in the Mayor's house again, instead of the other way around. How stupid she was, she told herself, hurrying towards her office, to think that he hadn't recognized her that night, or that he might not have known where she'd always been during these years. Or that he was here now by chance.

"Why don't you tell me about some of these pictures," he said, pursuing her. "Looks like you keep the good stuff up here— you know, where the public's not allowed. And why not, really— they wouldn't appreciate it. Dopes. What's this one?"

Francine turned to see the Mayor pointing at a canvas; he was still the guy who let the tip of his finger get too close.

"James Marsh Millicent," she said. "And don't touch, please."

"How about this one?" It was a murky, failed landscape. The Mayor tapped at it.

"That's a Bonicello," she told him.

"Bonicello. Okay, now there's a guy I've heard of."

She'd hoped to provoke him with this, but what could she make of his answer? He touched the painting again, this time tracing a line of horizon with his fingernail.

"You're missing your party," she said. "You should go."

"I'm in no hurry. You know how many parties I've been to? Hundreds and hundreds. It's nice up here anyway. I can see why you keep it to yourself."

The Mayor moved past her—he only seemed taller now, she thought—and went into her office. He let out an entitled sigh as he lay back and lifted his shoes onto the velvet chaise. In that moment, she saw her career for what it really was, a collection of small moves, old furniture and old habits, the last edge of her youth and possibility—and this crooked man lying across it.

"You've done okay for yourself," he said, looking up at the ceiling. "Perfect, all your fancy things here." He stood and walked around the room. "You did all right."

"I worked hard for it, too. I envied you. Did you know that? You always knew where you wanted to go and exactly how to get there. It wasn't that easy for me," she told him. "But now, well, it looks like you're going to prison."

"Hey," he laughed, "do you know something I don't know?" He moved to her desk, touching her papers, her glasses, her pens, her porcelain rooster. She saw her unease register in his face and the methodical trespassing of his touch. "Nothing's over. I haven't done anything I'm ashamed of." Her calendar, her mail, her sweater on the back of the chair. "And how about you? Are you still so good?"

"Your party's waiting for you."

"It always is," he said.

The Mayor's hand hovered indecisively over her things, and then he picked up the rooster and boldly put it in his pocket. He looked at her, waiting for her to say something. But she was speechless, furious and thrilled into silence, and he left the room. Here, still, was his greatest skill as a politician; he knew what to forget, and what to remember. And in this small criminal gesture, Francine saw that he still knew, he remembered, exactly who she was.

Later, she took the back steps to the kitchen. The Hunt-Paring kitchen slaves were generations gone now, replaced by an army of good-looking catering staff. On every surface there was untouched plenty—platters of fish, towers of fruit, mousses slipping in the heat. Tomorrow the room would be sterile again; life having come and gone from the house as quickly as the party. She went into the pantry where trays of tiny fruit tarts were abandoned on the counter, the cherries and blueberries staring up at her like glazed eyes. She called Sanford on the phone.

"How's Dag's last supper?" he asked.

"There's so much here," she told him. "And it's all untouched. Desserts, a huge bowl of shrimp on ice, mostly melted. Who were they expecting?"

"Everyone loves the Mayor."

Francine was struck by the party givers' optimistic miscalculations, when the end of the Mayor's career was written in the abundant and now wasting food. "Brie, strawberries. Glasses of champagne. I'm going to bring it home."

"I won't eat his food, I don't want anything of his in my house," Sanford announced. Francine could hear the dog snoring next to her husband on the bed. "Come home now. What do you need to stay for?"

It was her job, she explained. When she looked out into the garden, Francine saw the Mayor stumble badly into the pachysandra and the determinedly festive night. His back was against the Hunt-Paring's fence with its wrought iron H's as the city blinked and breathed behind him. She knew she could march outside and call him on what he'd done, expose his thievery of a trinket as his last pathetic act. But his vitality was still undeniable and unchanged, and now his pulse was quickening—Francine could see it in how his eyes drifted to where he might go next. She was excited by her decision not to say anything. After all, she'd stolen it first, and it was this beautiful riskiness that they had in common, after everything, liars and thieves that they both were.

THE AERIALIST

Forty years old and his first time at the circus. Glorious. Next to him, his girlfriend's son Jack flipped through the program whose vigorous line drawings reminded Hollis of a sex manual. A spotlight rose on the ringmaster. With a full moon ass rising in white satin pants, she adjusted the strap of her high-heeled shoe. Hollis had expected a man with a mustache. He expected a contortionist too, tiptoeing poodles, a guy shot from a cannon, but if he didn't get any of that here at the Single Planet Circus, it was enough to be with the boy under this white canvas swoop, the boy's hand resting on Hollis's knee. Just the two of them, like father and son. Which they weren't.

Jugglers tossed bowling pins, and a man in a grass skirt and pale chest sashayed around unappetizingly. Hollis bought caramel apples from a hawker. Four trapeze artists—called trapezoids, he told the boy, who at seven didn't get it but laughed anyway—arced through the air. Hollis's stomach swooned at the beauty, the angles of leg and arm, the slapping clasp of wrist. Their last-second grasps were charged with death's possibility. He sank his exultant front teeth into the apple, tasted the sweet, the tart, then the icy knife of pain that sliced his palate and lodged between his tearing eyes. He waited for his life to reel out before him, but nothing came. And what did that mean? Only how little he'd lived! His agony was fluorescent, religious. He was going to die. Drool slid down his chin.

"You sound weird," Jack said. "Are you sloshed?"

Hollis pointed at the half of his front tooth that was planted in the caramel like a tiny headstone. He couldn't watch what was left of the circus because the aerialists were like angels coming to take him home. His pain had turned him into a Baptist. Noise throbbed in colors behind his eyelids. When the show was over, there was a jostling climb from the bleachers and a nudge that made Hollis afraid his head was going to roll off his neck.

He and Jack emerged into the rosy summer night and walked to the car parked in Middletown's First Church lot. The boy twirled on the steps, cheered by the cicadas and a child's eternal summer. Hollis had never seen anything so beautiful, and had never felt such agony at the same time. Maybe this was life and now he'd experienced it. He didn't know what he'd do if the pain reared up while he was driving back to Providence, but he understood the value of his cargo nodding off in the back seat. Holy shit, he needed a dentist bad, and it was a Sunday night. If no dentist would take him tomorrow morning, he'd have to find an emergency solution, even if it was a drunk with pliers in a garage in Woonsocket. He urged himself toward distraction. The lines on the highway, the dusty moon, the horse trailer ahead of him with the view of a swaying chestnut rump and tail. Bonnie, his former wife. Perfect, he thought; he'd managed to land on the greatest pain of all.

She had fallen in love with someone else, but wouldn't tell him who, as if their marriage was a game of switcheroo. One night, meeting the sympathetic side of their friends at a restaurant, Hollis had been ravenous, but when his eggplant covered with a duvet of cheese arrived in front of him, he lost his appetite. He'd also lost the ability to say anything even remotely interesting, so he'd gone to the bathroom to examine himself in the mirror. He was failure itself, slump-shouldered and pasty. He saw something between his upper front teeth and he picked ineffectually at the splotch. Dental decay. Bonnie had never mentioned it, but there it was.

Joseph Bondino, DMD, walked into the bathroom while Hollis was leaning over the sink. The man took a piss without noticing Hollis. He was just that kind of smug, arrogant bastard. The walls were black granite, a Mafioso look, and Bondino was equally slick in a black shirt and ice-blue tie. Tonight, the man was far from the blur in a white coat and blue paper mask he and Bonnie had been going to for years.

"Hey, Doc," Hollis said. He'd become the kind of idiot who called doctors "Doc." Bondino turned his carnivorous head, snapped a paper towel and dried his overpaid hands.

"I need to ask you something." Hollis approached with his teeth bared. "See this?"

Bondino wouldn't look. "Call the office in the morning. The girls will give you some names."

"What do I need names for? You're my dentist."

"Let's be men about this, okay?" Bondino said, lifting his chin. "Now, excuse me."

Hollis's balls shotgunned into his gut. Christ. Bonnie was doing the dentist. He'd heard dentists were oversexed, and what was that joke about their always having their tool in someone's mouth? Stumbling back to the dining room, he saw Bondino with his wife, the poor dense cluck with her zuppa and bread-sticks. Just the thought of it now made the roots of his busted front tooth twist in pain.

Lil and her ex-husband Patrick were on the couch when Hollis and Jack got back. A fan half-heartedly churned the heat and a shared joke. It wasn't Patrick's night with Jack, but there he was once again, just hanging around. After almost a year with Lil, Hollis still didn't know what to do with all their post-marital chumminess. It wasn't hard to understand why they were still friends, their boy aside. Patrick was charming in a surfboard-ish way, the type you'd wrongly assume was dumb, with a blameless grin and eyes the color of an electrolytic sports drink. And Lil, the classic science nerd girl, who'd grown into her gawkiness without really ever having outgrown it. Every day she wore clunky black shoes, the kind worn by parochial school boys, so unsexy they were actually sexy. Scattered, optimistic Lil, with her disorganized giggle and gazelle legs. She took nothing too seriously. Once she had told Hollis that mistrust was the reason for the breakup of her marriage, which Hollis took to mean that Patrick had cheated on her. He could spot the rawness of that well enough in himself and he was sure he'd sensed it in Lil, too, from the first time they met, the way she evaded and drifted into grinning, wounded distraction. Patrick had all the swinging ease of a man with an irresponsible dick. Hollis was shorter, darker, with a stubbled chin, and jealous cock.

Jack ran across the room and tackled his father. Hollis hissed in pain; his vision became a singed spot where Lil's face was meant to be. He folded, hands on knees, and a line of spit reached to the floor.

Lil jumped up. "Hey, sweetie. What's the matter?"

"He hurt his tooth," Jack explained. "On a candy apple. He can't talk. Not even one word."

"You poor guy," Lil said, and ran her hand across his back. "Which tooth? Open up." Hollis shook his head.

Patrick, with the boy riding him like a knapsack, leaned in. "Let me look, man," he said. "Open up, don't be a pussy."

What could Patrick, a guy who owned a bike shop with erratic hours, know about teeth? Patrick's face nearly touched Lil's. With their thin noses and blond affability, they could be related. Lil lifted her upper lip as though Hollis, like a monkey, would mimic her. Which he did.

"Wow, you broke it right off," she said, sucking in a breath. "That must have hurt like hell."

"I can see his tonsils," Jack said, peering in. "They're all rubbery."

"They are kind of rubbery," Patrick confirmed. Hollis clamped shut. What he needed was something to annihilate the pain immediately.

"Let me call your dentist, find out what we should do," Lil said. Hollis drew a fatal blade across his throat, then pointed a gun at his temple. "Wait, you're kidding. Do you mean you haven't been to a dentist since that asshole Bondino? That was five ago." Lil's nose wrinkled. "I have to tell you—that's a little gross."

Hollis went into Lil's bathroom. The florid orange ball of Jack's bathing suit still lurked near the shower drain days after they'd been to Horseneck Beach. Lil didn't see things like this, but the unattended bothered Hollis. It was like Patrick hanging around, something unfinished. Lil rummaged through her medicine cabinet, tumbling bottles onto the counter. Everything but the aspirin had expired and she rained a pharmacopeia of pills into the toilet.

Patrick told her to stop; the medicines made fish grow boobs. "In the meantime." He handed Hollis a glass of scotch and a straw. "Bottoms up, you poor fucker. Then you're coming with me. I have something for you at my house. You can crash there."

Hollis sucked up the drink, and because prudence could not compete with pain, he followed Patrick out to the man's ancient station wagon. Patrick lived above his bike shop, across the street from a house full of summer school students sitting on the front steps smoking and flicking lit matches into the dusty yard. The

UNRAVISHED

apartment wasn't what Hollis had imagined—a place stuffed with the detritus of a boy-man. Instead, it was spare and worn, a little sad. His own luggish brick house was twenty-five minutes away. It had been Bonnie's choice, and then she'd saddled him with it like an old dog. He'd never warmed to the place that swallowed sound—and truth, apparently—and stood as an example of a particularly dreary period in suburban architecture. It was the wrong place for him, director of the city's preservation society, to live, a neighborhood where kids watched TV in the middle of the day.

"Take anything you want," Patrick said, offering up a display in his medicine cabinet. "Percocet, Vicodin, Tylenol with Codeine, Mylanta, Immodium, Sudafed." Maybe he was a hypochondriac or an addict. There was a bottle of antibiotics with Lil's name on it, a souvenir from their time together.

"I get it," Patrick said. "You can't make up your mind. I don't blame you." He took a pill out of a label-less bottle and handed it to Hollis, who didn't especially care what it was, as long as it worked. Soon he was having a hard time seeing the outlines of things, and found himself on the couch with Patrick blurry and squatting in front of him.

"Does Lil love me?" Hollis asked. His lips felt like inner tubes. He knew he had no pride anymore. "Does she still love you? I'm nothing like you. I'm loyal. I wouldn't hurt her. Do you still love her? Of course you do, I mean, Jesus, who wouldn't?"

"Hollis? You okay? I can't understand a word you're saying. Maybe you should stop talking."

"Is that why you're around so much? Do you want her back? Have you apologized enough for being a dog? I love her. I love Jack, too. But I can't deal with you. I'm not big enough for that."

"Christ, you're a mess. Wipe your drool. I'm taking you back to Lil's."

The next time Hollis opened his eyes, Lil was undressing him and Patrick was in the bedroom doorway. Hollis wondered if this was *Rosemary's Baby* revisited, sex with the devil, a trade for Lil. He'd do it in a minute, except that an erection seemed out of the question. He woke to a moment of midnight clarity, Lil's face pressed against his ribs. He'd ask her to marry him, but he wasn't sure she'd say yes, though he wasn't sure she'd say no, and soon he was alert to the fuzzy hot light of Monday morning. He was alone in the bed. Through the heaviness of an opiod hangover, his pain was exquisitely tuned to match his heartbeat. Lil had gone to work, Jack to camp, and she'd left him a straw on the pillow, hearts drawn on its thin wrapper. You had to love a woman who did that.

Hollis emailed his office that he wouldn't be in, and then looked up Dr. Shetty, the dentist he'd been to when he was in college in Providence. He realized that last night he'd dreamed about her filling his mouth with cotton hotdogs and wiping his brow with silk. After all these years, he didn't expect her to still be in business, but there she was at the same address, even answering the phone herself, and yes, she had time this morning to see him—which probably wasn't a good sign, because it meant that she didn't have many patients. If she recognized his name— and why would she through his garbling and the decades—she didn't say so. She'd be in her sixties now, or older, but he pictured her younger self in that purple sari and white coat, her serious, wide face in that same office with its non-clinical furniture and dripping sink, its smell of coriander and rubbing alcohol, its spider plant reaching towards a window.

He drove shakily to Pawtucket. Fortunately, the town, on the downside of progress for years, was post-apocalyptically empty in the merciless July sun, and he didn't come close to killing anyone. The apartment building that held Dr. Shetty's ground floor practice hadn't changed, its dim lobby stinking of laundry and onions. His heart burbled with apprehension; there would be pain, he knew her style. A young Indian woman in blue jeans and a pink tank top that showed off notable biceps let him in. Then he remembered: Dr. Shetty's daughter, a girl of five or six back then, who'd sat in the waiting room with him. Was this the same girl who'd put down her crayons when he'd put down his book as though she'd been taught to be a good little hostess to her mother's patients?

She had a poppy seed bagel in her hand and a smear of cream cheese on her upper lip. She was intensely beautiful, with not-so-friendly eyes. The empty waiting room had a desk, mismatched chairs and a plastic orange couch. Dr. Shetty's daughter, if he was right about who she was, handed him a clipboard with a sheet to be filled out. Her hands were calloused and red, the nails cut short.

"Been here. Twenty years ago." His lip flared to avoid contact with his gum. He sounded demented. He was blushing, sweating, trying not to stare. A single AC groaned.

"Too long ago," she said, took him into the office, and sat him in the chair. Her earrings were cheap gold chains that swung when she clipped a paper bib around his neck with a crisply bored motion. A poppy seed was stuck in her front teeth. Compared to this worn-out room, Bondino's office, with his slaphappy hygienists, was NASA, full of ruthless technology and the yen for other men's wives. Soon he heard Dr. Shetty and her daughter arguing in another room. He couldn't hear their words, but they were so fierce with each other that his shoulders rose to his ears. And on it went with great passion and piercing consonants until Dr. Shetty emerged from battle, and gave him the same vaguely disappointed look she'd given him two decades earlier. Hollis was amazed that she was now much closer to his age than she'd been back then. Older had looked old then; older looked young now, though thicker. She was no beauty, nothing like her daughter. She'd traded her thick-rimmed glasses for rimless ones and today wore a white coat over jeans and rubber Adidas sandals with graying white socks.

"I understand you were here once," she said, no trace of the recent fight in her smoothly accented voice. She pulled up to him on a wheeled stool and told him to open up. She lifted an instrument and his mouth slammed shut.

"I see," she said. "It hurts. How did this happen?"

"Caramel apple. At the circus," he slurred.

"Aren't you a little old to be going to the circus and eating caramel apples?"

"First time," he said.

"Do you think you're in a movie? A children's book? Are you a child? And what did you think would happen there?"

"Took a boy."

"Open. This one"—she tapped his bottom left incisor—"I worked on this, didn't I." She sat back, and allowed a small smile. "I remember—you were that silly boy who juggled pool balls to impress a girl. And how did that work out?"

"Married. Left me." He wiped spit off his lower lip. "For a dentist."

"Ah, she left you for a dentist." Dr. Shetty clearly found this amusing.

Juggling pool balls, his only trick as a college senior, Hollis had taken his eye off the yellow one for an instant to look at Bonnie, the girl he was in love with. A week before, he'd let her pierce a hole in his fleshy earlobe, using an ice cube she'd been sucking on as anesthesia. He'd worn one of her studs. When the pool ball fell, it snapped off his incisor so cleanly that the thing looked like an orange seed on the floor. Everyone laughed at first, including Bonnie, who then fled with the others. He fell deeper for her that minute. Even then, he'd confused the pangs of pain with the pangs of love. "Should have listened to your advice." It wasn't easy to speak. "You said that trying to impress girls never works."

"No." Dr. Shetty crossed her arms over her chest. "I never give advice. I didn't say that."

"And you wore a sari."

"You're mistaken." She paused. "That girl ran away when you were hurt and you still married her. Tell me, does that make sense? What did you think would happen?"

She shook her head. Back then, she had put her hand on his forearm to soothe his dental and romantic distress. She must have seen him as a foolish boy. What could she possibly make of his romantic life these days? He was still a foolish boy, still trying to squeeze a woman's love out of a tube. He looked into her eyes that peered into his mouth. They were the briny green of capers. Was there anything more intimate? No wonder people hated to go to the dentist; it was like having your soul excavated with a pick ax. He'd developed a ridiculous crush on her years before, which he hadn't remembered until a remnant of it rose like a tattered flag. Dr. Shetty placed a lead blanket over his organs and took X-rays. She said he'd need a root canal and brandished a needle of Novocaine. She told him to relax as she poked it into his gum with a pinch that made him wince. A warm, stoned stain spread through him, but when she tapped the shard of tooth, he shot out of the chair. Tears spilled down his cheeks. She clucked and gave him another boost of the stuff.

"Your sari was purple," he managed to say.

"Nonsense," she said. "Don't talk."

Dr. Shetty's daughter came in and they sat on either side of him. They snapped at each other in whispers. Dr. Shetty explained that Hollis had been at the circus and then she let out a dismissive puff of air that reached the bridge of his nose. His jaw was unhinged as she ground away in his mouth, but he wasn't really there. Dark hairs on the daughter's forearm lined up as she readjusted the spit sucker. Noise was everything. She chewed gum. Dr. Shetty gave him a curious look and he knew he was going out, that maybe his eyes were rolling to the back of his head. The pleasantly warm wander, the jerk of the foot, the leady body melting into the chair. The relief was blissful. His erection cheered on. He found himself out on the waiting room couch, his face stuck to the orange plastic. His t-shirt had ridden up and his soft belly was sticking out, the hairs in pasty swirls. There was a somber woman sitting in a chair, her black purse on her lap, staring at him. He ran his tongue over the temporary tooth. Pain beat away like a flat tire on asphalt.

Dr. Shetty's daughter appeared and blocked the woman's view. "You okay? Personally," she whispered, "I think you're on some strong shit. I've seen it happen before. Novocaine's not a great mixer. You were saying some totally weird stuff. You can't drive, you know." Her biceps twitched fetchingly. "You have someone who can pick you up?"

"Lil," he said, and handed her his cell phone before he went out again. When he woke, the woman across from him was gone and Patrick was at the front of the room, perched on the desk and talking to Dr. Shetty's daughter. Smirking, smooth Patrick with his cargo shorts and flip-flops and girlish ankles.

"You're looking a little damp there," Patrick said. "Need a bib?"

"Where's Lil?"

"Couldn't leave the lab. She sent me instead, you lucky guy."

"Don't you ever work?" Hollis pushed himself up to sitting. His head was a water balloon. He pressed his temples. "Christ.

What did you give me last night?"

Patrick and Dr. Shetty's daughter, those two flirting, vigorous beauties, found his question hilarious and laughed with their faces turned to the stained ceiling panels. Patrick squeezed one of her golden biceps. They sucked the air out of the room. Their cells yearned to collide; their attraction to each other was going to short out the AC. It was remarkable, enviable. Hollis didn't think that he and Lil had ever made those kinds of fireworks. The infatuated pair maneuvered Hollis into Patrick's car, and then stood on the sidewalk and talked while Hollis sweat and tilted the rearview mirror to see himself. The temporary tooth was an improbable white that made his other teeth look shabby. His face was puffy, his lower lip swinging loose. Dr. Shetty was still not a great dentist.

"Jane says you have an appointment next week,' Patrick said, when he got into the car.

"Jane?"

"Jane. That's her name. The dentist's daughter. She's gorgeous, isn't she? Did you see those arms? I want them around my neck, around my everything. And that voice. I think I'm in love."

"Don't be an asshole."

"No, I mean it. It's like we've just been waiting to find each other. And your tooth did it." He knocked Hollis on the shoulder. "We're seeing each other later. Can't wait." He pulled onto East Avenue. "Jane told me you had a boner the entire time. Way to go. I mean, why not?"

Christ almighty, Hollis thought, fall in love and fly away already, will you please?

The Novocaine still held at dinner, and Hollis's upper lip flapped as strands of spaghetti beat his chin. Jack laughed himself off the chair and onto the floor where he contemplated the underside of the table and twitched like a beetle. Lil tickled him with her bare foot. The boy's childhood was a formless thing, a cloud lit from behind that Lil let float any way it wanted. It made for a dreamy, inventive kid. Hollis could watch him for hours.

"Kiss me," Hollis said to Lil, when Jack had crawled out of the room. He puckered up as best he could. "I want to know what it would feel like to be someone else kissing you. And you kissing him."

Lil pressed her mouth against his then sat back. "So, what's it like?"

"Soft," he said. Her hair was gathered messily at the back of her head. "Room temp, a little parmesan-y, nice. So how does the other person feel about kissing me?"

She leaned her chair back, her chin lifting. "Who are we talking about now?"

"You."

"Okay, but who's kissing me then? I'm confused."

He knew she was playing with him. "Me. The guy who loves you," he said, and waited for her respond. Which she didn't beyond letting the front legs of her chair hit the floor. "Just tell me. Do you still love Patrick?" he asked.

"Come on, Holl. We've done this."

"Because I'm having a hard time with him being around all the time. It confuses me, if you want to know the truth."

"A marriage is not Netflix. I don't have to return the guy when I'm done," she said. "He's my son's father."

Another woman might try to assuage him, but not Lil. She was tough that way. "You didn't answer my question," he said. He knew the bind—how you could pine for the one who really did a job on you. Bonnie. Red hair, stubby fingers, cold, cold blood. Sometimes he'd wake with a perplexing sense of missing her.

Lil looked at him with a half-smile that let him know she wasn't going to answer. She pressed her lips to the top of his head "Whose brain am I kissing now?" she asked. "Because it tastes kind of insecure. It tastes like it wouldn't know love if it bit him on the ass."

He grasped her by the waist and pressed his face into her belly. He threatened to bite her ass. She ran her fingers across his scalp. It felt like love, didn't it? He thought of the rearrangement of atoms between Patrick and Jane. He went into the other room and lay next to Jack on the floor, their shoulders touching. The boy had turned off the lights and pulled the shades and shined a flashlight on the ceiling where his mother had randomly pasted glow-in-the-dark stars. Hollis would have made sure to recreate the constellations; it would have bugged him not to get it right.

"This is what space is like," Jack said.

"I see." It is what my feelings for Lil are like, Hollis thought, a light looking for some identifiable constellation to land on. He adored the feel of the boy resting on his arm.

"Where's my dad?" Jack asked.

Another beam of light looking for something to land on. "He had to work tonight," Hollis told him, knowing that Patrick was with Jane. Fucking by now, no doubt. "People need their bikes, sometimes even at night. It's very important work."

Patrick zipped into the drive-thru for a bag of donut holes, Jane's favorites. "Even though she's in training, she cheats," he said, clearly charmed. "She's like a kid who thinks that if no one sees her eat one, it doesn't really count. God damn adorable."

"Training for what exactly?" Hollis asked.

"You won't believe it." Patrick whisked his long hair behind his ears. He'd spent the past seven nights with Jane, only twice stopping by in the evening to wrestle with Jack for a few minutes. It was fine with Hollis that he wasn't around, but the boy's disappointment was tough to take. His flashlight was still lying on the living room floor. "The trapeze. She's an aerialist."

"That explains the biceps." Rain watered the Pawtucket concrete. Hollis's own life suddenly seemed too much lacking in that kind of whimsy.

"She's fearless. She was in dental school, but hated it, grossed out by bad breath and nasty things that lurk between your teeth." Patrick wiggled his fingers. "But her mother won't let her leave, won't even watch Jane practice on the trapeze. That kills her."

So Jane was courageous except when it came to her mother.

"Besides, people hate dentists, and who wants to be hated? Aerialists and bicycles, on the other hand, make people happy. Have you ever seen someone who's just bought a bike? Fucking euphoria. The best is when I fix someone's bike that's been sitting in the garage for years. It's like I've brought a past lover back from the dead."

Patrick slammed on the brakes as a dog ran out between the parked cars.

"That was too close," Hollis said. Infatuated lovers made lousy drivers. "Seriously, Patrick. Don't you have a job to go to? You didn't have to drive me." How had it happened, he wondered, that he actually liked the man, despite everything?

"What does a job matter when it comes to love?" Patrick laughed and fished a blue pill out of his shorts pocket. "Here. For your nerves."

"I'm not nervous." Hollis's bladder throbbed and his fingertips tingled. He hadn't slept last night imagining today's torture. "I just don't like pain."

"Just take it. Trust me."

Hollis took the pill. Patrick's theories on love had stirred something up in him. What did anything matter when it came to that? He could preserve a hundred houses of historical significance, and it still wouldn't equal Lil. Once again, there were no other patients in Dr. Shetty's waiting room. How could she survive like this? Patrick smirked at Hollis when the arguing voices of mother and daughter rose from another room.

"Tough relationship," Patrick whispered. "They're tigers, lions. Definitely some kind of cat. Very sharp claws."

Jane appeared, her jaw set at a furious angle as she performed her morning's duties, jabbing on the computer, snatching charts, yanking open the curtains to fill the room with the rain's ashen light. She wore running pants and a white tank top that revealed her seething chest. Patrick's face fell—she hadn't yet acknowledged him—and he looked like a boy the school bus had just zoomed past. But then Jane gave him a slinky kiss on the mouth and took the bag of donuts.

"Sorry," she said, and smiled contritely. "Just another blow-out with the boss. I needed a minute to get my head back."

Dr. Shetty leaned out of the office and motioned for Hollis to come in. He sat while she banged drawers and huffed around in her foul mood.

"That must have been quite a fight," he said. "You both seem pretty upset."

"What fight? What are you talking about," she snapped. "Open." She stared into his mouth for too long. Her fingers held open his jaw as if she were practicing mind control over a crocodile. She was going to hurt him today. She wasn't on her game.

"Jane," she yelled too close to Hollis's ear, and then frowned at him. "Is that man out there a friend of yours?"

"Friend? Not sure. My girlfriend's ex-husband."

"Well, I don't like him. He's a fool. And my daughter's a fool around him."

"Fools fall in love." Whatever it was he'd taken was starting to make him smoothly moronic.

"What does that mean?"

"It's a song."

"I know it's a song. But why is he here all the time? What are you doing with him anyway? It's wrong. It will confuse you. And you're already confused enough."

It was a funny thing about her; she could scold and be almost kind at the same time. Hollis felt corrected for his own good. "I am confused," he said, "but I thought you didn't give advice."

"That's not advice. That's a fact." She glared at the door.

"I remember when Jane was a little girl," he said, edging into wooziness. "And now she's an aerialist." He waved his hand through the air. "Like this. It's stunning to watch." He wondered if he was confusing the glorious art with the pain to come.

Dr. Shetty shook her head. "What kind of a thing is that? It's crazy. It makes no sense." She filled her needle with Novocaine. A few drops arced icily in the air. He didn't like the look of the needle and Dr. Shetty's maternal rage coming at him.

"Wait," he said.

She held the needle aloft. "A grown woman should not want to fly through the air. That's for children."

"All the more reason to do it. You and me; maybe we're just uptight." He questioned his own logic but went on. "Maybe we got old too quickly. Have you ever seen someone on a trapeze? You have no idea how exciting it is, and how elegant and brave." She approached him with the needle again; she was ready for him to shut up. "Have you ever seen Jane on the trapeze?" he asked, though he already knew.

"I have no interest in that. Open. I have other patients waiting."

"No you don't."

Dr. Shetty's eyebrows dipped as she jabbed the needle into

his gum. "I need her here." She shook her head and stepped back to watch him drift away on the warm current of his morning cocktail. "You wouldn't understand."

"She has to live her own life," he slurred. "Where is your husband, Dr. Shetty? Is he dead? Did he leave you?"

"This is *her* life," she said, as though she hadn't heard his question. She turned to the window. "When I first started this practice," she said, "I couldn't see the river because there was a building in the way. Then they tore it down and now look at my view."

"It doesn't usually go like that. You're lucky. It's a good sign."

"A good sign of what, Mr. Berger? It could be a bad sign, the city falling apart around me. Who's to say?"

Jane appeared in a white coat. He felt drunk with their problems. She hooked the spit sucker with its oceanic pull on his lip. Dr. Shetty struggled to take off his temporary tooth. She had both hands in his mouth and they didn't fit. His head smacked against the chair as her knuckles bore into his lower lip. She was going to rip his mouth right off his face. Pounding, yanking, prying with a metal pick. He couldn't feel the hurt, but he knew his body was storing it up for later.

"Jesus Christ! Stop!" he yelled. "Please, stop. Please!"

"What is it with this guy?" Jane asked her mother, and they laughed long and hard at his goobledygook, détente at his expense. He thought he would piss himself. When the tooth finally came off, there was a hole in the back of his head and he could see space through it. And there was Jack with his flashlight looking for the stars again, and Hollis was looking for his father there, long dead of a heart attack while riding Amtrak. Grief came on with a garden hose of tears. He thought his heart would crack open with all the pain a human could store, and what he really wanted now was for Dr. Shetty to put her arms around him and tell him he'd be all right.

He opened his eyes to see her feeding instruments into the autoclave. She moved with the rhythm of her chore. He said her name.

"You're awake," she said, turning to him. Her green eyes were red.

"Are you okay?" he asked. 'Have you been crying, Dr. Shetty?"

"A morning for tears," she said, and wiped her eyes with her sleeve. "You were saying some very sad things. Terrible, sad things. Silliness, probably. I don't know what you're taking, but you shouldn't. You have to go through life with a clear mind. Drugs are for people who already know they're stupid."

Her funny, bossy theories. "Take a minute. Sit," he said.

"Yes, maybe I will." She pulled up the stool. "Do you have children, Mr. Berger?"

"No." He felt perfectly clear-headed now. Lil didn't want more children.

"Then I'm not sure you can understand."

"Can I ask you something? You seem lonely."

"That's not a question."

"What do you think it means that a woman leaves her son's bathing suit on the shower floor for days and days?"

"I think," she said, "that it reminds her of something nice, something she liked. And she wants to think of it again." She leaned over him and unclipped his bib. "She's in no hurry to forget what's good just to move on to the next thing."

Hollis dreamed he was falling, his body banging on granite crags, but the noise of bone on rock was really something happening in the kitchen: the cord from the window blind being gobbled up by the fan. Lil was asleep, a line of sweat on her upper lip, and she didn't stir in the stifling air. Hollis knew it had to be Jack sleepwalking again—as he'd started to do frequently, maybe because he missed his father who was hardly around since the advent of Jane, maybe because of the heat. The apartment had to be a thousand degrees. They could have all gone to his place with its haughty central air, but he couldn't bear to bring Lil and Jack there.

Hollis pulled on some shorts and went into the kitchen, where Patrick sat on the windowsill. He was naked, illuminated by the stove light, his uncircumcised dick too comfortable. He was eating cereal out of the box and washing it down with a beer.

"Shit, did I wake you up? Sorry." He tossed back a handful of Cheerios as if they were bar nuts. "Those kids across the street from me finally caught their house on fire. The whole thing up in flames, a shit box to begin with. The smoke was killing me."

"Maybe you should put on some shorts," Hollis said. "In case Jack wakes up."

"So he sees me naked. No problem." He took a beer out of the fridge and gave it to Hollis. "He has a dick, I have a dick, so do you, I'm guessing."

"It's more complicated than that." Hollis paused. "You haven't been around much. Jack misses you. Lil's pissed at you. Anyway, why aren't you at Jane's?"

"Are you kidding? I'm not allowed to sleep in her mother's house. It just wouldn't happen. Ever. Her mom hates me. Jane doesn't even spend the night at my place because she knows her mother's waiting up for her."

"She's a grown woman. Shouldn't she be making her own decisions?"

Patrick gave him an aged look. "Those are her decisions. I want to show you something." He put down the beer and the cereal and held his palms under the light to reveal a line of translucent blisters. Two of his nails had been ripped down to the base. "She's been giving me lessons, on the trapeze. It's like nothing else. You have to try it."

"I don't even like escalators," Hollis said, and felt an acute envy for Patrick's ability to attach to his own thrill. Where was his own?

The door to Jack's room opened, and the boy stumbled across the hall to the bathroom. They listened to him pee in the dark. When he stumbled out again, he looked at both of them, but saw neither it seemed, and moved towards them, eyes open, but in a sleepwalker's trance. His feet crunched fallen Cheerios. The men were still, their held breath heavy with expectation; choose me. Jack veered towards Hollis and leaned his face against his belly. Hollis kissed the boy's salty scalp, and steered him back to his bed. He arranged the clip-on fan to blow air across the boy's bare chest. His affection made him teary. He didn't want to leave the room and face Patrick.

Patrick was on the couch. "How long has he been doing that?" he asked.

"A few weeks. I'm sure he thought I was you. Actually, I'm sure he wasn't thinking anything." His victory was empty and painful.

"Maybe. He likes you. You know I love him more than anything, right?"

Hollis nodded. Minutes passed silently as the ceiling fan whispered through the air.

"I have shit on my lungs," Patrick said.

"Shit on your lungs. What does that mean?"

"Spots. They're going to kill me, maybe, who knows? Fucking doctors. I have to start treatment next month. It's going to do a number on me, make my hair fall out. Do me a favor and don't say anything to Lil. I haven't figured that out yet. Or Jack."

"Jesus, Patrick." Hollis's body seized. There was a glacier behind his eyes. "Jesus. I'm so sorry."

He turned off the lamp and waved Patrick to join him lying on the floor. The flashlight was still there from days earlier, and he trained it on the ceiling's random stars.

"Lil's universe," Hollis said.

When he handed the flashlight to Patrick, the man shined it in the corners of the room, as though trying to force the angles to open. A chair's arm was a woman's gestures, the boy's sneakers, with their tongues and laces, like strange vegetation.

"Does Jane know?" Hollis asked.

"She's come to all the tests with me. Do you see how easy it is to fall in love now? When you know you never have to fall out of it?"

Hollis drove himself to his last appointment with Dr. Shetty to cement the new tooth. He was surprised to see two other patients in the waiting room, Jane tapping away at a keyboard, soft rock playing from an ancient boom box. She gave him an impersonal hello and told him to take a seat. Her lover was going to die and she was probably going to become a dentist. She wanted neither.

"Looks good," Dr. Shetty said, when she was done. She handed Hollis a mirror. The false tooth was still too white, a precursor of the ravages of age. He didn't think he'd mind; it would be a kind of calendar.

"We'll pick you up at 6:00," he said. They'd agreed on this when Hollis had called her the day after he'd learned about Patrick. Come see your daughter perform, he'd urged. She'd resisted, snapped at him, told him to mind his own business, and finally relented.

"I may not feel well later," Dr. Shetty warned now.

"You'll feel fine."

That evening, she was scowling outside her apartment building in khakis and a white blouse, her purse held in front of her, when Hollis pulled up.

"She looks mean," Jack said.

"Christ, she really does," Lil said, but jumped out to get her. Dr. Shetty assessed her coolly. Lil took one of Dr. Shetty's reluctant hands and pulled her towards the car, and made her sit in the front while she got in the back with Jack. Dr. Shetty smelled like Ivory soap, clean and serious.

"Hollis has told me lots about you," Lil said.

"I don't feel well," Dr. Shetty announced. Hollis exchanged looks with Jack in the rearview mirror. The woman had barely acknowledged the boy. "And I can't stay long. I have things to do."

"God, who doesn't?" Lil commiserated. "Doesn't it always seem like there's more and more to do? Sometimes I think if I ignore it all, it will just go away. It's a beautiful night though, isn't it? A beautiful summer night?" Lil was trying hard; she knew what she was up against.

They passed a closed computer repair shop, an empty Chinese restaurant, an overflowing dumpster, the DMV's traffic school with smokers hanging around outside. The sun lowering in a faded orange and pink urban sky.

"This is a bad neighborhood," Dr. Shetty countered. "Gone from terrible to even worse. You should do something about this, Mr. Berger."

"Yes, Mr. Berger," Lil said, putting her hands on his shoulders from behind. "You really should." He was slightly embarrassed by the way she kissed his neck.

"Yeah, Mr. Berger," Jack parroted.

"I'll see what I can do, " Hollis told him. "You think I should just blow the neighborhood up? Call it a day?" The boy nodded excitedly.

Dr. Shetty's face hardened—no doubt she thought he was making fun of her. He realized how much he wanted Dr. Shetty to approve of her daughter, and of Patrick, and how unlikely that seemed now. They left the city for roads bordered by stone walls and overhung with late summer's tired oaks and maples.

"We don't do this often enough, Holl," Lil said. "Just get in the car and drive, see what's out there, explore."

"I don't see the point if you don't have somewhere to go," Dr. Shetty said. "And you waste gas."

Lil had run up against the woman's brittle exterior, but she seemed determined to break through it. "I'm really looking forward to meeting Jane and watching her on the trapeze. It's not something I get to see every day."

"Maybe me and Hollis saw her at the circus?" Jack asked. "Did we?"

"No." Dr. Shetty turned in her seat to face him. "You look like your father."

The unmarked green metal structure where Jane trained was the size and shape of a small airplane hangar and sat at the front of a field in Foster. Inside, the space was cavernous and chaotic with scaffolding and cross beams, wires and ropes hanging from unknown points. Men and women in white tees and black leggings flexed and stretched. Foam pits covered parts of the floor. There was a low, serious din, what Hollis imagined murmuring monks sounded like. The unearthly light, bright enough and muted at the same time, seemed almost pious. Some kind of prayer was necessary here, a pardon for trying to fly.

Patrick appeared at the far end of the building. He was out of breath when he reached them, the ring of skin around his mouth and eyes first pale, and then hesitantly pink. His inner arms were bruised. He also wore black leggings and a white top. He swung Jack around.

"Wait until you see Jane," he told Dr. Shetty, as he kissed her horrified hand. "You won't believe how beautiful your daughter is up there. Not that she's not beautiful down here, but it's a whole other thing."

"None of this looks safe," she said, gripping her purse to her chest.

Patrick tried to ease the bag away from her. There was a short struggle, he pulled and she pulled back, panicked. She made a high, mouse-like squeak.

"What are you doing?" she demanded, giving her bag one last, victorious tug.

"I just wanted you to have a good time," Patrick said, and held up his hands in surrender. "I was going to carry your bag for you, that's all. I'm sorry."

"Why on earth would I want you to carry my bag?" Dr. Shetty demanded.

Patrick's face was strained as he pointed to the bleachers where they should sit. Jack, confused by the tug-of-war, clung to his father, but Patrick told him to stay while he found Jane.

"I'm sorry," Dr. Shetty said, when Patrick was out of ear shot, "but I'm afraid the man's a complete idiot."

"What? What are you thinking?" Lil said, fiercely. Her attempts to warm up the dentist were over. "Don't say that kind of thing around my son." She grabbed Jack's hand and marched to the bleachers. Hollis and Dr. Shetty followed.

"I shouldn't have said that," Dr. Shetty whispered. "That wasn't nice of me."

"No, it wasn't."

People began to climb onto various contraptions, and Hollis

saw that they weren't all young or even athletic-looking, but they shared a somber determination. There was something almost cultish about the place. Lil sat halfway up the bleachers, while Jack had gone to the top. When Hollis took a seat next to Lil, Dr. Shetty hesitated, and then she climbed up to where Jack was and sat near him, leaving a couple of feet between them. Hollis saw Dr. Shetty pass the boy a lollipop, the kind they gave you at the bank.

"She's kind of a bitch," Lil said. Hollis wondered if she'd noticed Patrick's bruised inner arms. "I'd hate to be like her."

Jane appeared and Patrick smoothed out the shoulders of her shirt. She climbed a ladder to a small platform. Safety lines snaked from her waist. She unhooked a trapeze and held it at arm's length. Two men who seemed to be instructors spoke behind cupped hands. Even before Jane had done anything, it was clear that she wasn't the usual student, that she was something remarkable. Others stopped to watch her. With a slight tilt of her body, she tipped from the platform, and for an instant, it looked as though she'd go down, despite the safety wires, but that was part of the thrill, the impossibility of the last minute save. Her body was an effortless undulation, a wave through the air as she swung from the end of one expanse to another. She hooked her legs over the bar and let her upper body and hair hang down. Lil, transfixed, grabbed his hand. Hollis was filled with a chilling, sudden sense of doom. He could not make himself turn around to look at Dr. Shetty; he was sure she felt the same thing he did as Jane's body drew parabolas in the air. It was too perfect to last. But maybe this strange inkling of disaster was not about what might happen to Jane, or even to Patrick, but to him. His teeth ached. He might lose everything, he realized, if he didn't act. He whispered Lil's name.

"Look at Patrick," she said. "He's in love. I was afraid it was never going to happen for him." She turned and waved at Jack. "I really did a job on him." She saw that Hollis didn't know what she was talking about. "When I was pregnant with Jack, I thought for a while that I was in love with someone else. Turns out I was only dazzled, but Patrick wouldn't come back. I'd hurt him and he wouldn't go through it again ever, he said. It's a huge regret of mine. I would do anything to take it back."

Hollis had never heard Lil speak without that distracting ruffling of her laughter's wings. "You were the dazzled one?" he asked. She nodded.

Behind them, Dr. Shetty stomped down the metal bleachers towards Patrick who was at the bottom of the ladder. Hollis couldn't hear what she was calling up to her daughter as she gestured wildly. People who'd been watching Jane stopped to watch the dentist instead. Jane landed on the platform and gazed down at her mother who was reaching up as though she could grab one of her daughter's ankles.

Hollis imagined that he was up there on that platform with Jane where he could view this newly rearranged world. He saw Lil's confession the way you feel the wind, and Patrick's longing, and the shit you can't believe you can live through, but feel more alive when you do. He saw Patrick motion for his help and he left the bleachers.

Dr. Shetty looked at him. She wouldn't acknowledge Patrick. "What kind of people are you that you do things like this, all of you doing what you want instead of what you should do?" she demanded.

"Mother, stop," Jane said.

Dr. Shetty allowed Hollis to take her out through a door at the back of the building. They were at the edge of a field of tall, gold grass. It was an improbable place Hollis had led them to, and they stood their together there in the strange expanse, the line of trees disappearing into the dark.

"It's ridiculous," she said. "I don't believe any of it."

"But it's beautiful, isn't it?"

He wanted to walk through the field with her—and there it was, possibility and all that brassy light and space in front of them, the last sun a yolky haze. They could touch the tops of the grass. He had the feeling that maybe this view had finally loosened her a little. Her mouth opened to say something, exposing teeth none too white or too straight, but then her silence was caught in the agency of the breeze.

COMPANION ANIMAL

When his wife told him to get out of the house that had been hers, anyway, long before they were married, Valdek Moore looked in the paper and found a semi-furnished, one-bedroom unit at Linden Pines. The development's name suggested an estate of elegant foliage, right for a term of penance, when it was really a clearing shaved into the scrubby flats of East Providence. Eight uninspired multi-unit townhouses were studded around a circle of asphalt while the noose of the cul-de-sac hung north of Route 6. On his first night in the single bed that still held the shape of its previous tenant, Valdek had felt a lift at having pioneered himself, at thirty years old, to a place he could never have imagined he'd end up. But by the next morning, what was new to him was already too old, and he came to the uneasy conclusion that Linden Pines was where people lived only because they had nowhere else to go, and for now, the same was true for him.

Since he'd moved in, Valdek had kept himself apart from his neighbors, but he knew some of their names from the cluster of mailboxes; there was Vasquez, Davis, Stahl, Peterlin, Lenning, Chin who lived above him with two poodles, and Mazelli whose uncurtained, sex-show bedroom window faced Valdek's over a narrow strip of knotty grass land-mined with dog turds. There was also the Molotovas, and on this October afternoon, he saw the daughter struggle to hang a string of Halloween pumpkin lights around her front door. A few times he'd said *hello* to her and the innocuous *What's up* because she was fourteen at most, he guessed, pretty in an underfed, impermanent way, and alone. He remembered girls like her on the fringe from his own high school days, rumors floating about them like auras, and their eager faces irresistible targets for rejection. Valdek leaned against the sun-warmed mailboxes and watched her, absorbed by how she tried over and over to loop the wire around a nail that was out of her reach, how the legs of the white plastic chair warped under her, how her tight jeans turned a lighter blue when she stretched. Hers was a child's compulsion, he decided; she refused to believe that what she wanted was not going to happen. On a day with not much else to do, it was strangely compelling to witness.

"Hey," she yelled, and gestured for Valdek to cross the asphalt towards her. "Hey, you. Can you help me?"

There was no one else out in Linden Pines, there never was, and she called to him again. It was clear then that she'd known he'd been watching, and that she'd been performing for him all along. Valdek turned, pretending not to hear her or see the way she waved like a woman flagging a passing bus as he retreated inside his dim apartment. He felt a little bad for ditching her, but he shouldn't have been staring in the first place; it was creepy enough that he tuned in to watch Mazelli go at his wife. He hadn't meant to provoke any connection in this place—invisibility was like being in a deep, timeless freeze—he'd only been looking for a letter, or anything from Frances, and his gaze had strayed. His face, with his mother's downward, foreign Slovak eyes and his father's wide American mouth always up at the corners, had been misinterpreted, and his long legs in black jeans and his empty hands had looked like the solution to the girl's wire-and-nail dilemma. He waited until she'd gone inside before he escaped to the hulking movie octoplex on Route 6. It was light when he left his apartment, and black when he wandered out of the theater, and for a few minutes in the disorientation of the dark he couldn't find his car. He had a feeling that he could be anywhere in the country at that moment, and still never know exactly where he was. Linden Pines, his neighbors, and the Molotova girl, he told himself as he wandered the vast lot, were words in a language he had no need to learn. He'd be leaving too soon for that. Frances, Franny, Fran, his wife of three years, she was his vocabulary, a taste of regret, but still sweet on his tongue.

Valdek's lower-level job at the Narragansett Animal Shelter was half a mile from the hospital where Frances, at forty-three, was Chief of Pediatrics, and one block from the Ocean State Family Planning Clinic and its chronic rash of protestors. Every morning, he drove by the same fervent group on the corner of Point and Friendship Streets, and though there was never any acknowledgement between them, Valdek hated his affinity with these people. But there it was, undeniable like the ever-expanding city behind them; they both spent their energy on things no one else wanted, and the caustic odor of euthanasia hung over all of them.

On this Friday, he was tempted to keep going towards the hospital to catch sight of Frances. He'd been sure the week, their fourth apart, was going to deliver her invitation to talk, but it hadn't, and he felt beaten down for having confused wanting something for believing it would happen. It made him think of the Molotova girl again, and how her chair was still lying in the grass in a gesture of disgust. The car radio predicted rain, and as he took the turn, Valdek saw that the sky that was already a tossing violet, not right for so early in the day. His view flashed black and white suddenly and he stood up tall on the brakes. A hooded protestor in a white rain poncho waved her poster with its picture of a fetus, faded like a water stain, in front of his windshield.

"You come barreling around this corner now like there's no one here," she scolded, and rapped his hood with her knuckles. "And we're always here. When are you going to learn?"

A joke came to mind as her poncho whispered ghost-like against his car; *What's black and white and red all over?* He couldn't imagine what else he might say to her, left breathless and wide-eyed by the near miss, but he pictured at that moment pinning her up against the chain link fence in front of Three Aces Lighting, his bumper at her knees. When he pulled into his building's yard a few minutes later, his hands were still murderous on the steering wheel, so he reminded himself of the mission for all who entered the animal shelter: to promote humane principles, stop cruelty, and alleviate fear. Already that morning, he hadn't done so well, and his heart flipped against his ribs.

An hour later, he got up from his desk where he'd been filling out an order slip for dog food to collect the first school group of the day—second graders from Spenser Avenue. His co-workers had chosen to devote their lives to working with animals, they didn't especially like kids, and so they'd gladly added this particular task to Valdek's collection of others. He'd seen these men and women, humorless advocates of abandoned dogs and psychotic cats, take offense when tiny palms covered tiny noses at the smell of turds dropped in terror, seen how they stiffened when sticky hands stroked fur in the wrong direction. Valdek understood the kids' impulses better because they were more often his, and wasn't it cruel, he often asked Frances, to tell kids not to touch what was most touchable? After all, he'd met her in this very building during that long August she'd decided it was time to pine for a dog—because she'd given up on ever having a baby—and ended up taking him home instead. He'd fallen in love with her slightly defeated confidence, the body and face she didn't much like, the way she looked at him like he was her last chance.

But he was a contagion to Frances these days, a man who'd had sex once with a woman who wasn't his wife, banished from the house, the dirtiest of all dogs. My mission, Valdek intoned again as he pushed through the lobby doors towards the children; to recognize the needs of companion animals and our responsibilities to them.

He gathered the second-graders, gave them his standard speech, tapping for effect the plastic tag on his breast pocket identifying him for the hour as Educator. He detected frozen waffles and the usual anxiety on their breath. Valdek walked backwards through the canyon of cages, the phalanx of kids following him. A fortyish teacher in front matched his steps so that they performed a kind of touchless tango. He moved to his left, she to her right with a smile that suggested she liked the way he looked. He heard the synthetic catch of her blouse over her bra, smelled her dry-cleaning, morning shampoo and flowery deodorant, and his stomach tightened and his prick roused. Since he'd strayed from the path of the good husband, sometimes what was least erotic turned him on, and he feared that his ultimate punishment was to end up a pervert, here among animals and children and teachers. He stuffed his hands into his pockets and tripped the rhythm of his step.

At the end of the line, a barrel-chested teacher gave him an impatient glance and corralled the kids forward. He was familiar but unplaceable, as though Valdek had seen the expression but not the face. The man's blue nylon jacket identified him as a member of a small society—weeknight bowlers, or a bar league maybe, or men who work with children, that slightly embarrassed fraternity. Soon, Valdek felt the group's ebbing of interest and the start of an inevitable surge flow through the children, the twitching and flexing of fingers, like the rustle to flight of small birds.

"No touching," he reminded them. "Hands in. You don't know the dogs and they don't know you, no matter how nice you are, no matter how many of you have pets at home. Now, how many of you think that cats really have nine lives?"

They looked at him expectantly, especially the teacher at the front, but did they really want to be disappointed by the truth? How many of you think, he wondered, that if you stick a finger in a caged dog's face he won't actually try to bite it off? He and Fran had seen it happen at the Phoenix airport last Christmas when they'd gone to visit her parents. The wail of the biter and the bitten were indistinguishable in the overcrowded terminal, and it had thrown Fran into a slump on a plastic chair, her thin knees tipped together helplessly. *Christ,* she'd said, *I'm supposed to know the difference between pain and fear.* The place on a holiday was full of babies being shown off to giddy, retired grandparents, and Valdek knew that this was what had really sunk his still baby-less wife. He didn't know what to say to Fran (though the thought that she was old enough to be a grandmother herself had occurred to him, unwelcome as an attack of food poisoning) and he focused instead on two planes that seemed inadvisably to lift off at once.

Halfway down the line of children he spotted a boy's hand form into a fist, that sly and beautiful packaging of thumb across knuckles. The kid reached out, but instead of a fist, inserted a finger between the bars of one of the cages. He had chosen the easiest of targets in the lethargic beagle, but the dog sprung forward in its final defense and growled in a demented, despairing way. Valdek grabbed the boy's arm and squeezed it hard, tightening his grip through denim jacket and Disney

World sweatshirt until the kid let out a wail.

"Don't ever do that again," he said, seized by some fury he didn't recognize. "Didn't I just tell you to keep your hands in? You want to lose a finger?" He was stopped by the boy's sudden springing up of tears—proof, like blood, of how deep he'd cut the kid. He was both acutely present—the feel of the boy's breath on his face!—and oddly absent; this wasn't him.

The dogs and children jostled each other and turned in noisy, agitated circles, while the teacher behind him breathed through her bright teeth, scared of her own bad judgment when it came to handsome men. Valdek quickly swept the group into the education room, and shut the door. When he'd figured out what to say, how to apologize, he would go in there and bring as an offering an old mutt the kids could sweetly molest. But for now, in the foyer just outside, he kneeled by the ancient beagle. The dog looked past him, vacant and dumb, one incisor wandering over the black lip.

"Hey. I want to talk to you." The teacher who had been at the back of the group came into the foyer. He sniffed loudly, the equivalent of a finger jabbed in Valdek's chest. "You overreacted back there," he said. "Big time." He had a booming voice, too loud for the space.

Valdek didn't look up as he worked at a lump in the dog's flesh, one of a new deathly scattering of them. "I'd just warned the kids not to touch," he said. "The boy could have lost his finger."

"Not likely. The dog's half dead anyway."

Valdek tapped the Educator tag on his shirt, his plastic shield of authority, if only for the moment. "Very likely, in fact."

"Bottom line: you don 't ever put your hands on my kids." The man paused to recollect his anger, and bounced on the balls of his feet in bright running shoes. "Understand?"

"Bottom line: don't threaten me. The animals and the children are my responsibility when you're in this building."

"Obviously, you're not safe around kids."

Valdek rose to look his accuser in the eye. He'd never been in a fistfight before, but he knew he'd do it now, even outweighed as he was. His opponent was huge, his jacket rustling with machismo. The idea of the two of them, teachers, nose-wipers and dog-food procurers, flailing away at each other made Valdek laugh. The man was puzzled, wondering if he was being made fun of, and then his face turned hard and menacing. The expression was suddenly so familiar it was as though Valdek had always known it. This fearsome aggressor, this unlikely protector of children and virtue, was Mazelli who lived in the next unit at Linden Pines. This was the man who screwed his wife with an efficient and cold enthusiasm, a nasty show Valdek had watched so often since moving in.

There was no sign of recognition on the other man's part when he said, "I'm going to report you. Get ready to look for a new job, you piece of shit."

And it's your bare, ugly ass I see every night, Valdek thought, but he knew it was useless knowledge, and that he was in trouble.

When Mazelli and his second graders left minutes later, Valdek tried to make some eye contact of apology with the boy, the unfortunate player who might be a player still if he continued to cry, but the kid refused to look at him though the downpour that had finally arrived.

Since he'd moved into Linden Pines, Valdek had begun to notice that the buildings appeared to huddle closer to each other the later it got. It was as if the days cast an obligatory, gray indifference over the place—the freedom to hide and ignore your fellow tenant was written into every lease, he imagined, like the instructions to haul one's own garbage—that packed up and went home when it got dark. Lights went on around the circle in a kind of assumed obedience, car doors shut, occasionally there was a disembodied voice, or the unmistakable crackle of a plastic grocery bag being lugged up the stairs. And that week, after his encounter with Mazelli, Valdek's window seemed to be a little closer to the other man's every day.

As he watched the sex begin, he understood now that the guy's routine was always a teacher's routine, fucking on week-nights between eight and eleven, scheduled in like library, lunch, and recess. It was 9:20 as Mazelli parked his small wife's feet on his shoulders and levered her hips off the bed. Valdek had never seen the woman's face, night or day, but he could tell even in the cheap erotic glow of a red light bulb, that she was as passive as an orchid. Mazelli was all cock and chest, his unbuttoned flannel shirt billowing behind him like he was a pantless ship's captain. His concentrated face with eyes rolling back turned occasionally toward the window, but he never saw Valdek there. When he was finished, Mazelli dusted his wife's legs off his shoulders and she rolled complicity onto her side, the crack of her ass straight as defeat. Valdek felt not at all excited by what he'd seen—limp, in fact, in brain and body—but only sorry and vaguely humili-ated for the woman and for himself.

Valdek drank a beer and considered phoning Frances. He wouldn't tell her about his neighbor's lousy technique, because what could she say—at least he has a wife? But he would tell her that at the moment he was watching the Molotova girl's pumpkin lights—when and how she'd gotten them strung up finally, he didn't know—short out from the rain in a series of exuberant sparks and small explosions. Fran would laugh when he explained that Linden Pines was the kind of place where parents encouraged their kids to fool to around with electricity and water. Finally, he'd confess to her how he'd grabbed the kid at work, and how he might lose his job because of it, how every day he expected it to happen, march right into his office and do him in. Frances might be sympathetic in a professional, imprecise way, but she'd have no sympathy for him specifically, and then what would he say?

He recalled, with a shame that was still remarkably unfaded after six months, the conference he'd been sent to where he'd met a woman who wore a (tarnished) silver cat pin on her brown jacket. Valdek had told the woman he liked her jewelry, and it was this dumb lie that had made him so aggressive and mercenary. She was young, too easily flattered and flustered by his looks and cruel smoothness, and he'd maneuvered her into the Sheraton's dark corner next to where the tongue of the escalator lay exhausted on the lowest level. It was one of those melancholy, defeated spaces where bad things happen, garbage collects, and drunks piss, unbearable in its uselessness to a man who knows he's become useless to his wife. Anger and sorrow had turned him on in bed with her, then made him sick by the time Frances picked him up at the Amtrak station the next night. He confessed while they were still parked, the new mall glowing like some imitation jewel at the end of the avenue, and she wiped at her tears behind her glasses. He knew that it was what he'd confirmed for Fran—that she'd made a mistake marrying him—that was so devastating for her, and not the act itself. In the end, there was no baby he'd been able to give her to assure her that she'd ever made a single good choice in her whole life.

Valdek looked up to see a woman cross the circle in an impatient trot, her shoulders lifted against inconvenience, the rain, and Chin out with his dogs. He wondered why she was out at all, what, or who she needed. From behind, she looked like the Molotova girl, but her body was a little more tired, and she passed by the dead pumpkin lights without seeming to notice or care that they'd gone dark. There was life in this place, Valdek admitted, and as he drank another beer, he heard the lines of connection tighten across the air and his chest.

"The guy put this in the wrong mailbox," the Molotova girl told Valdek when he opened his door one morning. Her knocking had thrown him out of bed, and his head was thick from too many drinks out with a friend. "This is *you*, right?"

She read his name off the envelope, the sound of it surprising in her mouth. To Valdek, an envelope with his name on it these days was a scary thing, possibly containing accusations and demanding accountability, but when he saw it was from Frances, finally, he felt instantly lifted off the floor. The word *saved* whispered in his ear. But he also saw that while she'd gotten the address of Linden Pines right, she had the unit number wrong. It was an easy mistake to make, but enormously discouraging. Valdek knew that this was the slipping knowledge of the small but essential facts of another person's life, slipping that would go on until there was nothing real or true left. He was fully awake now, firmly in his hungover body, his two feet on the slick wall-to-wall, and suddenly very aware of the girl who was shivering in the chill. The hem of her bell-bottoms covered her sneakers, and her hands, bright with cheap gold rings, moved in and out of her sleeves. She was prettier this close, with an assessing gaze that made him look away so that his eyes caught on the significant swell of her breasts under her yellow fleece.

"Your place is exactly like mine," she announced, having stepped fully into the apartment and run her eyes over everything in it. "But they're all alike, I guess." She looked out the window at her own unit. "Decorations help—that way you always know which one is yours, especially at night when they really look the same. I got my little pumpkin lights up finally. No thanks to you, by the way."

She moved through the room with an air of suggestion and entitlement that was part woman—how she brushed his things with her fingertips—and part child, as if her parents had never told her a single cautionary tale about going into the apartments of strange men. Valdek put the counter between them and a cold cup of yesterday's coffee and Franny's envelope in front of him.

"I'm Lena," she said, with an odd assertiveness. "Lena and Valdek." She lifted her hands in front of her face and thought for a second. "Kedlav and Anel. That's us backwards." She looked longingly at the drink he moved to his mouth, as though she wanted not just it, but insatiably, everything she laid her eyes on. He sensed there was something decidedly off and needy about the girl; she was both compelling and, if he were smart, to be avoided.

"I don't drink coffee," she told him. "Not usually, anyway. My mother's was born in Russia. We drink tea."

"Want some tea then?" he offered, but she shook her head.

Lena sat on the arm of the couch that another tenant's nervousness had scratched bare. She told him that her mother worked the night shift at the laundry at St. Joseph's Hospital, that she slept during the day, and that she'd just gotten a used Impala. The girl spilled facts carelessly, whisking them around with her glittering hands, and they piled up in front of Valdek, thin and of unclear intent.

"So what about your father?" he asked.

"I don't have one. I mean, obviously I do, but I don't know where." Lena glanced at the low ceiling as Chin's dogs raced back and forth. "I see those dogs all the time, you know. He lets them poop on the grass and he doesn't clean it up. You should say something."

"Why should *I* say something? How about you?"

"Because he lives in *your* unit." She kicked her heels at the side of the couch, smug with her understanding of the rules that he clearly lacked. "And you should put something up on the walls, too. It's kind of ugly in here. No offense."

"I'm not staying very long."

"You're leaving?" Lena seemed disappointed for a second and then gave him a flirtatious but skeptical look. "Yeah, sure. We'll see about that."

"I'm married," he said. "Actually, I have a house in Providence. This is just for a little bit." He was surprised at his impulse to tell her anything or speak any part of his life—true or not—but the need to announce that he wouldn't always be in Linden Pines, that there was somewhere else he needed to be, was overpowering. "We're working some things out."

Lena shrugged. "Well, my mother happens to think this is the greatest place on earth." Her pounding heels drove home her disdain of the notion. "She's fucked, though."

"What do you know about Mazelli, the guy who lives—"

"He lives there." Lena waved her hand over her shoulder. "He's a pig." She laughed, and a faint discoloring crept up her neck. Did she also watch him at night? "He's a teacher, or something like that." She hesitated. "So what else do you want to know?"

Nothing, he told her. He didn't know how she knew anything when all he ever saw in Linden Pines were fragments of interaction so brief and strange he sometimes thought he'd imagined them. Unless of course, he realized, they happened just like this—inside, undetectable, and unreal. Lena picked up yesterday's paper from the floor and began to read as though it were something she did in his place all the time.

He opened Fran's envelope, slicing the seam with a kitchen

knife. There was only a piece of paper wrapped around a business card with her lawyer's name and number on it. What was there to haggle over? Her money and her house were always hers. He had nothing really but what she'd given him. And soon I will be divorced, he told himself; she won't take me back. A dizziness crept up his spine and lodged at the back of his head.

"You have to leave," Valdek said suddenly to Lena. His teeth were ice cold against his tongue.

"God. What's *your* problem?"

"Thanks for my mail, but you have to go now."

The girl unfolded herself from the couch in a yawn of inconvenience, and the newspaper returned to the floor, open to what she'd been reading, a bright ad for a giant toy sale of picnic tables, baby pools, inflatable chairs. She left his apartment, and he watched how she lingered in front of Mazelli's as though she were trying to decide whether to go there next. From the way she slipped her hands into her sleeves and held herself, Valdek knew there was nowhere she had to be. And if she needed something from him—well, he'd cut that off. That night when he saw Mazelli and his wife going at it as usual, Valdek remembered the way Lena had pointed over her shoulder towards the man as though she owned him and all of Linden Pines.

On Halloween, Valdek watched Lena with her drooping shopping bag move clockwise around the circle. He'd had only three other kids all evening, and when she'd reached into his bowl of candy, he'd known it was her behind the Betty Rubble mask by her hand of confused jewelry—a claddagh ring, a gothic serpent with glass eyes, a tiny gold-plated ankh on her thumb— but neither of them said anything. She went inside her apartment and a few minutes later reappeared in a different mask, something rubbery and unidentifiable, and walked towards him.

"I've seen you before," he said to Lena. "Isn't this called double dipping?" She looked at him through ragged rubber eyeholes and then lifted the mask from her flushed face and rested it on her head. A cloud of tangled hair hovered over her forehead. "Aren't you a little old for this? Don't you have some friends to hang out with?"

"It's just a goof," she said, defensively. "There's nothing better to do." She unwrapped a lollipop and put it in her mouth. "I'm stuck here, as usual. I'm a loser, just like you."

"Don't hold back," he said. "Tell me exactly what you think."

The candy moved inside her cheek, like a dreaming eye. "I thought you were moving."

For the first time since he'd come to Linden Pines, Valedk could hear the grind of traffic on Route 6 through the denuded trees. It seemed a bad night to be alone. "So, where's your mother tonight?"

"I told you already, she works nights. Anyway, she doesn't get Halloween at all, thinks it's totally weird that people dress up and eat candy. Did you see my pumpkin lights are broken? I know she did something to them. I'm so mad at her." Two lines, like tiny blades, appeared in her forehead. "I hate her."

It seemed almost cruel now to tell her about the natural conspiracies of weather that had caused her lights to spark out. They were inches inside the doorway, Lena with her tough-girl stance, when the lights in Mazelli's apartment went on. Lena caught her breath just as he caught his. Valdek stepped back from Mazelli's view, and she stepped in and almost against him. He had *his* reasons for hiding, but was shocked to see a shade of the deepest unhappiness fall across her face. Her fingers twisted tightly in the handles of her bag, her eyes became platinum with tears, and she seemed at that moment entirely lost. He didn't know why exactly, if it was talk of her sabotaged lights, or her depressingly un-American mother, or if it was some acute understanding of the shittiness of her life.

"You know how long it took me to get the lights up? And now they don't work? Why didn't you help me that day?" she demanded.

It was a moment of thrilling clarity for Valdek; the pure human sound of her misery, the cold air in his nose, the perfect peak of the roof above them. He didn't want his life to be just circumstances and after-shocks anymore, and knew he could turn Lena away then, or not, and that a choice was a rare and beautiful thing.

"I'm sorry. I guess I'm not very good with children." She snorted in agreement. "Let me take you to the shelter where I work. We'll go see the animals." He knew this was reckless, that you didn't put girls in your car and drive them away. Lena's mother might be careless with her daughter, leaving her alone all night, but he wouldn't be.

"I'm not supposed to leave," she said, but already he knew she would.

It wasn't until they were halfway to Providence that Valdek realized he wasn't heading towards work at all, but towards Fran's house on Lyman Street. He steered with one light finger, the mood lifting and buoying with the moon. Lena's chatter and the careless scent of candy filled the car. He'd never seen anyone eat the stuff the way she did, clicking it against her teeth and letting the wrappers collect at her feet. When they had reached the highest span on the Red Bridge and reflections of the city lights drifted in the water, Lena didn't notice. Valdek glanced at her knees drawn up and parted, at her thin, too tight pants, at her sneakers resting on the dashboard, and wondered what she was looking at if not the lights. He felt an urge to touch

Lena's tangled hair, her hand, even the rubber mask on the seat between them.

"Your mother leaves you alone a lot," he said.

"She has to. Besides, everyone knows."

"Everyone knows what?"

"If something happens," she said.

"If something happens," he repeated.

He was tempted to ask her, this girl who got into the car of a man she didn't know, what she imagined that something might be, but they'd arrived at Lyman Street by then, and he parked in front of Fran's house. Even in the dark Valdek saw that it was in the process of being repainted and repaired. A group of kids in costumes waited at the front door, and when Frances didn't answer, they moved on. He imagined Fran, no great fan of the holiday, staying late at the hospital and checking her watch so she'd know when it was safe to go home again.

She had torn down the rose bushes that sometimes caught on her sweaters, replaced the feisty vines with a row of tight-assed boxwoods and the sagging fence with a wall of cedar. It was an old and majestic house, the place always needed a hundred repairs, and the idea of selling had sat like a dented can at the back of the cabinet, one that's too old to use but can't quite be thrown out. When they'd met, Frances had already lived there for over ten years; she had a history with it. It seemed to Valdek now that he had entered one door and then she'd let him out by another. It made him feel as though he'd died.

"This is where you work?" Lena asked, sitting up in her seat. "This is where the animals are?"

"No, this is where my wife lives."

Lena was undeterred by the detour. "My mom would die to live here," she said. "She's fixing it up, your wife, I mean, before you come back."

Valdek was touched by her attempt to tell him what he'd like to hear. He saw that Lena was captivated by the activity outside while the two of them were locked inside watching. "Want to get some more candy as long as we're here?"

She was tireless and drawn to the houses with the brightest, biggest decorations, sure of her passions and bluntly acquisitive of everything, furniture seen through open doors, pets, children, potted plants, even the shoes a man had on. He wondered if she imagined her future decorated with the stuff. The people who had been his neighbors cast cool glances at Lena, and something only a little less chilly at him. What must it have looked like to them when he moved in with Fran, the woman who'd previously joked to anyone that *Oops! I forgot to get married and have children?* They would not have imagined that *this* marriage, older woman to younger man, money to nothing, was something that was going to last, so would they have even noticed when he left?

"Let's go to the animals," Lena said. "I'm sick of candy."

"We will go, I promise." Valdek began to walk towards Fran's backyard. "I just want to see one thing first."

What had Frances done with the land? There had been mounds of nature before; a squirrel skull lodged in the soil, a patch of genitalia-like mushrooms that sprouted after too much rain. Valdek had grown tomatoes, and a summer ago, he'd presented the first ripe one to Frances who'd eaten it with salt. She'd claimed it was an act of faith to grow food within sight of the skyline, the train station and the housing projects, and he liked that he'd succeeded at something she'd always assumed was impossible.

Now the ground was flat and pounded hard, the bushes cleared, and the view sharper than before. Lena leaned against the fence and stared at the city, her neck arching above the collar of her puffy coat. Valdek knew from the way she urged herself against the fence that she was delighted by the lights, but there was something disquieting about her pleasure. Minutes before, he had put on her mask to make her laugh, and now he knew that the taste in his mouth, an earthy peppermint, was her breath that had condensed there.

He forced down a speeding erotic current in his body. He wanted to get away from the girl in his wife's yard, and climbed a stage of scaffolding on the back corner of the house where some clapboards and a small square of roofing were being repaired. He'd always suspected that this spot was the source of the leak that bloomed on the ceiling above the bed where he and Franny slept. In the damp, it was prone to rashes of mold, while in the summer, it peeled like her sunburned shoulders. He'd never done anything about it because its repair never seemed urgent. But it *had* bothered Frances a lot, apparently; he was barely out of the house before she had it fixed. With him gone, the place was all hers again. He put his cheek to the house and inhaled the scent of new paint. The zipper of his jacket pinged against the metal scaffolding.

Valdek looked into Fran's bedroom. On the other side of the door, a ladder blocked the hallway where the paper was half stripped. What he saw was that Frances hadn't bothered to push it back to accommodate her life, to say *I still live here and you're just a temporary inconvenience.* Instead, she must have squeezed around it every time as though she wasn't really there for this undoing—this erasing of the time she'd been with Valdek— but she'd be back for the redoing, the reclaiming of her old life. It seemed to him then that his sleeping with the other woman had given Frances an easy way out of a marriage whose terms he hadn't entirely understood—or fulfilled.

"You should come down," Lena said. "You could fall or something."

Her face was offered up to him like a plate of sweet offerings he could easily take. Christ, Franny, he whispered, let me in: am I not enough for you? Lena sat on the grass and bent her head towards her chest, her legs straight in front of her. She flexed her feet and pulled at her toes, tilting herself into a triangle so that her body levered off the perfect turf of the yard. And Valdek knew looking down at her then that Mazelli didn't have a wife at all. Mazelli had Lena.

"Can we go now?" she called up.

He didn't know how he'd missed what was so clear; the lines of her body in Mazelli's bed that were the same lines he'd watched as she hung her lights, the arching of her arms when she wanted something impossible, the way she'd dodged the man's view earlier. He knew he was reaching into air when he took a step, and still he did it. Valdek saw the house rise above him, then the moon, and then Lena over him as he landed on his back. His heels and fingers wedged into the ground. The scaffolding knocked against the house.

"Are you all right?" Lena crouched by him. "I told you that would happen." His head ached and his spine felt encased in ice. "She's going to see you lying here, and she'll never want you then."

The girl was beautiful in her sympathy for him, and her hand with those rings hovering over his chest was a gesture more intimate than he'd ever seen her make with Mazelli.

"Your mother shouldn't leave you alone at night." He touched her cheek. She was pure sorrow. "You're way too young."

She felt her face where he had. When she stood, she was unsteady, her self-possession gone. "Stop saying that. I'm not a child, I'm sixteen. Can we go now? If you're not dead or paralyzed, then will you get up?"

Later that night as he walked across the moonlit circle to the Molotova's apartment, he recalled how Lena had fallen asleep on the way to the shelter. He'd touched her hand curled on the seat, surprised to find how chapped her skin was, like a boy's. Her eyes had been distant with disorientation as she stood close to him and he unlocked the shelter door.

Inside, the smell of mournful animal was hot and meaty, and she'd put her hand over her nose as he led her past the cages to his office, where he'd had the old beagle sleep every night since he'd grabbed the boy and squeezed his arm.

"Is this one yours?" Lena had asked. "Pretty sad-looking dog."

Valdek had hoped the dog would die there, drowned under the weight of her own tumors and far from the horrors of the cage. The dog had been brought in a while back because she'd bitten someone; she was no companion animal. Valdek knew then that he would quit his job, even if Mazelli was likely to be too powerless in his own guilt to accuse him of anything. (He couldn't do right by the boy he'd hurt; that was a scar.) Lena had touched the folds at the dog's neck. But an animal is nothing to a girl who sleeps with men, Valdek had thought. She'd looked at him then, confused and tired, and as on the day he'd first been caught staring, it was clear she knew exactly what he understood. And wasn't she asking for his help now?

Valdex was sure that if he watched, maybe not that night, but the next or the next, he would see Lena with Mazelli again. He would call the police, report the rape of a child going on next door, and watch as they dragged the man's ass out of the apartment, his pants puddling around his ankles like drowning humiliation.

Valdek rang the bell and waiting as the string of pumpkin lights scratched against the siding. After a few minutes, a face appeared in the inches between chain and door. For a moment, he thought he was looking at Lena; a dimmer light wouldn't reveal the lines, the older skin and eyes that made mother different from daughter. Behind her, the television was on and the sliver of room was discouragingly just like his.

"Yes?" she asked.

"I live there," he told her. He glanced back at his own black doorway. It was almost two a.m., the dark still had a forbidding hold on the place, but if this woman thought his appearance at this hour was strange, or even frightening, she didn't show it. That she'd answered at all surprised him, but she was incautious like her daughter.

"I know. Do you want something?" He heard the bedrock of her foreign accent.

"I know your daughter," he told her. "I want to tell you what's going on. That man, Mazelli, across the circle—she goes to his place when you're not here."

The woman's fingers curled around the door. "No, she's here, asleep."

"Not now," he said. "When you're at work. She goes to him."

"She's asleep." She gave him a dull, puzzled look, and her shoulders lifted in a familiar way. He remembered a woman crossing the circle in the rain.

"No, when you're not here." His voice rose in frustration. He'd begun to scare her, and she moved her weigh against the door, the inches narrowing. "Do you understand what I'm saying? That man is sleeping with her."

"Go away. We're asleep now." Her head shook with a tiny tremor, but he could tell from how she averted her eyes and defiantly retained her right as a non-native speaker to misunderstand what she wanted that she already knew all of this. Lena's jewelry, her mother's Impala, this shitty apartment for a night of body. It occurred to Valdek that Mazelli paid for it all. People made bargains and used each other all the time, hopefully and willfully blind, and this was just one of them. He and Frances had made another; the terms had been clear enough.

There wasn't anything more to say to Lena's mother—though for the briefest moment he considered the geometry of being with her, of moving in—and she pushed the door closed. Valdek knew there were a thousand other places he might live now. It seemed both a lonely and invigorating truth. In the meantime, he'd bang on his window until Mazelli finally saw him, just to let the man know he was there watching.

NATURAL WONDER

Once, when she'd been walking in her neighborhood, a car had stopped for directions to Alsop, the psychiatric hospital perched above the Blackstone River. How to get there was complicated, the man already so lost in the tangle of leafy streets that Tess hadn't been sure where to start. Begin at the beginning, wasn't that the trick? So she'd asked, "Do you know where you are?"

The man's smirk emerged from a fog of cigarette smoke. "Lady, if I knew where I was, would I be going to the nuthouse in the first place?"

They'd had a good laugh as the sun twitched behind the trees. She'd told the story to Eli that night, but later she wondered why she'd found it so funny. This was a few years before Ben did his own time at Alsop—and there was nothing particularly funny about her son droopy behind those metal doors. She was like that lost man now; did she have any idea where she even was? Her daughter had given her directions to the ski house up in the gullet of Vermont, precise distances, route numbers, and sharp turns, but they left her cold and without imagination. If Tess had been giving directions, she would have included the ice-encased apple orchard and the tennis courts like giant cribs blanketed in December's snow, sights to make you feel the long trip was worth it.

She was headed to Gorham, but where was she in relation to anything else? It wasn't like saying come to Paris, or Detroit, or the bedroom, or come to me, something she and Eli hadn't said to each other in a very long time. She'd meant to look at a map yesterday, but instead she'd gone out to buy a salami for Margot, a decision that now seemed ridiculous and striving. She could smell the thing stinking in the bag next to her. Take me, she would say to her daughter, take my sopressata, forgive my failings as your mother. And then she would add: your father and I are splitting up. Margot wouldn't take it so well.

She was certain she'd never been to this part of Vermont before, and yet here was a sign for Millboro, a town she'd spent a weekend in with Eli years ago. She was alarmed by how she'd gotten her geography wrong, as if it wasn't her memory that had drifted, but the land itself. She took the exit out of curiosity, a need for gas, and no hurry to get to her daughter's, but nothing was familiar, not the gleaming Exxon station with its vivid declarations of snacks and sodas, not the stand of pines behind the idle school buses, not the way the land dipped away like the bowl of ladle. But there was that July weekend she hadn't thought of in decades; fireflies, gin with curls of lime, two young couples so fat with the notion of endless time that she was embarrassed now by how little they knew. She considered calling Eli and saying, *guess what?* And, *guess where I am?* And, *guess how fast time goes?* But he would recall the weekend one way, she another, and where would that leave them but blinking into the familiar and sad silence between them?

Frigid air needled her skin as she pumped gas. There was a low roar, and a train of snowmobiles crested the snow and parked at the other set of pumps. The riders were fearsome in steroidily leather outfits. No, she wouldn't call Eli; that's not what they did anymore. The weekend had ended badly anyway, with the men fist fighting in the moonlight like insomniac pugilists. Memory did not preserve marriage like a child's tooth in a small white box. What she needed to consider now was everything ahead of her today—her formidable daughter, her son-in-law of a year, Kirk. Tess had told people she was looking forward to two nights at the ski house, Kirk's real estate booty from his first marriage, at the base of Wantusket Mountain, but really, how could she be. Margot could be like an ice pack you placed on your pain; flip her over and she might be even colder. And then there was the news Tess was bringing her. She glanced at the line of snowmobiles and left.

It was just after noon when she found the house, but already hints of evening were falling like ash. She didn't think her Mini, unlike the massive SUV at the top of the icy driveway, was going to make it, so she parked on the road and hauled out her bag. She hoped that someone would appear in one of the graceless A-frame's windows, but there were only reflections of the mountain it bowed before. Halfway up, she fell forward on her hands. Her knees smacked the ice and a sour taste rose from under her tongue. She wanted to rest her forehead on the ice for a moment, but she was a fifty-three-year-old in a green parka riding down on all fours; best to enjoy the slide. On her next try, she reached the house, knocked, and went inside, snow-blinded and rushed by humidity. It was like breathing in a swarm of gnats. In front of her was a steaming hot tub on a platform, and in the cauldron, like two overdone birds, were Margot and Kirk. Chlorine's stink banged through her sinuses.

"You made it," Margot said, her shoulders rising from the water. Kirk waved a beefy, dripping arm. "We thought you probably got lost."

"Nope. Perfect directions," Tess said. "Very exacting." Sweat was already collecting under her breasts and she took off her coat. "You didn't tell me there was a hot tub. I would have brought my suit."

"I did tell you," Margot corrected. "I guess you forgot."

At one point in the fully blossomed years of Margot's acidic adolescence, Tess had decided to swallow rather than spit out these small untruths and accusations from her daughter, restitution for having given her Ben as a brother. If someday they found a gristly knot in her gut, it would be made of acquiescence and guilt. Margot looked cooked, her short hair forming apostrophes on her forehead. At twenty-four, her features were already thick like Eli's peasant mother. She had none of Tess's thin tension. Kirk, fifteen years older, had the alien coloring of thinned-down carrot juice, and enthusiastically big nipples that bobbed on the water's surface like pool toys.

Tess asked him how the skiing had been that morning. Her question didn't require answering, but what could she do but nod at the fleshy son-in-law she barely knew? She assumed there was some fiddling going on under the water while Kirk talked avidly, because Margot was starting to look disconnected.

"Hey buddy," Kirk said, removing his paw from the erotic depths.

Tess turned around to the palest child she'd ever seen. There was the suggestion of a bird's hollow skeleton beneath the bloodless skin and popcorn colored hair. He had red-rimmed, fetally lashless eyes, the faintest mouth like a cranberry juice stain.

"And who are you?" she asked. He was wearing a dirty white turtleneck and corduroy pants with a high elastic waist. All that was missing was a dunce cap.

"Ryan," Margot said.

"You didn't tell me—." Tess caught herself. She'd known the boy existed, of course, the ten-year-old output of Kirk's first marriage, but she definitely hadn't been told he'd be there.

"Say hello to your grandma, Ry," Kirk instructed. "Be polite, buddy."

Grandma—but she had nothing to do with this strange kid.

She smiled at him. "Call me Tess, ok, sweetheart?" She talked to him like he was a rock, but there was something so absent about him it was like speaking to the box where you placed your drive-through order. You never knew if it went through.

"Hey, want to jump in, pal?" Kirk asked. "Take a soak, soldier?"

Buddy. Pal. Soldier. None of those idiotic, virile tags fit this wisp of a kid.

"But no peeing in the hot tub," Margot warned. "I mean it."

"I don't do that," he said, and mumbled *dumb-ass fucker lady* so Tess could hear.

"Do you ski too, Ryan?" she asked. She wished he wouldn't stand right behind her, like a stalker.

"I have a cold." He exhaled tepid, sour milk breath as evidence.

"But you're learning how, right, pal?" Kirk encouraged.

The boy gave his father a primal and blank look, and pivoted back to where he'd come from, a room abandoned except for a plaid chair and a television jammed in the corner. Margot stepped out of the tub, her black suit slick like mercury, and threw a towel across her shoulders. The fronts of her thighs were glistening slabs of ham. She led Tess to a wood-paneled bedroom in the back, the flow of green indoor-outdoor carpet uninterrupted. The house was wedged into the side of a hill, and the bedroom's lone window was black with snow that pressed against it.

Margot sat on one of the two single beds. "Just so you know, I didn't know Ryan was coming," she said. "A so-called last minute emergency with his mother."

"It's fine. He's cute. It will be fun."

Margot's eyebrows lifted. "Cute? Not sure about that."

"Yes, cute. All kids are cute," Tess said. "In their own way."

What did her daughter, with her small and pinched sympathies, know about being a stepmother? What had she ever learned from Tess who strained at the seams with mistakes? Margot worked in the public affairs office of the American Heart Association, an incongruity not lost on Tess who sometimes developed the warning signs of a weak ticker when she was around Margot—the tingling of regret, the hardening of pride. But she loved her daughter fiercely and leaned down to kiss her forehead.

"It can be complicated, exes and steps and all that,"Tess said. A long marriage had buffered her from the things her divorced friends had had to contend with, stepchildren whose overnight bags held not only pajamas but also other women's contempt. "You get used to life being unpredictable with kids. In other words, plan nothing." She laughed. Or plan everything, Tess wanted to add, just so you'll remember how you once imagined your life was going to go, even hour by hour.

Margot stood and looked at the wet spot she'd left on the quilt. "It's weird, you being here without Dad. I wish he'd come too." She paused. "It's like he's dead."

"That seems a little overblown," Tess said. "You know he had to work. The world of the paper box beckons." Her daughter could take away her breath like no one else, and then leave her gasping. Dead? How could she tell her now about the split? Later, she thought, I'll tell her later. She extracted the salami from her bag.

Margot smiled and held it to her nose like a flower. "You're the only mother I know who travels with a salami,"

"And don't you forget it,"Tess said, and kissed her daughter again. She tasted of chlorine. On the other side of the wall, Tess heard Kirk urging his little soldier, his ghostly comrade, to join him for a soak.

When the others had gone for an afternoon ski, Tess stared at the shaved pudendum of the mountain through binoculars. She tried to spot Margot in the red suit she'd vacuum-sealed herself into, etching her way down the slope. Tess didn't get the appeal of skiing, had never believed in the heroism of wind-burned faces and the bravado of broken bones. For years, she'd watched her family get expensively whisked up mountains, and she'd felt only grateful for the solid ground under her boots, though she'd sometimes imagined Ben flying off the gondola or a ledge just for his supposed fun. She wandered around the house, noting evidence of Kirk's first family everywhere, as if they had only gone out for a while; the ugly duck motif in the kitchen, the dusty funereal silk flowers in a mug on the back of the toilet, a flannel dog bed when there clearly was no dog anymore. And of course, the boy, the palest evidence of all. At lunch, he hadn't been allowed salami or nuts, or ketchup, or strawberries, or chocolate—there was an exhaustive list on the fridge—and he had pushed around his crustless white-bread and butter sandwich. Behind Kirk's coaxing him to eat, Tess had picked up the man's deep fear of his kid. She knew it all too well. It wasn't hard for children to find exactly where their power lay with their parents and pitch their tent there.

Tess went to her room and unfolded herself on the bed. What she wanted now, in order to fight off a mid-afternoon sleep, was to recall that weekend in Millboro, but getting there meant pushing aside books and boxes, battered cake pans and old coats, her kids' artwork and sneakers and medical records, the dusty impulses of a long marriage. There'd been an old Cape house, a pond crowned by cattails, and a clipped field that ran up to a line of mountains, wooden chairs that sank into the ground as the evenings went on. There'd been that shit, Gerald, Eli's new friend and fascination that summer, and Gerald's girlfriend, a beautiful, studious woman, entirely nameless now. The pictures came to Tess in disorganized snaps, which was the closest she could come to describing what middle age was really like. The past was all there still, but you weren't sure how to organize it anymore into a story that made sense.

After dinner, Kirk massaged his wide lower back and traced on the dark window the way he'd come down the mountain earlier. Tess liked him enough, she decided, though she might not be hard pressed to admit that he was a blowhard. He was rich from commercial real estate, and apparently nothing was prettier to him than a building's empty shell. She told him about the abandoned dress shop near her office, and how the sun passed through in the mornings like a nurse visiting the terminal ward. A dress shop? He didn't get what she was talking about, or why she found the decline both sad and beautiful. Margot, reading *Newsweek*, likely understood all too well her mother's romantic notions and dismissed them. Standing at the cold glass, Tess began to understand why her daughter had married Kirk and married so young. He was a perfectly uncomplicated refuge, a little dull and dense. And yet, there was the most complicated boy in this picture Margot had also gotten in the deal, who, next to Kirk's fleshy finger reflected on the window, was curled on the couch. His knees were pulled up to his chin.

"You okay, Ry?" Kirk asked. He leaned over his son, but kept his hands behind his back. Patterns of gas flames from the fireplace played over the boy's face. "All right?"

Tess put her palm against Ryan's forehead. His eyes squeezed as if her touch hurt. "He is a little hot."

"Because he's in front of the fire," Margot said. Her tone was unlovely. "He's fine."

Kirk looked from child to wife to child to wife, an unconfident volley. Tess sat next to the boy. It had been years since she'd felt the perfect heft of a child's head in her lap. She couldn't say she felt affection for him exactly at that moment, the warmth of his skin against her palm, but the kid who wasn't loveable was the one you had to go all out for. The love was sludgier, richer maybe. She looked down into the shiny spiral of the boy's ear. What's in there, she wondered, who's home? Soon, Kirk scooped up the boy and carried him to the sleeping loft.

Margot closed her magazine. "Ryan makes himself sick, you know."

"Come on," Tess said. "Children don't do that. They can't."

Tess leaned forward to whisper. "He goes over to another kid's house and he gets sick, and on field trips, and at school so he has to be sent home. And sometimes when he's with us. Kirk doesn't see it."

"Maybe the boy just wants the world to stop for him until he figures it out," Tess said. "He seems lost. He needs love in the meantime." In the silence, she knew she'd angered Margot. After all, they were not talking about Ben, as Margot would point out. History was not reruns.

"I try," Margot said. "I really do. It's not easy."

The admission astonished Tess, and she considered that maybe she didn't know Margot as well as she thought she did. Wasn't that part of her family's problem, that they were all stuck in their old stories? Margot might well understand about the split, after all; she had grown up some. They averted their eyes from each other and listened to Kirk pleading with the boy to get into his pajamas; Tess imagined it could go on forever, and the boy might still prevail. It depressed her. She kissed Margot goodnight and went downstairs to her bedroom. She fell easily into the tropics of sleep, but woke at 4:30. For a minute, she thought her bag on the opposite bed was Eli, zipped up with everything familiar stuffed inside. She could open it, root around in the contents, but still wouldn't know what she was looking for. Or she could ask, *are you awake, E? Are we really doing this? I'm terrified.* She yanked the bag to the floor. Someone was walking around upstairs, thwacking the refrigerator door shut, and then it was quiet, but she knew she wasn't going back to sleep. She didn't mind how this early waking could make her day endless, but she wasn't always prepared for how possibility suggested itself to her as a naked proposal in the light of these uncertain hours. It had been possible, she'd discovered at a time just like this, to consider the end of her marriage. Ben had exhausted everything. It had seemed possible to have the half of life left to her feel like something that could be whole again.

She put on her bathrobe. The hot tub moaned under its plastic blanket as she passed. Upstairs, she looked at the mountain. Machines zigzagged across its face as showers of manufactured snow caught in the orange headlights. She heard the steady mouth-breathing of the boy above her in the loft. It was on her way back to her room that she saw him asleep on the kidney-shaped dog bed in the corner of the kitchen. He fit perfectly on the flannel, hands balled under his chin, tail tucked between his legs.

The morning was sunny and punctuated with the staccato of things dripping, which apparently was not great skiing news for Kirk, who appeared after breakfast in his obscene tube of ski clothing. He went out to pack up the car, but Tess sensed there was something else beside irritation over slope conditions going on, that his exit and Margot's position at the head of the table were planned. Her daughter fiddled with the uneaten triangles of Ryan's toast.

Tess opened a decade-old Vermont tourist brochure she'd

found in the downstairs bathroom and tapped at a faded picture. "While you're skiing, I'm going to see the world's largest frozen waterfall," she said.

Margot gave the page a cursory look and then they both turned to watch Kirk load up the car. "I have a favor to ask. Ryan doesn't feel well. Will you stay with him while we go skiing?"

"You know he slept on the dog bed last night?"

"We'll just be gone a few hours. Back after lunch."

"A dog bed, Margot. The boy slept on the dog bed." Tess wasn't sorry to see Kirk, the fugitive father, slip and land on his ass as a pair of skis slid all the way down the driveway. "Did you hear me?"

"I heard you, but what can I do? He likes it," Margot said. "I made his lunch. Put him in front of the TV or he won't eat. And don't let him have chocolate. You know where the list of bad food is, right? Nothing but the sandwich, or he'll puke."

Ryan appeared above them, leaning on the loft's railing while earphones fed him music. His hair was a nest above a triumphant smile. The boy had it all over Margot and Kirk, had them perfectly hog-tied. Tess had to admire the way he banished them to the mountain and how he sang along to lyrics to he surely didn't understand. He got what he wanted—when he had nothing he needed, it seemed. Out in the driveway, Kirk warmed up the car as the wipers swung in escape across the windshield.

Pitterpat Flow is one of the world's greatest natural wonders, Tess read in the brochure. *From November to March, visitors will be able to view the miraculous power of water in its stilled state. Some fifty feet high, the Flow is a frozen picture in time.*

She didn't believe a word of the hype, but was interested in the intersection—if there even was one—of the lie and the truth. She would take the kid with her, and when she was ready to go, she climbed the ladder to the loft. On the bed amid a sea of clothes and babyish stuffed animals, was the boy with his headphones still on. His eyes were closed as he played with his stiff little penis. She gulped with amusement, and some small measure of embarrassment. Why bother the kid now?

On the other hand, she thought, he can give it up for a while and we can make something of the day. She rattled the ladder, and soon he appeared at the top. "Get dressed," she said, motioning him to take off his earphones. "I'm taking you to see one of the world's greatest natural wonders."

His expression hinted at a challenge. "I can't go. I'm sick."

"Even sick people can go. Especially sick people. Says so in the brochure. Do you need help getting dressed?"

He waved her away and soon reappeared in the clothes he'd worn the day before, the white turtleneck with its timeline of purloined food. She helped zip up his awful lavender puffy boots. Girls' boots, she decided; his mother wasn't helping matters. The boy was fidgety in the car and it occurred to her that he should probably be in the back given his weight, but she didn't move him. She was beginning to like his strange presence next to her. She told him they were going to see a frozen waterfall.

Ryan opened and closed the heating vents. "If it's a waterfall, it's moving so it can't be frozen," he said.

"Ah, smarty-pants, the brochure says differently. And I believe everything I read, don't you?"

"Do you have a husband?" he asked.

"Yes, his name is Eli. He couldn't come because he had to work."

"I'm hungry."

This struck her as a perfectly reasonable response. She realized that she'd forgotten the prescribed sandwich. Maybe she could find something harmless for him; mashed potatoes, oatmeal, a banana, saltines, snow. Foods that matched his color. She gave him an Altoid, which he spit into his mitten with great drama. Soon she took a road that ran parallel to the highway. On either side were fields of untouched snow, a few houses set far back. Occasional buildings appeared, signs of life, but no actual life itself. The Family Restaurant turned out, despite its benign name and frilly curtains, to not be a particularly homey place, the bell on the door signaling the few people nursing coffee to look up and stare. The boy took a booth facing the sanded lot.

"Bacon cheeseburger with french fries and a coke," Ryan announced to the waitress and slapped his plastic menu shut. "And that will do it."

Tess laughed at his swagger. She considered overruling his order, just in case, but in the end, she asked for the same, though she wasn't hungry. "You're a funny guy," she told him. "Do you know that?"

He asked her for a pen and began to scribble on the place-mat that advertised local businesses: a maple sugar museum, the birthplace of M. Cotter.

"You're not really my grandmother," Ryan said, his pen obliterating the Tru-Value logo.

"That's half true. I'm your step-grandmother. My daughter is your stepmother."

He looked up. "Who's your daughter?"

"Margot." Her water tasted as though it had been pulled right from the frozen ground. "Remember? She's married to your father."

"I know that." He rolled his eyes and sighed. "Stupid lady."

Had she expected him to like her because she was the champion of troubled little boys everywhere? She felt stung. Their food arrived with lettuce and tomato that Ryan dropped on the table. He concentrated on the descent of ketchup from the bottle, and when too much flooded the meat, he removed the sludge with a finger that he then wiped down the front of his shirt. Tess pushed a napkin towards him. He ate in feral bites, pushing in the fries. A single red spot pulsed in each cheek. Ketchup, a particular poison. God, what else? Why had she let him do this? To prove that none of it was true? A cold flow of worry ran through her.

"I'm done," he said, and pushed his plate away. "I have to pee."

He slid out of the booth. People at the counter watched him because he was, in his own way, entirely unforgettable, a little boy, a shrunken old man. Tess looked out onto the parking lot just as a filthy crust of snow fell off her back fender. The sun was high and thin; she could almost imagine spring here, waiting in this booth for it to arrive. She took out her cell phone and called Eli. She wanted to tell him where she was and who she was with, but she was dumped to his voice mail. Splitting up had not been his idea, and it had taken her forever to convince him that it was what they both wanted and needed, that Ben had left them worn out. Eli fought and his fury was a lightning storm. And then he'd called her from work one day to say ok, and behind him she'd heard the clatter of the folding machines; he'd chosen to talk to her from the factory floor with its well-tuned industry, its loyalty and agency, its perfume of glue and cardboard dust. She'd spent half her life there, too. Decorative paper boxes; it was what the world needed, they'd discovered together. She didn't expect now to feel such regret, but she missed him with an ache.

Ryan had been in the bathroom too long. If he didn't come out in a minute, she'd have to get him. And if he wasn't all right? The waitress came over to take their plates.

"Are we close to Pitterpat Flow?" Tess asked her.

The girl had never heard of the place, nor had the two men sitting at the counter, but there was only one road it could be on—and Tess was on it. She felt oddly conspired against, as though they were leading her down a dark alley. Ryan appeared with the triumphant, feel-good look of a boy who has pumped the soap dispenser a few thousand times and pulled a few hundred towels from the silver box. The front of his shirt was wet, plastered against his thin chest and sesame seed nipples. He'd tried to scrub off the ketchup.

Outside, the temperature had dropped, and in the car, the boy slipped inside the warm nest of his coat. They passed the occasional yard sale, sleds and skis stuck into the snow like athletic grave markers. Set back on the left side of the road was a deserted hut with a faded sign for Pitterpat Flow. The lot was unplowed, the structure an unreachable artifact, and she drove past. She imagined plaits of ice, the relic of a faster fall. That would have to do. She couldn't imagine the trek through the snow, and leaving the evidence of her footprints.

"I have to pee," Ryan said.

"Listen," Tess said. "I know all about little boys and their needing to pee. You just went; you can hold it now."

But he wiggled and thumped at his crotch until Tess stopped. He wouldn't go in the open, though they had yet to see another person, and insisted on climbing into the thickness of the woods. Tess followed his sickly purple boots and turned away from the sight of his pants pulled down and his bare white bottom. She wondered if his father had ever taught him a single, useful thing. The air was sharp with balsam, and alive with the soft plop of falling pine cones. She stood where the woods ended above a field, dried stalks punching up through the snow in cold protest, and in the distance, a series of red barns and outbuildings. This was the goat farm Gerald had walked them to one afternoon that weekend. She recalled the organic odor and how Eli had been too embarrassed to milk a goat. She had found her way into Millboro; she'd wanted to see it again, and why not? She was allowed. It wasn't a bad thing to remember. A rumble made her turn to spot the purple boots and the boy struggling with his pants, and then back to see a line of snowmobiles plowing through the field. The procession bounced and zipped and flew. It looked exhilarating. The boy galloped up to her.

"I missed them," he cried. His face was twisted with despair now that the caravan had slid into the distance. "Shitting fucker. Shitting, shitting fucker."

"You'll get other chances, I promise," she said, but he was as despondent as an ancient emperor. "You have to move quickly when you hear them. You'll think you have forever, but then they're gone."

He stomped back to the car, still swearing. Did he always get what he wanted? His disappointment was palpable and adult. Tess drove by the goat farm and towards where she thought the house had been. Ryan said she was driving in the wrong direction, and shook his head like an irked spouse. The curve was too long, and what appeared first was the Blue Wales Motel that had been under construction back then. The place had an old face now, the shutters drooping with palsy. Gerald had wanted Eli to invest in it with him, but Eli's money and her own was already in the box business. Gerald had said that Eli was too young to be so tied up and tied down, his balls in a vice. Eli had given her, his new wife, a contrite look.

"I've been here before," she told Ryan, who claimed he felt sick. Tess put her hand on his forehead. "You shouldn't say you're sick if you're not. When you really are sick, no one will believe you."

"I almost died once," he said. Her hand was still on his

forehead. "When I was born, I had to stay in the hospital for a long time. I couldn't eat because I threw up everything. I was this tiny little guy who almost died for days and days and days."

You were this tiny little guy who almost died. She could hear the line being told over and over. This is what families did—they turned their lowest moments into stories to live off, to mark their survival by. Remember the window Ben smashed, remember Margot's bloody nose and the raw scratch down her back, remember the stunning ferocity her children had brought out in each other, the violence they inflicted.

"But you're not going to die now," she said. "That was a long time ago, and now you're fine. Healthy and very, very smart. I think you have great powers."

"Bullshit," he announced, but smiled.

Farther down the road was the same white Cape house with the mountains as backdrop. Gerald had wanted to buy the place, but she didn't imagine for a second that he actually had. Bullies didn't' win. She pulled up in front. The door was open as a woman tried to push a reluctant cat out with her foot. When she saw Tess' car, she used her book as a visor and squinted into the white distance. The cat squeezed back inside. Tess thought about driving away.

"Are you looking for something?" the woman yelled. The cold thinned her voice. "Are you lost?"

It was Poppy, Gerald's girlfriend. Gone for years and that red, sexy name was there instantly. The shock of seeing her was like seeing the actual flower in the snow. Tess had assumed that Gerald and Poppy had split up at the end of the summer.

"Tell her no," Ryan whispered.

Tess leaned out. "My husband was a friend of Gerald's. Eli. Eli and Tess? From a long time ago?"

Wind rolled across the snow banks, whitening the air and

the retrieval of memories. "Eli and Tess? From a hundred years ago? My god, come in." She waved with her book. "Come in!"

"I don't want to," Ryan insisted. He pressed a hand over his stomach. "I don't feel good."

"Remember? You're fine. There's nothing wrong with you."

He scuffed up the front walk behind her. Poppy was still beautiful, half-gray now, still had the longest legs. Glasses hung from a beaded string. The intervening years did not for one second lessen Tess's notion that Poppy was another species of woman—elegant, desirable, emotionally impractical. She felt wan and generic next to her, just as Eli had appeared solid and stiff next to Gerald's lean and hectic height. Poppy and Gerald had been a magnificent-looking couple. Gerald had gone without a shirt much of the hot weekend, enormously strong, exuding conquest and a smell of sex and sweat. Tess had been overheated with erotic envy.

"We can't come in," Tess said. She didn't want to see Gerald. "I just wanted to say hello."

But Poppy insisted as she looked at Ryan and absently touched a small diamond in her ear. A woman without children, Tess decided, a woman all to herself. They shed their coats and boots, but there was nowhere to leave soggy clothing, not on the pristine Shaker bench that held a stack of books and a wine-colored leather bag. Tess's damp socks left prints on the bleached floor, but to take them off seemed too intimate. Already she was stalling—why had she agreed to come in anyway? Her attachment to the past struck her as dangerous. Now and then was likely to slam shut and she'd be caught in the middle, her fingers squeezed in the hinges.

The kitchen was no longer cramped, but airy with a full wall of windows that looked out onto the field silvered with mist and the pond with its fringe of reeds. Gerald got just what he wanted: the house, the woman. Poppy's brilliant green eyes had only faded a little. And Tess, so smug in her marriage that ancient weekend, was the one driving around now like someone who was entirely lost.

"Amazing." Poppy turned the gas on under the kettle. "After all this time. There are people you imagine you'll never see again, and then you do. And it just blows you away."

"I'm surprised you remember me," Tess said.

"But you remembered me, didn't you?" She glanced at Ryan on his stomach in front of the fire. The cat slithered around his head. "Life gallops—children with children—while it still feels like last summer. God, I sound like an old lady." They laughed companionably.

Where do we begin? Tess wondered. She took the cup of tea Poppy offered. She'd begin at the end—today. There was the goat farm, the frozen falls, her son-in-law's house, her daughter, the boy who wasn't really her grandson.

"And Eli?" Poppy asked, tentatively.

"Eli's fine." Tess looked into the pale brown water in her cup. "So Gerald actually bought this place. He always struck me as the kind of man who would get everything he wanted in life."

Poppy smiled. "Not at all. This is my house. I've had it for almost fifteen years. I come up from the city when I can." Her eyes cinched at the corners. "Gerald died. You knew that, didn't you?"

Tess had been picturing someone who didn't exist.

"I hadn't talked to him in years," Poppy explained. "We were married for one, divorced forever. I always felt bad about that weekend. Gerald was a fool, his own enemy. He thought people were behind him, when really they were much farther ahead."

Tess didn't think Poppy knew that the men had fought.

"How did he die?"

"Fell off a ladder. It would have killed him to know that something so banal did him in." Poppy seemed embarrassed by her own smile.

Tess looked at Ryan. She had an impulse to pull him onto her lap. There was the familiar drone of snowmobiles and a line of them appeared from the left. They edged the pond on the far side before they disappeared. Digging above Ryan's upper lip was the disappointment that she'd failed once again to call him in time. Having dashed to the window, he now showed her his bottom teeth like a dog.

"I hate those things," Poppy said. "If I could, I'd buy the land and keep them off with a shotgun." She let her head fall to the side and she pushed around the skin on the back of her hand.

"We should get going," Tess said.

Poppy hated to ask, but would Tess help her with something outside before they left? She opened a closet stuffed with winter gear, the browns of men's coats, enormous boots, gloves for working hands. There had been men in the house, some Poppy might have loved, but none who remained. Poppy handed Tess a pair of heavy socks. The cold was alarming, the sun falling fast over a path tamped down in the snow that led to a small shed. Poppy had been trying to work the door open and get to the firewood, but had managed only to pound the snow against itself into an immoveable icy wedge. It would have been better to dig in the first place, but it was too late now. The small ineptitude of a woman living alone surprised Tess.

Poppy's breath came out in pink, determined clouds as they rocked the door back and forth. Tess smelled the lichened wood inside, and saw through the inches of open door, seams of light falling over the logs. Gerald had told Eli that Poppy was sexually uptight, that he was going to dump her at the end of the summer because he needed someone who could really fuck.

Eli, furious, told Tess this in their bedroom across the hall from where Gerald and Poppy slept. She was struck by how innocent her husband was in some ways, and how the look into others' lives made them both self-conscious. They didn't know anything about fucking. The next morning they'd watched Poppy, breezy in a sleeveless dress, scrambling eggs, while Gerald ground into her from behind. Poppy had leaned back, her spatula poised. Eli had watched them, too. She wished now that she'd asked him what he'd been thinking, and that she might have known her husband best in that moment.

"Gerald was a bastard," Tess said.

Poppy stopped pulling on the door. "No, that weekend, maybe. I think Eli brought something out in him, some kind of panic or competition probably."

"He said not nice things about you."

"Oh, he was always saying something awful about everyone. He thought it was motivating." Poppy seemed cautious, her gaze far off, and Tess knew she shouldn't say any more. "Don't tell me, ok? I don't want to know what he said." Poppy shook her head. "Shit. I can't believe I'm crying."

"I'm sorry. I don't know why I even brought it up."

"It's ok. It's just that I haven't thought of him in a long time, that's all." She shook her head and led them back to the house.

Tess would have liked to sit down for a minute, but Poppy didn't take off her coat and told Tess to keep the socks. She was clearly ready for them to leave. But Ryan was not in front of the fire. His boots and coat were still in the hall and he was not upstairs. Tess looked at the field and saw the last sunlight gild footsteps toward the pond.

She heard the noise and saw the snowmobiles' lights cut through the cold. She knew the boy wouldn't let himself miss another chance to see them. She ran through the snow with her feet barely rising above the winter line. Poppy was behind her somewhere, saying something, asking something. The boy wasn't smart. He was scared to death of himself. He would be struck, tossed into the air, and struck by another machine down the line. She was a careless, breathless woman and he was the color of the snow, an endless season, a sun always hidden behind clouds. Who would believe this was how both their lives would end?

She fell back into the reeds. The purpling sky rose above her. The machines passed and faded into ribbons, and then she heard sounds of absolute, exhilarating pleasure from the boy. He'd made a seat for himself in the reeds where he was close enough to smell the fumes and have the snow spit on his face. He was enthralled, his body pulsing with excitement. Tess turned to Poppy who stood to her left. At first Tess thought she was meant to take the offered hand, but when she stood, Poppy slapped her hard across the face. For a moment Poppy froze, and then ran back to the house. Tess didn't feel anything, but she thought she might shatter.

"Did you see?" the boy asked. His face was wet with snow. "I saw the machines. I saw them close."

At the house, Tess sat the boy on the bench and told to him not to move. She went upstairs to find Poppy. Her cheek burned; she'd apologize. She looked into the room where she and Eli had slept. On their last night, Eli's disappointment in Gerald was suffocating. She'd woken to the sound of the men outside and looked down at them through the bars of the headboard. Gerald was naked, his chest luminous, his penis thick, Eli in shorts that cut into his unyielding waist. Eli swung ambitiously at Gerald who stumbled back, then forward, and landed one in return. One thrown punch each, then they were done, stepping back, hands up in truce. Not fighters really, but they wouldn't ever talk again.

Poppy appeared in the doorway. "I hit you."

"You were scared. It's okay."

"I'm not apologizing." Her hands were in her sweater pockets. "I wasn't expecting any of this. I didn't invite it. Would you leave now?"

Poppy went downstairs first and stood at the open door, indifferent to the cold air rushing in, and Tess and Ryan rushing out.

It was dark now, hours late, and Tess pulled into the Blue Wales lot to call Margot and Kirk. Margot would have called her father already, furious and worried, and Eli might have broken the news. But she couldn't find her phone, not in the yellowed light of the car's interior, and she knew it could be anywhere really, on the Family Restaurant's sticky seat or in Poppy's field. Ryan, sated with excitement, had fallen asleep. The fake fur of his hood moved with his breath, and tiny beads of moisture caught on the fiber's ends.

Tess drove too fast and the car swerved on patches of ice. Thirty minutes later, idling on the side of the road in front of Pitterpat Flow, was Margot and Kirk's car. Tess pulled up behind it. She would apologize; no harm done, except some worry, but for that she was very sorry. She knew what it was like to worry. She left the car running and got out. The SUV's tinted windows were infuriating, prolonging the freeze as she stood there like a penitent. She clicked the glass with her ring. The window went down to reveal not Kirk, as she'd expected, but her daughter, alone.

"Where have you been?" Margot demanded. She pressed her temples with the heels of her hands. "Is he okay?"

"He's fine." The air was perfect now, a cold silver bell.

"That's it? That's all you're going to say? He's fine?"

The day she and Eli had taken Ben to Alsop, Margot had

waited on the steps of the house with this same rage when they returned. "Where is my brother? Where did you take him?" she'd asked. Tess hadn't heard her daughter's fear then, but she heard it now. Fear and some kind of difficult love in that rage. Tess moved the boy to Margot's car. She told her daughter that she'd been to the place, even the room, where Margot had first been imagined, an amazing thing after Eli's fistfight. An amazing thing now on this foreign, snow-bound road, but Margot was saying something to the boy, leaning over him, her face hidden in the depths of his hood, and she didn't hear her mother.

LOVESICK

From an opposite bench on the boat's lower deck, Bowman watched his wife Claudia place her hand on his stepdaughter's belly, and he knew that what grew there was not simply a baby, but his own uncertainty. Soon, a line for the snack bar blocked his view, and he saw bodies in their happy procession, coffee cups and foamy Buds held aloft early in the morning. He looked like these other day travelers on the Harbor Queen in his salmon-colored golf shirt, Nikes without socks, and the extra pounds that had arrived with his forty-third birthday, but he wasn't nearly as sure-footed as they were. An instant of Claudia was revealed in the sway, and seasickness suddenly rose under his tongue like a dirty word.

He took the stairs to the airy upper level. The trip had been her idea. They'd had such a good time when they'd been before, she'd said, laying her hand on his stomach. Her coyness had made him embarrassed for both of them because they hadn't had a good time at all, and she knew it, too. But a crease from the pillow was still mapped across her cheek when she asked, her nightgown had fallen off one sweet, freckled shoulder, and though he didn't entirely understand what she was asking, why she'd want to go back, he'd felt too much in love with her to say anything but yes.

That visit, four years earlier, came back now to Bowman in the same way moments of childhood humiliation revisit the grown man; fully lit, and reanimated by expectation that things will play out differently this time. Hope made his knees loosen without warning. He noticed that the red benches were arranged like pews and the silvery sky was a dome above the Harbor Queen, up where the air was carbonated with prayer. The woman next to him was wearing white high-heeled sandals, impractical, optimistic shoes, and her eyes were closed in her own romantic invocation.

In every direction there was boundless ocean and no horizon, and Bowman felt the rise and drop of the boat beneath him. The water had been choppy the last time too, but seasickness hadn't even occurred to him then. He and Claudia had been married for only two years at that point, and he'd still kept an anxious eye on his thirteen-year-old stepdaughter Mariah, a girl who was a gift to him when his life seemed so perilously giftless before. She'd laughed as the boat rolled from side to side, her sneakers rose from the deck, and her hair lifted. When he'd had enough of imagining she was about to be pitched overboard and sucked into the purple waves, he'd pulled her back. She'd teased him about it, and it had shocked Bowman, this hard, sassy affection she had for him. He'd never known anything like it. Claudia had been up on deck too that day instead of down with the morning drunks and the diesel fumes. She was just pregnant then, luminous and sleepy and inward. Bowman had whispered to her how Provincetown, as it burned into view, glittered like a rich host, and he'd let his mouth linger by her ear which smelled a little like new mown grass.

The woman in the white sandals left the upper deck and the boat slinked into the harbor until its final, rubbery bump against the dock. Bowman was the last to get off, and he moved towards Claudia and Mariah standing on the dock, the day already simmering with only the feeblest of July breezes at his neck. Mariah's face was wide, her mouth dark-berry. The sun melted in her inky hair, reminding him that her real father was a Pequod Indian, a bum, and a bastard who was not around and never had been. It reminded him too, uneasily, that his wife's past would never be entirely known to him. When and where had she made love to the guy?

The monument behind Claudia bent in the heat's distortion, its triangular point skewering a single cloud. She was pale where Mariah was dark, abbreviated where her daughter was generous and unavoidable—and he was big enough to fit them both in his arms. It was the similarity of their expressions that amazed Bowman; today the look was indulgent but also slightly impatient with him, as if wandering off was something he tended to do all the time, when he was nothing but reliable, predictable. But if Mariah said everything that came into her head without caution or consideration (had sex the same way too, apparently), Claudia was a tight package, lifting only an occasional corner to reveal what was inside. Today she had a thick, sensible smear of white zinc on her lips and an itinerary in her head.

"Where'd you go?" she asked. Their feet sucked at the tar of MacMillan wharf as they walked towards town.

"Checking out the view on deck," Bowman explained. "Getting some air."

"Queasy," Claudia suggested. "You're a little green around the edges. You should have eaten breakfast."

"So, did you see anything up there?" Mariah asked.

Bowman would have liked to surprise her curiosity by saying that he'd seen something extraordinary—a dead body in the water, or someone shooting up near the life preservers—but he hadn't. On their left, they passed the fidgeting lines for whale watching tours and deep-sea fishing expeditions. Bowman hesitated, and in that instant, a brochure was slipped between his fingers. I could easily be lured away today, he thought, feeling the pull of bad judgement and the blue-green tide.

"What do you girls say?" Bowman asked, waving the brochure.

Mariah bumped his shoulder with hers. "Rip-offs, Bow," she warned, redirecting him. "Don't even *think* about doing that crap."

She wore his Celtics basketball shirt over a bikini top. It hung loose at her skinny arms and pulled like a neon green skin over her belly. Nineteen, he thought, with no husband, no boyfriend, not even a fucking father for this kid, just a few college credits and a full moon of baby rising over the waist of her bicycle shorts. Christ. Knocked-up; Claudia hated when he used the word, but there it was to be used for just this occasion. (She'd been eighteen and knocked up once, too, she'd informed him—as though he could forget that detail.) In the spring, Bowman had begun to turn away from the sight of his ever-expanding stepdaughter, even as they talked and he offered her orange juice, a bagel, advice she'd ignore. Evenings, he retreated to the cool of the garage, with its all-business male adornments and the neighborhood viewed through an open door. He wasn't sure of the true nature of his snappish discomfort with the pregnant Mariah—when he adored her—but he was fearful of its suggestion that he was a disappointed man.

"Maybe we'll go next time," Claudia consoled, nodding towards the whaling boats, "but not today. I thought we'd climb the monument this morning, before it gets too crowded."

"Me? Climb? I don't think so," Mariah said.

"That's how I feel," Bowman added, patting his own stomach.

On Commercial Street, fumes from the foot-long hot dog pit blew at Bowman, rousing his seasickness again. He knew Claudia wouldn't buy anything for herself on this trip—she was tight with money, left over from her years as a single mother—but she would explain away this deprivation by declaring there were no deals in a tourist trap like this. *She* wouldn't be taken. A few waxy wads of salt water taffy, maybe a fan of postcards she'd end up doling out to her second graders in the fall. But right away, she marched into a crappy-looking souvenir shop. Bowman waited outside and watched the thick parade of people. Last time he'd been in Provincetown, disease had decimated the place, blown through town like the final, great party of the century, leaving the streets echoing and scattered with garbage. The men who'd wrapped arms around each other's waists did so not out of affection, he'd decided, but loss. And in the midst of this, he'd allowed himself to imagine pushing his baby down the street on his next visit. There was nothing cold-hearted or selfish about it. His kid would be evidence of Bowman Starr's—of life's—determination to survive. Now the place was packed once more with all types of body, and everywhere people were dodging, putting things into their mouths, gorging themselves on sweets and flesh and free AC. Childless, baby stroller-less, he was suddenly ravenous, crossed the street and bought himself a three-scoop mint chocolate chip ice cream cone.

When Claudia reappeared, she cast a disapproving eye at Bowman's ice cream, and then showed him the tiny shirt with a glittering picture of a clam on it. Impending grandmotherhood had caused her to develop wildly bad taste, and the house was filling with her stockpiles for this kid, stashes of pastel in drawers and closets.

Bowman handed his cone to Mariah who'd been eying it acquisitively, and absently picked at the sparkles on the shirt with his thumbnail. "Looks like a girl's shirt to me," he said. "You so sure this kid's a she?"

Claudia took the shirt back, examined it, and folded it as

small as an English muffin. "What difference does it make? I think it's adorable," she said, but by the way she turned it over in her hand, Bowman knew she was thinking she might have made a mistake. Why, he asked himself, had he felt the need to say anything at all, to stir her doubt?

"That's bullshit," Mariah announced, her mouth glossy with his ice cream. "Your shirt's pink. Are you a girl? Are you gay?"

"It's salmon, not pink," he said.

"I'll give my boy a tutu if he asks." She licked the ice cream with a long, swiping tongue. "You have to let kids do what they want, be who they want. You can't stifle their self-expression."

"Excellent idea. I say let them make all the rules and call all the shots," Bowman said, surprised to find himself angry and sarcastic. "You let me know how it works out. Did you ever read *Lord of the Flies?*"

Mariah rolled her eyes, tossed the still full cone into the garbage, and walked ahead. She was proud of the way she looked, too proud, belly thrust out, hair swinging defiantly, pissed off at him. Her ankles were swollen from last night's Chinese food. Her pregnancy was like the kids' game of sticking a pillow and two oranges under your shirt. Claudia hiked her bag high on her shoulder, a Sherpa.

"Nice job," she said. "A great start. Why do you have to be like that?"

"Do you see how crazy this is?" Bowman asked. "Does she think anything through? Does she understand consequences? For chrissake! Look at her."

"I am looking at her. Is there something to be done now?" Claudia asked. "What I was hoping for today—" she stumbled. "What I was hoping for coming here," she said in a tone instantly hardened with warning, "was a day when you're not angry at her, because this baby's coming whether you like it or not. It's done. It's your choice from here on."

She turned to look at the narrowest space between two buildings and a slice of water and then took off after Mariah.

The first time he'd gone to Claudia's apartment in Mount Pleasant, there was Mariah, hidden. Until that evening, their dates had been informational, the necessary laying out of habits and histories in neutral places. That night they'd talked softly—the daughter he had yet to meet was asleep down the hall. Bowman admired the clean, practical efficiency of Claudia's life, her place, and the way she managed. He imagined she was so careful with things that they never wore out, an imagining that was mostly infatuation and little awe. That Claudia lived on the least-secure first floor, her door festooned with locks and chains, seemed to Bowman a vulnerability even she had not been able to avoid with all her self-sufficiency, and it made his heart pound to think he could fix this much for her, put her in a house with two stories and a bedroom overlooking a yard.

Claudia's feet had urged against his thigh as they sat on the couch. He touched her lacquered nails, the one on her baby toe as small as a seed. Occasionally she laughed and told a story on herself, but her face profiled in the silver light from the television was always purposeful. It didn't bother him that she wanted to find a father for her daughter, that she was tired of doing everything alone, that she had a mission. Until then, he assumed his chance for a family had wasted all its opportunities on cheap rides and thrills; romance had left him mystified, and his bachelorhood made him suspect in every way the older he got. Later, as he pressed Claudia against the wall just outside her bedroom, he said he was in love with her and he thought he felt her control crumble under his hands. But he was wrong.

"Stop." She pushed him away, her palm against his chest.

"One thing."

"Yes, you are the one thing," he said, finding himself hugely romantic all of a sudden. Why shouldn't he finally be able to say these things? What was there to lose? She opened the door to her daughter's room where the girl was asleep, facing them.

"Just so you know, you can't spend the night," Claudia whispered.

This introduction of her child into their groping was confusing. He didn't know what to say; he'd never slept with a mother before. Claudia ran her hand down his back, suspended one electric finger at the fork of his ass. A dim light from the kitchen moved restlessly on her cheek. A jewel had been revealed to him in the form of the sleeping kid, and he understood then that someday she might belong to him, too. He urged Claudia's hand to continue, and decided, this is a woman who doesn't really need me—look at her life alone, tidy and economical, and rich in ways mine isn't— but maybe simply wants me, and in his mind, want was something much more rare and valuable.

"Let's get you a new bathing suit," he said to Claudia when he caught up to her, moving his hands to her front, tucking his fingertips into the waistband of her shorts, his mouth in her hair. She had stopped in front of *BodyBody*, a store whose windows were filled with pale, headless mannequins in neon suits, their nipples like gumdrops. He pressed himself into her, hopeful again, sorry for being a bastard.

"I don't want to try anything on now," she said, but by the way she leaned back into him, he knew she wanted to be convinced. "It's too hot for that, don't you think?"

"You'll take your clothes off. You won't be hot then."

When Mariah, who had stopped a few feet beyond, walked

back to them, Claudia moved so that Bowman's fingers slipped from her. "We're going to buy your mother something nice," he announced. "Something glamorous and sexy. Pink with zippers, gold, maybe, something impractical."

"You can't actually swim in any of these things, you know. They fall apart instantly." Claudia reapplied zinc to her lips and examined her reflection in the window. "God, I look ridiculous. Oh, what the hell—here goes." She passed her bag over her shoulder to her daughter and went inside.

Bowman and Mariah followed and sat on a bench. The girl sucked in clipped, shocked breaths, and when her knees banged together, Bowman heard the sound of bone against bone. It made his stomach surge in fear for her.

"You okay?" he asked. Sweat glossed the skin below his eyes and above his lip. "You're breathing funny."

"Don't look so worried. I'm fine. It was probably the mint chocolate chip," she said, fanning her face and smiling at him. "Totally disgusting."

"I wouldn't know. You chucked it, remember?" Drips of ice cream dotted her shirt front as if someone had drawn the eyes and nose of her unborn baby. "Look sweetheart," he said. "I'm sorry I haven't been so nice recently."

"Incorrect. You've been a total asshole."

"I know, but just tell me one thing, will you? What the hell are you doing having a baby?"

Mariah let out a high, endearing laugh. "Now you're asking? Isn't it a little late for that?"

She looked towards the dressing room as though she were about to reveal something she wasn't sure she should. "Did you know I wasn't at all positive what I was going to do at first?" She hesitated. "I know you think I don't think about things, that I'm flighty. That I'm too young."

"You are too young." Bowman watched Mariah rub an ancient scar on her knee, one she'd gotten long before they ever knew each other.

"I was going to have an abortion. I even made an appointment." She patted her stomach. "I mean, do I need this? I got to the place and everything, but Mom wouldn't let up, crying, begging me. You know how she can be." Mariah looked at her feet, resigned to giving in to her mother. "But you know this already, right?"

Bowman shook his head.

"Come on, I know Mom told you. Maybe you just blocked it or something," Mariah added lightly, as if to skip over this vast canyon they'd just come upon was simple and even delightful. "Anyway, it doesn't matter. I'm happy about it now."

"Happy," Bowman repeated, a useless word. Something dull had invaded him, as if he'd always been hunched on this bench watching his life take place without him. No, there hadn't been any discussion with him about this baby or an abortion, just the fact of it presented to him along with pork chops and rice one night by Claudia, and later all manner of logic from her. *It's Mariah's decision*, she'd said, *and she wants this baby very much. I have nothing to do with it.*

Bowman watched his wife's feet shuffle under the dressing room door as she bent to take off her shorts and then again to put on her suit. When it caught at her ankle, she stopped, her hands clutching the silver material. It seemed that she stood forever in that awkward pose and Bowman knew self-consciousness had crowded into the tiny space with her and said no new suit for you, nothing special, you deserve nothing. Especially since you're a liar. He pictured her naked body, the hard ladder of her ribcage, the knuckles of her backbone, tiny breasts, pubic hair the color of toast, a body hardly changed by motherhood, it ad happened so young for her, too. She pointed her foot and slid the bathing suit off again. It was unnamable, this slither of cloth against his wife's skin. He felt no particular yearning for her at the moment, just a surprisingly familiar sense of disappointment.

"We tried to have a kid for awhile," Bowman said to Mariah while Claudia was still in the dressing room, her feet now affixed to the floor as if standing still would enable her to hear everything.

Mariah nodded. "I know. She told me. Didn't work."

"I don't know why it didn't happen," Bowman said. "A big, fat fucking mystery."

The unexplained. Even today that cruel whisper of possibility was in his skull. Claudia had allowed him to discover her babylessness month after month in the form of an open box of Tampax sitting on the back of the toilet. His hand rubbing her back—that was Bowman's wordless acknowledgment of the disappointment they'd shared. And if she sometimes turned away from his comfort still well, why should he force her to say something when there was absolutely nothing new to say? There was no baby for them. The end. The unexplained.

Claudia hadn't wanted to see a doctor, or have any tests done, but he'd had himself checked without telling her and had the results sent to his city hall office in Records and Licenses where he was the recorder and filer of everyone else's fortune and misfortune. The report said nothing was wrong with him. The entire procedure made him feel like a criminal, his balls accessories to the crime. In the weeks after he got the results, he was determined to tell Claudia, but he developed a tiny stutter, and a habit of evasiveness she didn't seem to notice. He began to understand that there was possibly another truth to be revealed if he told her—that Claudia didn't want a child with him—and what would he do with *that?* After a while, he'd managed to convince himself that he had no business wanting a baby so much anyway, that it was freakish, a misfiring in his brain of some sort, a feminine, feathery side of his heart he shouldn't expose. A man with a wife and daughter and career was not supposed to ache for a child at end of the day when he stared up at the ceiling, when he felt his sleeping wife's hip roll against his.

"Not such a mystery," Mariah said. "She just couldn't do another baby." Mariah patted his knee, a placating, chilling gesture. "But she's always saying how crazy you are about kids—and that you'll be crazy about this one when it's born. That this is a good thing for you—even if you're a prick about it now."

"She couldn't do another baby," he repeated, spotting his wife who had left the dressing room. Until today, he hadn't been sure if it was failure or loss they'd suffered together, but now he was sure it was deceit he'd suffered alone. He'd been angry at the wrong woman.

Claudia's face was flushed. "I tried them on and didn't like a single one of those suits. I don't know what kind of body they're made for, but it's definitely not mine." She glanced from Bowman to Mariah. "What's going on? What are you two talking about?"

Bowman looked at her as though she might offer some truth, but she was the one whose ghostly white lips were parted in expectation of an answer.

"You, actually," he told her. "We were talking about how you decided Mariah should have this baby because you didn't want one yourself."

"Oh, Bowman," she said, "it's not like that." Her voice was placating, but her face contracted, like a flower by a cold window.

"You could have just told me," he said. "It wouldn't have killed me."

They lost Claudia or more precisely, as Mariah pointed out, Claudia had lost herself when she pushed out of the store. There were thousands of places for her to hide in this town. Bowman didn't think he'd been wrong for what he'd said to Claudia, yet it didn't seem right that a man should ever let his wife disappear. He turned every few seconds to see that Mariah was not so much accompanying him on his foray up Commercial Street as she was dogging him, her face pained like a child's aware she's had some part in her mother's abrupt leaving. And of course, he had implicated her too in the crime—"we were talking," he'd said, forcing the conspiracy.

Everything on the street appeared mismatched, the leather store next to the candle store, perfume next to candy. There was the alluring blue of the bay nine-tenths obscured by tackiness and baby carriages. And there was always someone striding regally against the flow of people, determined to have the crowd part for him and his bare and hairless chest. Bowman envied the bravado. Halfway down a set of stairs that led into a basement store, Bowman stopped for the shade. He was overheated and seized by a brilliant moment from the last trip, when it had seemed necessary to pull Claudia into this precise spot of cool.

Mariah stood above him on the steps. "My feet are killing me."

Bowman shut his eyes. Claudia, always private, had been reluctant at first to kiss him in this semi-public place, but his gesture, brought to life by the news that she was pregnant, was not something he'd wanted to control. He had become the kind of man who kissed his wife in restaurants and at parties, who lived in a continual fog of expectation and gratitude. His fingers, his cheeks, even his prick had tingled. When Claudia's mouth finally softened, and he was able to explore it with his tongue, she tasted both sweet and sour. He had been ignited by happiness.

Maybe that's all she'd had in mind when she'd brought him back here today—recalling that moment—but she'd been wrong to think it mattered. When Bowman opened his eyes, he saw that Mariah was watching him with a peculiar mix of sympathy and anger. Her fingers drummed against her belly.

"Forget it. She'll be fine. We'll meet her at the boat later," she said, and took a step up towards the street. "I need something to drink. I'm dying here."

She led them to the Bell Deck, a dark bar set back from the street in a clapboard house. Above the door was a painting of a ship's captain in a yellow slicker steering a wheel and the words, *And I have asked to be where no storms come.'* Mariah pulled the door's rope handle and disappeared into the yeasty smelling dark. At this pre-lunch hour, the place was empty except for a single man at the bar. The Bell Deck's nautical theme looked tired in the light coming through salt-dusted windows; its best face, if it had one, was at night. So was the bartender's who gave them a cool, unfriendly snap of his chin. When they sat down, he rang a small bell above a row of bottles, but made no move towards them.

"What do you think that bell means?" Bowman asked Mariah, and wondered if she's brought him to a gay bar on purpose. She shrugged while he felt compelled to talk and talk, to cover up his discomfort being there. "What's a bell deck anyway? The bell's probably some kind of code for tourists—one ring to raise the prices, two for shitty service, three for salmonella."

"Yeah, probably." Mariah rested her hands flat in front of her, as if drawing gloss from the wood. "Excuse me," she called to the bartender. He turned around, glancing quickly at the man at the end of the bar. "My father here thinks your bell is some kind of secret code."

The bartender was indifferent. "What can I get you?"

Mariah ordered a gingerale, Bowman a beer and a cherry for his step-daughter's drink.

"You should eat something," he said, after they'd sat silently for a while. He sensed a slight desperation in the way Mariah wiggled on the stool. The bartender rang the bell again but ignored them. It wasn't menace Bowman was picking up from the place, but the distinct possibility of shame coming towards him. He smelled it all around like the sour stench of the dishwasher drifting from the kitchen. The beer slunk into his stomach. He jolted at the alcohol behind his eyes and the inadvisability of drinking on a empty stomach.

"My god," Bowman mumbled. "What an idiotic place this is. No service?"

"I get it." Mariah said, fiercely alert all of a sudden. "The bell means you're one of them. You know, a *fag*. You're a fag in a pink shirt—one ring means you're looking for a blowjob. Two means—"

"For chrissake, cut it out. What's wrong with you?"

Mariah looked at the glass in her hands. "Look, Mom not having a baby doesn't have anything to do with wanting. She got some infection when she was pregnant with me that scarred up her insides. She's known it forever, since I was born. There was no way she was ever going to get pregnant again. She should have told you."

Bowman was strangely calm, as though the wind inside him had just died down. He heard the parts of his mind file into order, the waves in his stomach lie flat. Claudia had lived recklessly once; she'd fallen for the wrong guy at eighteen and after that, she'd lived safely, but always orchestrating and evading. The man had only been around long enough to get her pregnant, but he'd left her with her whole life; this daughter.

"I shouldn't have told you any of this," Mariah said. "I promised her I wouldn't, I swore."

Though he knew he should feel some sympathy for his wife and what she'd suffered, he couldn't. "Why didn't she tell me?"

"Ashamed, I guess," Mariah said without looking at him. "And she didn't want you to leave us. She didn't really understand why you would want to be with her in the first place, a woman with a kid, and she thought if you knew, that would be it. But God, Bowman, what would be so bad about you loving this baby instead?"

His earlier nausea came back with surprising force as though it had only been gathering strength all this time. It tipped Bowman off his stool, pushed him to the door with the rope handle, and led him to the alley behind the Bell Deck with the dumpster and the puddles of milky-looking water. He leaned with his hands on his knees and threw up a morning's seasickness, and with it, a family's lode of lovesickness.

He mounted the blistering hill to the monument where he bought a ticket outside the gift shop. He took the stone steps up and focused on the predictable, rhythmic strain he felt in his thighs as he climbed. At the three-quarter mark sign, he stopped at a wide window cut directly into the stone. He could see everything from the gloriously windy height, the town spread out below, the cut in the dock where the Harbor Queen would arrive and leave again. He knew he was should also imagine he could see his wife and stepdaughter together down there, but he didn't want to. He was aware of people moving behind him, a blend of voices on the stair's twist. He pressed his hands into the stone on either side of the view, tested his weight against the belts of chain that held him back from the temptation to slide himself over and take a thoughtless, delirious soar on the summer air.

He was responsible for no one, and his stomach finally felt clean, a hollow, gleaming space inside him. He had no interest in his demise.

On the boat ride home from Provincetown four years earlier, the sun had slipped behind the clouds in the afternoon, the temperature had fallen and the air was needled with moisture. Claudia, shivering in a sundress, had touched her head, then her stomach in a confusion of discomforts Bowman believed were about the baby. She had gone down below, leaving Bowman and Mariah on the upper deck to stuff themselves on a half-pound of fudge. When she didn't come back, Bowman went to look for his wife, leaving Mariah with instructions not to stand too close to the railing. He found Claudia coming out of the bathroom, wiping her hands on a paper towel long after they were dry. She was pale, and had tucked her hair sharply behind her ears as if she'd been examining herself in the mirror.

"I should have brought a sweater," she said, as if that were the full text of her uneasiness. Bowman wiped his own sticky hands on his pants. He intended to wrap his arms around her. "Cramps," she explained. "I have a little chill, that's all."

She rubbed his arm and looked out the wet window that was so low to the water it seemed possible a fish might look back at her. Bowman waited for her to say everything was fine, that these cramps were part of pregnancy, queasiness, the weather, the stench of the boat, but she didn't. She was edgy to go to the upper deck and check on her daughter, but Bowman remembered now that she had stayed down with him instead. It must have been her way of holding on to him, not to deprive him of expectation, but not to tell him the truth that there never had been a baby and there never would be. He'd only understood what he'd wanted to, shocked now by hope's ability to blind.

On the final quarter of his ascent, the dusky spiral of the stairs ended in a cool, stone room punctuated by windows and the gleaming brass of coin-operated telescopes. Scraps of garbage swirled in the windy corners. Up here, there was only the woman with the white sandals from the boat, and she was bent into one of the telescopes so that the backs of her thighs, where her dress rose, were taut. She'd taken off her sandals and abandoned them near the top step. Her heels were dotted with blisters like pearls.

There was a thickening to her middle and bare upper arms, a density of flesh that reminded Bowman of himself. She'd spent the day alone, he guessed, but there was something in her tossed shoes and swirling dress, her messy hair, that was still determined.

"What do you see?" he asked, but she didn't hear him as the whistle of wind swallowed his voice. "What do you see?" he shouted again and took a few steps towards her.

The woman didn't move from the telescope at first, and then swiveled her head to look at him over her shoulder. If she recognized him from the boat, she didn't let on.

"The view," he said again. "Did you find what you were looking for? I saw you on the boat earlier, on the way over." He moved so that he was only feet from her.

She seemed to calculate his size and the fact that they were alone registered on her face. All the clues that drifted between strangers were sucked up in the wind's vacuum. She was afraid of him.

"I don't mean to scare you," he said.

"Then leave me alone, please." Her voice was surprisingly clear; she'd only pretended not to hear him at first. She moved to pick up her shoes and hesitated as though trying to decide if she should put them on before fleeing down the stairs. She turned to look at him again. "Get the message? I'm not interested."

"That's not what I meant," he said. "I wasn't trying to—" He stopped; not trying to what, exactly?

The woman disappeared down the dark mouth of the stairs, her bare feet slapping the stone. Not trying to pick her up? Not trying to make her feel desirable? He wondered if this heart-sick confusion was what desperation felt like. He touched the telescope she'd been looking through and the eyepiece was still warm. The instrument hummed as the minutes she'd paid for wound down. The huge bulk of the thing, with its sweet odors of metal and oil, was poised at Bowman's chest, the barrel of it pointed down and over the town.

The lens was still open, but he didn't want to look towards the pier where he figured his wife and step-daughter had gone to wait for him though they had hours before the boat came. In a few minutes, he knew he would also see the woman with the white sandals moving towards the uninterested protection of the crowds. He was sorry to have ruined the day for her and forced her to face the fact that she was alone. He didn't know what he would say to his wife when he finally met her on the wharf later, but he hoped now as he put his eye to the telescope, that it might lead him through the mysterious chambers of the human heart back to her.

COLD-COCKED

Harris was a college freshman then, twenty years old in a grey tweed jacket, corduroy pants, and leather shoes with laces. In 1980, his hair was short and parted as if he went to church, which he didn't. There was nothing disco-era, or any other era about him; he dressed like his old patrician father. His eyes were uncertain and almost colorless, and he worried that they were too close together for him to be good-looking. He had okay height, but not the body he wanted, a pair of black driving gloves, but no driver's license, and no coat in the seventeen-degree night as he waited on the deserted platform of the subway station at 11:35 pm. He claimed he never got cold, but now he suspected that being out here at this frigid hour—coatless, no less—wasn't the smartest thing he'd ever done. Still, he didn't ever want anyone telling him what to do or what to be afraid of, even if he was the one doing the telling to himself. After all, he was a sophisticated city boy—from another city—and he knew how to handle himself. A flame rose from the gold lighter he stole from his father's bureau drawer as he lit up, holding the cigarette between thumb and forefinger. It was quiet enough in the empty station that each drag sounded like surprise. The platform was lit like an empty stage in a dusty school auditorium— resigned, scuffed, but still hopeful.

He had ridden the bus from the house of the girl he was interested in and busy finger-fucking—she was a senior in high school, lived with her parents, and wore a hair-thin gold chain with a tiny cross. Here, at the end of the bus line, the subway station was above ground. To his left, the tracks both emerged from and disappeared into the dark tunnel. Amazing how fast the neighborhoods on the outer rings of a city changed, he thought, from hard-won private property to lopsided, scabby apartment buildings no one cared about, to the projects here and hard dirt expanses dusted by insecure security lights. The scent of the girl was on his upper lip from where he'd swiped his acrobatic finger, sweet before dinner, salty from later in her flowery bedroom. Harris liked to believe that he believed he was hot shit, but he knew he was flabby, silvery white under his clothes; he knew how weak and foldable he really was. His chest was pudgy and cautious, his heart was a shell that rattled around on a windowsill, and his dick listed to the right like the miserable building on the other side of the tracks, the one with lights on and no one visible. He was battered, defective, he detested himself, and now he admitted that he was uneasy out there on the platform, and that no one in charge of this city's transportation system was going to give a shit that the last train had actually stopped before 11:30, rather than midnight. He flicked his cigarette, an ember on the tracks. But no one would mess with him, he knew, because he gave off the twin lights of empathy and suffering, despite his aristocratic patina and expensive education, though sometimes at night in his dorm room bed, he was all poverty and need and rolled around helplessly, his legs caught in the sheets.

He'd waited so long for the train to take him back to campus that it had begun to snow large, unhurried flakes. That he was seeing the snow before anyone else pleased him; just this one beautiful thing was his alone. People were coming up the stairs to the platform now, their voices smacking the frozen metal risers. He knew they were drunk white boys; he'd been a drunk white boy himself often enough to know how consonants lost their edge, how footfalls wavered. There were girls' voices too, that pitch of excitement and fear females thrilled to. Harris glanced at the group that moved amoeba-like, changing shape but staying as one, all seven of them deep in their hooded parkas.

Clearly, higher learning was not this group's thing, he decided. They were like barking dogs, raw and idiotic. Harris couldn't help but lift his chin, something his father did, a vestigial superiority. The girls were being teased in an increasingly aggressive way—their squeals sprinkled the air with bruised drops of apprehension—but what was their choice now, to abandon the group and walk home alone at this hour? He also heard in their voices their own dormant brutality. They were not like the girl he just left, pink-painted nails and moist behind blue panties.

Three decades later, I'm terrified for Harris on this subway platform. My mouth is full of brackish spit. I imagine he sought comfort in the smell on his upper lip, but now it was not the girl he detected anymore, but a peppermint-oatmeal stink that was underneath it, his father's soap, the scent of dread and disappointment he lathered himself in. His father had always assured him that he was a fool and a failure.

"Hey, asshole," Harris heard.

At this, the dimmest color, the panties' palest blue in his mind faded away. The tracks were polished and carbonic. Harris thought about the black and white documentary he'd watched in philosophy class earlier. The final scene was of a retreating Citroen, a hedgerow, a stone wall, and the sound of squealing tires, breaking glass and shearing metal, and the narrator's heavily accented voice giving the line Harris had been repeating ever since: "At zee age of forty-six, Albert Camus is *dead*." Harris whispered it to himself and flexed his fingers in their leather gloves.

Last week, a boy my oldest child had gone to grade school with died in a house fire along with his girlfriend and their baby. They were eighteen. A month ago, the son of someone I know, home from Afghanistan, hanged himself from a pipe in the basement. Tonight, on Halloween, out with five other boys, my youngest child, fourteen, ran into a gang and was cold-cocked. A fist smashed the side of his face and eye socket, and knocked him to the ground. The concrete scraped his cheek raw. One of his friends, beaten around the head, is in the ER. Their candy was stolen. That's what I had to tell the police when they came to the house and asked if anything was taken in the "incident." Their candy was stolen, I said, as though this was the crime, Skittles and Milk Duds and Milky Ways the cause of violence that visits boys. It all begins with something small and godly you can hold in your hand, something someone else wants. One cop took notes while the other looked around as though I was hiding the truth in the dirty dinner dishes and scattered pieces of homework, as though my son holding a bag of frozen peas to the side of his face was making it up. *We ran, we ran, we ran*, his friends said, a breathless chorus of misgiving and relief as they wondered if they should have fled or stayed to help their two felled friends. They'd never know the right answer, not even when they were my age, though the question would appear to them with increasing weight and frequency; did I do the right thing by saving myself first?

My cold-cocked son is too old to collect candy anyway. Tonight, at the end of his childhood, he describes the moment he was hit as "everything went white." He's fascinated by his mind's ability to protect him this way. He says that he'd known when he saw this bunch of hooded, much older kids coming towards him—fifteen or twenty of them, he claims, though by now in his head, there might as well have been a battalion—that the encounter wasn't going to be good. He didn't run, he tells me, as if to prove he is no coward. This cowardice is what men and boys fear most—more than their own terror, more than the damage done to them, and this is how they tell stories. There are kids still out on the street going from house to house begging candy, but I've turned off the porch light, Halloween over forever.

Before he went away to college, Harris lived with his parents on the shoddy left side, second and third-floor apartment that had once been part of a grand, single-family house. The scratched inlaid floors ended in mid-pattern where dividing walls had been put up for profit, and the ceiling fixtures didn't hang in the centers of rooms anymore. The windows were off too, some banked into corners, others unreachable. The apartment was full of chipped antiques, swipes where polish met failure's dust, but also an expectation that things would get back to better any day now.

Harris's father, a lawyer, had been passed over years before, but ambition clung to him like clots of earth: useless and dry. His figure cut like a pen line, his head a formal gray serif. That his face revealed nothing when he looked at me, his only child's high school girlfriend, unpolished and in overalls, revealed everything. Harris's mother had shaky hands, and when she talked about the hostages in Iran, which she did all the time, her voice was at a high pitch of concern. Her skirts were sometimes stained or the zipper was broken, and she wore chunky necklaces that fell on a deflated chest. She was often tipsy by late afternoon, going on about the Ayatollah from her faded armchair, while city buses roared past outside and Harris and I escaped upstairs. Harris's room had the unsympathetic feel of a guest room with its single, tightly made bed and bookshelf of travel books his non-travelling mother read. There were no signs of his teenage life—a stereo, or posters, or the kind of sentimental junk that filled my own room. He'd lost his boyhood stake in the place when he'd gone away to boarding school at twelve, and it was still not his when he'd come back at seventeen. He was a year older than anyone in our class, having appeared as an aloof mystery out of nowhere in September of senior year. He never seemed to work and still excelled. He knew things that the rest of us had never even heard of.

At times, he was strikingly focused on me, focused as he kneeled between my legs and parted my flesh, and I kept an eye on the unlocked door. Focused when we fucked. He asked me too often what I liked, what felt good. Beyond that embarrassing scrutiny, there is no feeling I attach now to those afternoons of sex, but there remains the sensation of my fingers pressing into his flesh, much like my fingers pressed into the flesh of my babies' upper backs. It was the profound awareness, each time, of another body. Below us, the kitchen television was turned up so Harris's parents could listen as they sat in the amputated living room with their drinks and bowls of green olives and Spanish peanuts.

One late afternoon, while Harris lay naked on the bed smoking and I was getting dressed, it occurred to me that in their immutable routine, his parents were waiting for something—not to happen, but to be over. It was May then, a month shy of our graduation, and the windows were open to the warm, sulfurous city air. Harris's penis lay on his wide thigh, condom in the trashcan that had a picture of a foxhunt on it. I asked him if his parents ever went anywhere, did anything, saw anyone.

"I don't know if you've noticed," Harris said, lazily, "but my parents don't leave. They're always right down there." He pointed at the floor.

"Your father goes to work," I said.

"You're being too literal." The way he dragged on his cigarette looked practiced and sinisterly French. I could not make the gesture jibe with his lumpy nakedness, his thin pubic hair, the way his penis had shrunk to a knob. He was inelegant. "My parents don't have friends," he said. "They only have people they've met."

He pushed his cigarette butt through a hole in the window screen he'd made with a pencil. The screen was full of them. There were only a few remaining fringes on the bedspread he could twist and yank off—and thread those also through the screen. He watched me pull on my overalls.

"You should get some different clothes," he said. "You look like a farm girl."

"You're just a snob."

He shrugged and smiled. "I love you, you know."

"Shut up." I laughed at the idea. I didn't love him and never would, though I was grateful for how he looked at me with his own deep gratitude. I threw a sock at him.

"Don't make fun of me." His face had turned ancient and sober. "Do not do that."

I was startled by his sudden seriousness and how I'd clearly hurt him. Harris knew something adult—discontent, longing—something I didn't. When I opened the door to dodge his disappointment—and my own in myself— his father was there, taking up the light in the cramped hallway. I pulled the door mostly shut behind me. One overall strap hung at my hip.

"Please tell Harris that it's time for dinner," he said. His eyes moved to what was behind me—Harris on the messed-up bed—and he pushed the door open with his fingertips. He sniffed the air as he angled toward the room. "Harris, have you been smoking?"

"Of course not." Harris was still propped up on one elbow, a kind of coy, naked pretense of innocence. "The window's open. It's coming from outside."

"You're not allowed to smoke."

"I know that. And I don't." Harris's belly puckered as he sucked his bravado in. He worked to stay steady, but he was shaking. I could tell he wanted to cover himself, but wouldn't.

His father refused to lower his eyes to his son's nakedness. "What's that hole in the screen?"

"It's a hole in the screen," Harris said.

His father turned. "You need to go to your home now," he said as he went downstairs. Harris had rolled onto his back, another cigarette already in his mouth, one arm behind his head as though he was victorious.

Twelve years ago, I ran into Harris in a restaurant. We hadn't talked in almost a decade by then. He'd grown a mustache, which made him look dated and hard to please. His suit didn't hide the bulk he'd put on. When I went to his table, it took Harris a few haughty seconds to acknowledge me. Then he pushed back his chair and stood.

"Here you are," he said, after an airy hug.

I laughed. "Were you expecting me?"

"Always."

In this awkward and stagey moment, his lunch partner said goodbye and left. The check had been paid, the final crumbs pushed around. Harris invited me to sit down and we recited the foamy details of work, families, spouses—I was surprised that he and his wife were still together, but didn't show it—his twin boys at the same celebrated boarding school he'd been to, a small victory in that, he said, as though he knew I'd still understand exactly what this meant. He ran a finger around the rim of his coffee cup, and in that gesture, his mood plummeted, taking the air with it.

"I'm miserable." His face was suddenly slack and gray. "That's the truth."

He'd once said I was the only person he'd ever told what happened that night on the subway platform, and I sensed then that this was still true. I was sorry that I hadn't turned around when I'd spotted him in the restaurant; I knew I could only fail him again. Because what had I done years ago when he'd been in real trouble? I'd cut him off, too stupid and afraid of being pulled down by his misery. I'd told him he needed to get some "help," an idea I had that someone could fix his sorrow. I'd stayed quiet during his weeping sessions on the phone. I was a girl back then, adept at pretending that what I didn't hear or think about didn't exist. But age had taken that talent from me. My face flushed and I fanned it with my hand.

"Hot flash?" he asked. "God, you're getting so fucking old."

I smiled with equanimity and forced myself to ask what I didn't want to know. "Why are you miserable?"

"My girlfriend broke up with me. Dumped me, yesterday, over the phone."

"But you're married, Harris. You're not supposed to have a girlfriend in the first place." My voice had the helium rise of self-righteousness.

"Christ. That doesn't mean I can't be upset about it." His tone was rough, and his tongue ran over his front teeth in challenge. He stood and buttoned his jacket. "Listen, I have to go."

"Come on, Harris," I said. "Don't do this. Sit down. I'm just not sure what I'm supposed to say."

"Obviously, that hasn't changed." He told me to be well and left. He was still without a coat in winter, but at least now his concession to it was a black knit cap that made him look truly directionless. That was the last time I saw Harris.

One rare afternoon when his parents were away, Harris invited over some people from school. We drank his parents' booze, ate their peanuts, blew the red tissue skins off our palms. Eight of us crammed into his bedroom, the window open to let out the pot smoke, cigarette smoke, the noise. A few of us sat on Harris's bed, and at one point, our backs against the wall pushed the bed away and sent us flying, heels over heads. We laughed, stuck like bugs, and when we righted ourselves, Harris dropped to his knees and ran his fingers along the ugly blond gouges the bed had made on the floor. We were silenced by how he tried to erase the scrapes with a spitty finger.

"All of you should just get the fuck out," he barked. The others scrambled; they'd been unsure about him anyway, and this just confirmed that he was too strange to ever be a friend. I kneeled next to him.

"My father's going to kill me." Harris stared at the wounds as if he could will them to heal.

"No he won't. It's just a couple of scratches. Who cares?"

"You don't know anything about him," he said, almost protectively.

I suggested we go out and buy some stain, and he let me lead him out of the house. He was distracted, his feet in his untied shoes slapping at the cobblestones, his oxford shirt billowing. I'd never seen him untucked like this. It was a spring evening, a week left of school, and the sidewalks were crowded. People sat on stoops, walked their dogs, nothing unusual. Harris and I hadn't spent much time out in the world together—we were either at school or tethered to his room after it—and being away from the house gradually lifted him. He pointed out ornate lintels above us and pansies planted at the bases of trees, a car he liked, the dogwoods past their time. I wondered why we hadn't done this before, why we'd stayed in the house he hated. Beauty caught Harris's unguarded eye out here and he was unbound. But we were too late—the hardware store was closed.

Harris's was resigned now to what was going to happen.

"I don't get it," I said, as we trudged back. "Your father doesn't say anything about what we do in your room, he sees you naked on the bed, he obviously knows you smoke, we drink his liquor, and you're not worried about any of that, but you're worried about some scratches on the floor?"

"Because he can talk about a floor, about scratches. That's something he can point to—that kind of fuck-up." The streetlights blanked out the moon. "As opposed to talking about me, the real fuck-up."

"You're not a fuck-up," I said, and touched his arm.

"You don't know."

"Then tell me."

"You really want to know?" He stopped on the sidewalk. "I got caught *in flagrante*. At boarding school. It means I was getting a blow job."

I clapped my hand over my mouth to cover my sudden laugh.

"I know, it's really hysterical. Go ahead, laugh some more. Hysterical too that I got expelled. They threw me and the other guy out the next day."

"The other guy?"

He eyed me chillingly. "Yes, the other *guy*. A boys' school."

I was afraid I'd laugh again, but not because I found it funny.

"I was hardly the only one doing it," he said. "I ruined things."

"What are you talking about? You didn't ruin anything," I said. "It's such a stupid thing to expel someone for."

He stopped and faced me. "A stupid thing? I broke the

rules." He picked up an empty soda can and while I thought he was going to throw it into the street, he dropped it in the trash, always the good citizen and the bad son.

His father had been to that same boarding school, he told me, and his grandfather, too, and a tradition had ended with his dick in some boy's mouth. Was this the shame that blanketed his family in wet wool and lead? Was this the fall that made his mother obsessed with hostages, turned his father into a ghost? Harris had been sent home, put in the third floor guest room, and told to stay there, enveloped in the shame. He'd missed an entire year of school. He said he read a lot and thought about killing himself every day.

"I would have run away," I said, ducking his terrible confession.

"No, you wouldn't have." His voice was sharp with disdain, and at that moment, he looked at me with his father's gaze of disapproval. He unlocked the front door and entered the dimly lit remorse of his house, leaving me on the sidewalk. I rode the subway home, and when the train rose briefly into the open air, I knew that his father must have had a hole in his chest before Harris had been born, one that allowed the world's disgrace to find its way in. He had always been on the verge of collapse. Harris was just another bad wind. I was relieved that very soon Harris and I would be done with each other, gone far away, the summer over.

At twenty-eight and in business school, Harris got married in the city where his wife was from, and back where he'd grown up and where I still lived, his parents threw him and his bride a party. I hadn't talked to Harris in years—years of purposeful forgetting on my part about what had happened to him on the subway platform that night—and I was surprised to get the invitation. His parents had some friends now apparently who half-filled the fusty marble foyer of a private club. Each time the door opened, a blast of summer heat hit the guests. The party had the feel of not quite making it to an upper floor, where it would much rather have been. Harris's mother held my hands in her cooler ones. Her dress was new, the tag still hanging from the armpit. Did no one in her family look at her long enough to notice? I introduced her to Theo, the man I would marry in a year. When she gave me a commiserating smile, and I understood she was soothing me for not being the one Harris had chosen. Her happiness was brittle.

Harris's father was lofty in his bowtie and jacket, and his cheeks were a gin-infused pink. When he saw me, was he remembering the day he'd seen his son naked on the bed and me half-dressed, or did he still see nothing? The party was to celebrate the marriage, but also, it seemed to me, to show this world of theirs that Harris had endured. In his parents' minds, the full force of tragedy had been averted, but I knew they didn't know about how their son had been shown his own death that winter night on the platform, how he'd wanted it and begged for it.

Harris introduced us to his bride Marguerite, a tiny, doll-like redhead, as though she were a prize bird. She was cosseted in contentment and hairspray. Harris looked at home in the club, dressed like his father, full of the jocularity of the older men. He treated me with a kind of jovial blandness. He didn't seem like anyone I ever would have known. He slapped Theo on the back as a fellow man about to enter the bind of matrimony. Before we left, he pulled us into a corner and stirred his scotch with a finger.

"Here's my advice to you," he said. "Take something to do on your honeymoon. It's fine for the first couple of days, but after that, it's all dead air." He slapped Theo on the back again but wouldn't look at me. I wondered what he'd done with all his sadness, how it was possible to swallow it down.

Theo and I burst onto the sidewalk, amazed by what we'd just heard; we knew the darker side of marriage would have nothing to do with us and we felt sorry for doomed Harris and his feathered Marguerite. For us, it turned out not to be the honeymoon that came with dead air, but our twentieth year together that rose up, gasping for breath.

With his good grades, Harris went to the college of his choice, despite claims from his father that having been tossed out of boarding school would follow him around forever. The day before he left, Harris gave me a pair of earrings. They weren't my style, though I see now that they were Marguerite's, plain and unimpeachable, as though he'd already conjured up the perfect wife.

One early Saturday morning in October, two months into my first semester at college, the monitor at the dorm's front desk called to tell me that Harris was in the lobby. I went bloodless and rushed the boy who had been in my bed fleeing down the back stairs. I pulled up the bedclothes that refused to give up their intimate heat. Harris was smoking in the common room, his legs crossed like this was a men's club instead of a women's dorm.

"What are you doing here?" I asked. I hadn't even said hello first.

"I took the bus last night. Ten hours. Came all the way here to see you." He reached out to touch my face, but I pulled back.

"Why?" I asked.

"Why? Because I thought it would be a nice surprise. I wanted to see you. I miss you."

I couldn't say I'd missed him. We'd never officially split up, but in our few phone conversations after that night of the gouged floor, our break seemed obvious and understood. I was angry now at how he was pretending otherwise, putting his arm around me. He reeked of smoke and bus fumes, while I stunk of guilt. He said that everything was fine at school, but the fact that he had no overnight bag spoke of a desperate impulse.

"This isn't how I imagined it," he said, when I took him up to my room. He examined the top of my dresser—change, pens, papers, and absent the earrings he'd given me—my roommate's unslept-in bed, mine clumsily made. "I thought it would be nicer."

We went out to get something to eat, but he'd spent all his money on the bus ticket. I couldn't make myself ask if it was roundtrip. He slept for much of the afternoon while I studied and silently urged him to wake up and leave, and later, we went to a party outside. The night was thin with cold, heaving with the rising hum of anticipation, of all those kids thinking that this was real life, and that they'd been chosen for it. Harris and I sat on a low brick wall. I didn't want his tweedy arm across my shoulders.

"I like seeing all these people looking lost and lonely," Harris said, nodding at the crowd, which didn't look lost or lonely to me, "and having everyone see me with my arm around you and being jealous because I have a girlfriend and they don't."

"When are you going back?" I asked.

"I get it," he said. "I'm leaving. You've made it pretty clear that's what you want."

He waited for me to deny it, but I didn't. I didn't want to know why he had come or how acute his loneliness was, and soon he pushed his way through the happy crowd and I lost sight of him. He'd walk miles to the bus station, and who knew how long he'd sit there in a hard plastic chair before he boarded for the ten-hour ride back.

When Theo comes back into the kitchen, I tell him I've been thinking about Harris.

"I never told you how he was attacked when he was in college." The Halloween candy-seekers are still loud on the street. "They were going to kill him."

Our son is fine, his pummeled friend is back from the ER, and nothing really terrible has happened. The story Theo tells me now is about a nighttime fight of his own, young men slugging it out in a cramped corridor. There's still exhilaration in his voice; it's a thin saga, but fat with pride. Boys make fear into myth and myth into their autobiographies.

Harris phoned a few times after that fall visit, though I never called him. Once, he'd wanted to know if I'd broken up with him because of what he'd told me had happened at boarding school; did I think he was queer? The next time, he told me that he had started seeing a girl, a high school senior, the daughter of someone his father knew who lived way out in the suburbs. By December, he had stopped calling entirely, until a February morning, 5:30 am.

"I was beaten-up last night," Harris had said. His voice was flimsy.

"So what happened to him?" Theo asks now, but I'm only just beginning to allow myself to picture it tonight, after so many years. "Tell me what happened. And why did you never tell me this before?"

When one guy said, "Hey, asshole," Harris turned, though he knew he was an idiot to do so. The girls had left by then. He shivered and peered down the tracks to see if the train was coming, wishing he had something to wrap his hands around. His stomach folded into itself, a ruined dinner trying to escape. He wondered what the hell he was trying to do by seducing a high school girl anyway. And one that lived so fucking far away from campus. He was done with her, he decided.

"Wait," I'd said. I'd pushed off the remnants of sleep when he'd called that early morning. The sky was still black between the blinds. "Are you okay?" He sucked in a sob. "Did you go to the hospital? Did you call the police?" He refused to do either. He was in his dorm room, he said, had class in a few hours and needed to shower. He wasn't making sense.

"But you have to do something," I urged. He wouldn't speak. "Harris, you have to tell someone. You can't just pretend nothing happened."

"I'm telling you," he said.

"But I can't help you," I pleaded. "I'm here, you're there. What can I do?"

"Just listen to me." A fading whisper.

"I can't hear you."

"They took my clothes. They left me on the tracks. I wanted to die," he said. "I'm okay now." He hung up, and when I called back then, and for days after, he wouldn't answer.

But when he called me after that, it was always very late at night. Our conversations circled around how he couldn't eat or sleep, how he'd stopped going to classes, how he hadn't told his parents. He wanted me to share his misery. He asked me to help him, I tell Theo now who is looking at me like he doesn't know me. Everything about that night was white for me and stayed like that for thirty years, until tonight, I say, when I needed to see Harris survive and walk away.

In his last call, Harris asked me to come see him, but I said no.

My son wanders into the kitchen in a pair of too small pajamas that reveal his impermanent ankles and wrists. The blue bruise and red blood on his cheek brighten as he attacks his father from behind in a chokehold, all love and lordliness. They tumble into a wall. The house shivers. This is fake violence, what they do when one catches the other unaware or when love is right there on the table, and if this is the shadow of brutality they're tangling with, where and what is the real beast?

"Stop," I say. "Just stop."

My son looks at his father and smirks. "What's her problem?" he asks.

The group approached Harris. The leader had a deprived face, a ragged mouth shadowed by a thin mustache. The others were all skinny legs, with underfed, dopey faces, empty forms, Harris thought, people filled with nothing. They were drunk and pissed off about everything, and why shouldn't they be? Look at their lives, Harris told himself. They knew they could take this pale and pudgy shithead without any trouble.

Harris sensed it coming. He'd been waiting for the attack his entire life, and now maybe this was a bit of a relief. He was strangely relaxed as he narrated for himself the story of what was going to happen next: robbed of his watch, his money clip with his initials on it, same initials as his father and grandfather, robbed of the gold lighter which wasn't really his to begin with, punched in the face, spit on. He could stand that much; they weren't going to kill him. He was sure of that. But he wondered why he couldn't hear what one guy was saying to him, even though they were only inches apart. There was a rush in his ears, maybe the train coming in an oceanic roar of salvation, but it was just his blood. He thought maybe he'd read this all wrong, maybe now they would kill him. If there was no one around, no one in the windows across the street, and it was still snowing, why not go all the way? To them, he was less than nothing.

Or maybe he was something, and that made the killing valuable. Someone put his hands on Harris's shoulders from behind, yanked back, pressed a knee against his spine. Rips began at the arms of his white button down shirt, under the v-neck sweater, the tweed jacket. He took a step back to lessen the pressure, but now he was on his heels and dragged like a mannequin. Let go, he sprung forward onto his knees. His protest was a few lukewarm drops from a kinked hose. They punched at the soft muscles of his privilege and the baked ham served at the girl's white-clothed table. This was drowning without the water. His face was against the concrete. He couldn't remember the fall. The pain he felt was happening in another country. There were a million polka dots of gum on the concrete, streaks of heels, hairs caught on preserved snowflakes. A steady breath blew up from the tunnel, stinking of piss. A knee ground into his back, others on the back of his thighs. He wasn't going anywhere, he told them, they didn't have to hold him down like that. His shoes were yanked off and bounced onto the tracks. Then his pants were pulled down, exposing his boxers with the peppermint stripes, the ones his mother still bought him and called "drawers." Then those were pulled off and floated down the tracks. He pretended he was Albert Camus, but why would Camus be in a shithole like this without his boxers? Harris was only himself, pure Harris stripped naked, robbed of his clothes, and left there. Shame was just a state of mind, he told himself. He'd gotten over it before plenty of times. This wasn't so terrible. It would be over soon.

This was the dream everyone had, the nightmare of finding yourself at school, or at work, or on a train platform without your clothes. He could already see himself, a white jiggly figure running down the first street of houses he came to, covering himself with some newspaper when he rang the bell. No one would answer because it was too late, but maybe they'd call the police. That's the best he could hope for. The worst had already happened. People would be horrified, but they'd laugh too the way people laugh at horror, and he thought if he were inside one of the houses and saw a guy like him on the doorstep, he might laugh too, not because it was funny, but because someone else was having your exact nightmare.

And then the guys stopped. Harris's skin sucked at the concrete, his balls retreated into his gut. His ass was white—he hated how it had dimples and dark follicles, an inexpertly plucked chicken. And when they rolled him like he was an old carpet towards the edge of the platform, his hands flat over his face, he felt like he was rising. Except that he was falling and he smacked the tracks. Nothing hurt, but everything was shattered. The steel was warm under him. He wanted his mother's anxious kiss of vodka and peanuts, wanted the frayed end of her bathrobe. He recalled the taste of sour milk.

"Train's coming!" one them yelled.

Harris lifted his head to see them scramble towards the edge to peer down at him. He felt the train's vibrations in his body. As though he'd just had a dream that had a single, repetitive thought—*I am still here*—he got to his knees. The guys yelled at him to hurry up, to *come on, shithead, get up!* They offered him their hands to pull him up as they shot glances down the tunnel. He knew they wouldn't let him die. They were frantic, urging him to come on, wiggling their fingers, swearing at him to *hurry the fuck up*, trying to save him. He believed that they loved him, and his own love took up where the pain left off, and he crawled towards them. He would somehow rise. But they fled in a cloud of laughter and self-congratulations, the white of their sneakers like blind spots in his vision. They'd left him and it was quiet. And this was where Harris stayed, frozen on the tracks, on his knees, without pants, to wait for the train to kill him. He wanted it, and when it didn't come, he cried at his failure.

He told me that when he'd finally lifted himself onto the platform, he found his pants on the stairs and walked the entire way back to campus. He watched the sun rise over a parking garage, and the thin batting of snow melt off the streets. It was his fault, he said, he shouldn't have been on that platform to begin with.

I didn't entirely believe his story until tonight. I thought he'd only wanted sympathy. It doesn't matter if it's true anyway. On my front porch now, one undeterred group of kids pounds the front door even though the light is off. They batter away at it. I'm not going to tell them to stop; they'll eventually go away. I've pictured it now; Harris, all bluster and ruin, had stumbled his way home, cleansed, lightened, but not really alive.

THIS IS YOUR LAST SWIM

They left their beds unmade. Little piggies, the dean of students thought, lovely, entitled, doomed piggies. She missed them. She was in Hollis House, one of the two girls' dorms, in a corner room on the second floor, with both the windows left open as if to invite the blur between outside and inside. Had the girls imagined their room being taken over by spring, its rampant vines and exuberant critters? Squirrels nesting in their beanbag chairs, bluebirds pulling threads from their cashmere sweaters, mice in their uggs?

Mimi picked up a silk scarf with red and gold horsey designs—stirrups, saddles, riding crops. She had been given one just like it at the end of last year by a student's family. The silk made a cold, slithering hiss as she wound it between her fingers. Outside, the birds jabbered away—she'd never heard them so insistent¬—then there was the crack of another gunshot somewhere in the forbidding distance, then silence soon corroded again by the oblivious birds. She knew the pattern by now.

The scarf wasn't her style—she wasn't even sure she had a style, or if khakis and collared shirts and topsiders were more of an anti-style—and she'd kept the thing in a closet at home along with all the other loot she'd been given during her nine years at Whitehall School. Junk she'd never use—a crystal salad bowl, a set of Italian espresso cups, gold rimmed and delicate, old lady jewelry and beaded bracelets supporting breast cancer research and childhood obesity eradication. She saw in those gifts how others imagined her life to be—bedecked, leisurely, aesthetic, on the correct side. Wrong. Wrong.

Too late now, but she'd always had in mind that she'd donate the stuff to an organization that would morph it into peanut butter and bags of rice for the world's starving. Hints of coercion had made her preserve the gifts in their original packages, but she didn't hold the giving against the parents. They just wanted everything to be right for their kids; their intention wasn't wrong, just clumsy. Too many of them thought money fixed everything—though it was amazing just how much money did fix, especially at this school. She tied the scarf around her neck, cowboy style. In the mirror festooned with feathers and photos, she looked exhausted and diminished, indistinctly middle-aged, but distinctly terrified, her skin plagued by pale patches and angry capillaries, her eyes glassy as though she were underwater. She wondered if she could hang herself with the scarf, if it would hold.

She recalled how some of her colleagues, like accountants, discussed the booty families had given them. They knew how much things cost because they'd looked up the scarves and pens and wine glasses online, totaled the gift certificates. She was embarrassed to see them doing this, the strident French teacher in his high-waters and flexing buttocks, the one-legged chemistry teacher, the woman who taught American history with a speech impediment, the three of them not incidentally also the quickest to punish students or erupt in some sanctimonious affront she'd have to deal with.

If the world wasn't about to end—amazing how she was able to let the thought tumble around in her head like striped socks in the dryer—she'd suggest that they put an end to this gift-giving entirely. It had the stink of the mildly unethical, like leather car seats or foie gras. Her proposal wouldn't make her any friends among her colleagues, but she didn't care. She didn't know where her streak of self-righteousness came from, though sometimes at night, alone in her low, unimaginative suburban house, she wondered if it wasn't just loneliness doing the hard-edged talking. Really, what did she care if they counted their gold pieces by candlelight? What did she care if it made them feel that they were worth something more?

But why had she wasted her time giving it any thought? The world was going to end. No question. There was no date, but in any case, very soon-ish. Anyone who was sane believed it and those who didn't were the zealots and the crazies these days. The same people who'd predicted the end a few years ago now didn't believe it was going to happen, so they'd begun long-term projects—baby-making, house-painting, dog breeding, reading *Moby Dick*. Lucky them if they blithely dismissed the truth. She moved away from her reflection, and felt a pinch of guilt, even under these pre-apocalyptic circumstances, as she went through the girls' bureau drawers, pawing through piles of thongs and satin undies and lacy bras. Curiosity compelled her, and she needed her senses to be sated all the time. She picked through their tangled jewelry and their pounds of makeup; a hundred different lip glosses, under-eye toning crèmes, blushes and palettes of eye shadow, mascara, pencils, bottles of nail polish, nail polish remover, Q-Tips, cotton balls, bottles of perfumes bearing the first names of celebrities and adjectives: Margo! Sinful by Patrice, Sly by Sylvia. She spritzed herself with Joyous! An overpowering stink of Splenda, vanilla, and chemical musk that she recognized as the scent that lingered in the hallways of the school, the library, her office, and on the sheets she'd slept in last night. Scent of the year: Raw Food! Gay Marriage! The End of Civilization! Mother's Sorrow!

Mother's Sorrow! would smell like a baby's fontanel, and flowered wallpaper fading in the sun. She checked her cell phone again; no service, of course, and service never again. The world had simply stopped working—no electricity, no TV, no phone. No police, no ambulances, no judge and jury, no burglar alarms, no army, no law, no supermarkets. If it weren't so horrible, it might be unfathomably marvelous. She tightened the horsey scarf around her neck. The birds were quiet all of a sudden. Had she become so used to the gunshots that she didn't even hear them anymore?

An unexpected explosion of mourning for her son flew out of her mouth and flapped around the room. The birds began again outside like a thousand clattering pick-up sticks. What was Jesse doing at that moment? Was her son thinking of her? She could not get to him, and he could not get to her, but could their minds meet in space if they concentrated hard enough? He was probably dragging his size-13 feet through the streets of Kabul in a dust storm of existential disorder—always this mixed-upedness with him, this moroseness since he was a little boy, a look of dulled panic on his wide, pacific face, dehydration on his narrow lips, grit on his eyelashes and army uniform and gun. Maybe he alone had known that this was how the world was going to end; he'd always been too aware of doom, of brevity. She could not hold his hand or touch his cheek to help ease him into the final passage. She could not gulp the scent of his sweaty scalp under his high-and-tight-and-ready-to-fight buzz cut, smooth the craters left by his rapacious acne, clean his glasses with the hem of her shirt. She had never been able to reach him, not really.

She closed her eyes. Someone was inviting Jesse in at this moment, offering him tea and a smoke and maybe a sweet—out of the heat, three blank, mud walls, a covered, mumbling woman. Who knew what would happen next? Her mouth filled with rust and she tugged off the scarf. Dig. Dig and sift and sort and inhale. Mother's Sorrow! Dig, she told herself, dig and sift through these silken things and do not think of your child.

Her hands went into the mess of abandonment: Birth-control pills. Wires and cables. Crest whitening strips. Tampons. Pringles (Sour Cream & Onion). Flip flops, sneakers, sandals, high heels, chocolate Kisses, candles (against the rules), two flasks, both full of vodka (really against the rules). Lotions, hair goo, leave-in conditioners, rinse-out conditioners, feminine-odor spray, feminine-odor wash. How much did it take to be a sweet-smelling 17-year-old girl these days? The two who had lived in this room were dopey and pink-skinned with flat, gleaming hair, girls who when separated from each other were mute and lost, but put them together and they were trouble, unafraid, and unrepentant. They reminded her of some married couples. Of the kind of married couple she'd once been half of, a combustible, cruel mix together, inert substances apart. Where was Paul, now? Probably having a beer, or ten, and a blubber, and recalling a cowardly prayer from his Catholic days.

Last night had been her second alone on the campus after the mass exodus from Whitehall on Tuesday, and she'd slept down the hall in one of the singles, those rooms meant for the emotionally fragile, the allergic, the strange, the talented. In every room she'd been in since the grand flee, she'd turned on the TV, the radio, the computer, the lights, hoping to catch an intermittent burst of electricity, any news, or a message from her son. Nothing.

During the day, she'd eaten when she was hungry, which was always—taking food from the dining hall kitchen and from what the students had left behind. She'd been dieting her entire life, and how good was a meal now of Snickers and Snapple, or bags of barbeque flavored chips, tins of cookies. I've been in love with you all my life, she whispered to the chocolate chip, the pretzel, the Cheez Doodle. She hated the word "model" when it was used as a verb, as in Whitehall-speak: "We must model healthy choices for our students"—which meant she had to be in good and abstemious shape, had to jog on the school track, had to keep a basket of apples in her office, eat salad for lunch. Bullshit. She was always wanting; it was the bedrock of her life. A woman's appetite and its denial was an underrated marvel, a drive that could rule the world. It could power its own nuclear reactor.

Beyond the open windows, past the flowerbeds bursting with obsessively spaced daffodils and felted pansies under a gauzy sun, a breeze taunted the surface of the Harrington Family Pool. For the first time since she'd watched the parents and their tear-stained kids run from the school, the despondent teachers clawing to get home, she detected another heartbeat on campus, and she froze. The proximity to nonexistence had returned her to basic biology, and she sniffed the air, all salty reaction and self-preservation. Her fingertips prickled as a tassel of fear brushed her neck. A question came at her with a whap: Would she rather be alone or with someone else in these last hours and days? *I suppose*, she whispered, *it depends on who that someone else is.* Her heart stomped against her ribs. She smelled herself badly in need of a shower. She wanted a weapon to fend off rape, murder, sadism.

A sand-colored dog emerged from the elms. His muttish, predatory head was down and determined, his tail straight out. His gait was the other heartbeat she'd detected. She wondered if people, made desperate enough, always began to imagine others, if this was the most primal instinct of all. That she didn't actually like being with people much made her imagining a kind of final, sad joke. It was a joke too that she should be a dean instead of a solitary gravedigger or a shelver of old newspapers or dented canned goods. But students, teenagers, high schoolers were an impermanent, febrile species. They could be good, mean, impossible, stupid, exuberant and overcast, hopeful beyond belief, and she loved them. Most of them, at any rate. And then they were gone in June, graduated, replaced with others who slipped into the same clothes and same roles. When she received wedding invitations from long-past students, she never went. She tried not to think of them.

She'd done a good job here as dean, she supposed, never had to confiscate a weapon, or come across a suicide (which she feared most of all and knew would be the end of her), but she had collected plenty of drug paraphernalia—pills and pipes and bongs and little Ziploc bags of pot. Among other things, she was the school enforcer, yelling at the girls when their tops were too tight or their shorts too short, at the boys for just being obnoxious and violent, something clearly very few could actually help. Half of the students were boarders, the other half day students. Two days ago she'd watched them scatter—cramming into cars, including hers, which she'd given away to a boy on scholarship who lived at the other end of the state—and make their way home for their last days, leaving their lives intact here, all their precious stuff exactly where they'd dropped it. Little piggies.

The dog appeared again, nose to the ground, and then slunk around the corner of the chapel. Mimi appreciated the remaining daylight, as she feared being pursued in the dark most of all. That was pure terror. Absolute, suffocating, terror that would make her fall to her knees and present the vulnerable back of her neck as an offering. Death was inevitable, but those moments just before? Get it over quick. When she'd trawled the boys' dorm rooms yesterday, she'd been looking for a weapon, but found none. There were bottles of Ritalin and Adderall, airplane nips of booze, porn and more porn, and the ever-hopeful sheath of condoms. It seemed a universal truth after her room excavations that all boys believed they could have sex at any moment, and all girls believed—or was it hoped?—they were desirable.

She moved down the hallway, stepping over things taken at the last minute and then dropped just as quickly. Who needed a blow dryer when the end was imminent, and you couldn't use it anyway? Books everywhere—textbooks and copies of *Ulysses* and *The Great Gatsby,* Norton anthologies of poetry, their thin pages ruffling like vain, wasted feathers. No one wanted to take poetry into their last remaining days, despite what everyone had always claimed about those deathbed recitations, those jagged lines of absolved grief, those useless couplets.

Beyond the front doorway of Hollis, the campus was vast and dazzling—150 acres on a hill above a quaint and useless town at one end, and a lake at the other. There was an art center, a squash pavilion, a chapel, indoor and outdoor pools, dorms and academic buildings. If the world were not about to deliquesce into a sticky glob, you could appreciate the grove of elms shading benches named for dead alumni, and the student center with a vending machine that spit out baby carrots, and beyond the tree line of modesty, the winking shores of Lake Wanskatuk. But where to go at this minute, at every minute from now on, was the question.

Eat. She would eat, stuff herself with food instead of fear. She made her way to the dining hall, zipping up the pink hoodie she'd taken from one of the rooms. It said *diva* too tightly across her large, fallen breasts, and it smelled like bubblegum. She went through the foyer with its giant fireplace, its rows of coat hooks with abandoned backpacks hanging like cured hams, and into the polished hall. Wooden tables, long as runways, were set with neat bouquets of napkin holders, and salt and pepper shakers. The room stunk of dishwasher, a sour milk, fish stick, and bleach stench that had impregnated the walls and the self-referential banners that hung from the rafters. Windows on one side of the room faced the central quad, empty and emerald. She pushed through the swinging doors into the kitchen. Yesterday she'd gone into the cold locker, no longer cold, and discovered that everything had gone bad, blood from defrosted chickens dripping onto the floor. She'd fled, gagging. The knives were in a locked cupboard. She'd need a crowbar to open it, but where was she going to find that? She pulled an industrial-sized can of chocolate pudding off the shelf, grabbed a loaf of white bread, and brought them, a can opener, and a giant spoon out to one of the tables. When she'd opened the can, the sharp edge of the lid glinted like bluefish teeth. What if the lid sliced open her arm, not sideways (as the experts knew), but from the elbow pit to the palm, right down the artery like she was halving a cucumber, and she bled to death? Who would wonder how she'd gone and what her expiration had looked like, what her final thoughts were? And wasn't that the whole point of dying? To have others contemplate your end so they could finally contemplate what was left of their own lives?

Only the tip of the spoon fit into her mouth, but it was a good mouthful, and the chocolate squeezed through her teeth. It tasted perfectly artificial, the idea of chocolate, the essence of smooth. She pulled a stack of bread slices out of the bag and poked out their soft middles, forming the dough into a dumpling. It was something she'd been forbidden from doing as a kid by her mother, and urge persisted like some erotic itch all these years. She dipped the dumpling in the pudding and ate it. She wasn't sure she'd ever experienced such a flash of satisfaction. She was sorry she had not insisted on pleasure every day of her life, and that she'd felt there was too much to be sorry about all the time, too much to deny herself. The trick of life, she was beginning to see, was not to collapse under the weight of regret, but to toss it up like a wedding bouquet, and say goodbye to what had been.

Her stomach pounded from the sugar and shadows began to fall outside. It was likely later than she thought, and the young leaves curled in response to the dropping sun. Silence was one thing, but the dark was something else entirely. She'd never seen such electricity-free night before and she hadn't exactly been in the mood to appreciate the stars or the moon. She'd only become scared of the dark as an adult. After her ex had moved out of the house, the dark had seemed harder to breathe in. And then Jesse had left, and there were nights so black that turning lights on only made it worse, but still, those nights were not half as terrifying as these.

She detected footsteps again, unmistakable now. Her wits were as acute as cavities touched by tinfoil. She felt the footfalls, soft-soled and intent, in her throat, and she dropped under the table. The steps halted just outside the dining hall door and then came in. Some shifting, the menace of the indecisive, a few more steps, and a squeaky stop. She saw the shoes—brilliant white, decades-old Reeboks, pale, freckled ankles, the bottoms of stiff blue jean capris. Peds with yellow fuzzy balls.

"Who's here?" the voice demanded. "Show yourself."

Always with that fucking ridiculous tone of authority, that air of unimpeachability. Incredible that she couldn't let it drop even now. The head of school, Pat Kneeland.

"Who's there, under the table? Come out right now. Do you hear me? Come out."

Mimi unfolded up, but stayed kneeling. "Pat," she said, offering her open hands in surrender. "It's me, just me."

Pat's face pinched. "Mimi? What are you doing here?"

"That's an interesting question," Mimi said, and gazed at the rafters. She deeply disliked the woman. "Let's see. I don't know. Proctoring the SATs?"

Pat's makeup was cakey—and for chrissake, why makeup

at all?—and cracked as she disapproved. "What I mean is," she said, "why aren't you at home?"

People claimed the woman read up on effective communication techniques in her spare time, but if she did, she'd missed all the important nuances—like warmth, like a subtle touch, like humility, like elasticity. She was a blunt tool, a solid instrument.

"Someone stole my car," Mimi lied. She'd handed the keys to the terrified boy and wondered now if he even knew how to drive.

"Who stole your car?" Pat demanded.

"If I knew, do you think—?"

"—No, it doesn't matter." Pat's gaze lowered to the scripted diva on Mimi's sweatshirt. "Hard to imagine, though, that one of our students would do that."

What was hard to imagine was that they found themselves, two women with a wary, distrustful affiliation, here together. The underside of Pat's chin was exposed like the belly of a cat, soft to touch maybe, but potentially an incitement to bite.

"I thought I was the only one here," Mimi said. "I assumed you'd gone home, too."

"Home? I live here. As I have for the past sixteen years."

"Yes, I know, but I thought family, maybe, relatives. Somewhere else." Her conjecture felt cruel, but she wasn't sorry. "Some place that isn't here."

Pat's brittle, almost translucent reddish hair was flattened on one side, as though she'd been lying on it for days. Her face was not unpretty, but it wasn't beautiful, either. Handsome, was what Mimi's father would have said. At sixty-three, she was efficient and smooth, like a ball-peen hammer.

"You hungry?" Mimi asked.

Pat pulled out a chair. She gave the pudding and bread a distasteful glance. "This is all you could find?"

Mimi hated that everything the woman said sounded like a

scold. "You'd prefer vanilla?" she asked.

Pat put her hands flat on the table. "I'd prefer not being in this situation at all, if you must know."

As if Pat were the only fucking one in it. As if this could all be blamed on someone's ineptitude. "Well, yes, there's that," Mimi said. "Me too."

"Actually, I think I would," Pat said. "Prefer vanilla, that is."

Mimi went back to the kitchen, got another giant spoon and tin of pudding, but hesitated at the swinging doors. She'd always been uneasy around Pat, resentful for sure, but wasn't it absurd to feel that way now? Why the pretense of a pecking order anymore, the self-censorship, the acquiescing? Mimi wasn't going to be asked to "consider what she wanted to do with her career," which was Whitehall-speak for, *you're shit-canned, you're dead to us.* She handed Pat the spoon. The woman turned to the window every few seconds.

"So. How are you doing?" Mimi asked. She saw the skin bunch on the back of Pat's post-menopausal hands.

"Ask me a better question."

Like, why are you so damn chilly? Like, why do you need to put people on edge? Like, why is it still okay for you to lord? Because here was the problem, that hard, humorless front that made you want to back away, even now, when Pat was, for the time being, the only other last person on earth.

"A better question," Mimi said. There was only one question left—how will we end?—but she wouldn't ask it. Pat could never soothe her.

Pat dipped a tip of the spoon into the pudding. She deposited a dollop onto her tongue, then turned to the window again.

"What are you looking for?" Mimi asked. "What's out there?"

Pat finally swallowed. "Vanilla isn't terrible."

"I saw a dog on the quad earlier. It spooked me—something about the way its head was angled, like it had already gone wild and it was looking to kill," Mimi said, aware that she was talking too fast. "Can animals really become feral that quickly?"

"I've never really enjoyed pudding, the texture of it," Pat said, putting down the spoon. "Slimy stuff."

Oh, to be stuck with anyone but this woman! Who the hell didn't like pudding? At the start of every school year, before the students arrived, when the excruciating faculty and staff ice-breakers and teambuilding exercises were in full, mandatory force—tug-of-war, scavenger hunts, everything but circle jerks—Pat participated, wearing this same pair of goofy pants and these same antiquated sneakers. She'd approached tug-of-war like a heartless surgeon, whisking her hands together when her team yanked the other across the line and onto their knees, and then feasted on a Diet Coke. In another game, Mimi had heard Pat reveal the name of her childhood dog, Pippy, and the name of the street she'd grown up on—Winston. That was her stripper name. Oh, ha, ha, ha, ha. It was a dumb, dated game; people only pretended to like it, their expressions slightly alarmed at Pat's laugh that was as convincing as plastic flower petals.

"How about some bread?" Mimi pushed the loaf toward Pat. She wanted to grab more of the soft innards and roll them into balls, but held herself back. Shame. Shame! It rushed her, as hot as the first time she'd been caught. She clasped her hands together. "Or would you rather have whole wheat?"

"I'm not concerned about my fiber intake at the moment." Pat unwound the bread's crust.

Was that actually a glimmer of humor? Mimi wondered.

"I saw you walking around earlier," Pat said. "And the day before."

"I thought I was alone."

"I know you did, the way you kept looking behind you. I was in the residence."

"So you were watching me?"

"I wasn't watching you. I was looking out and you came into view."

Had Pat heard the same gunshots as she had? To ask Pat why she hadn't left the residence, why she hadn't called out to Mimi, was to ask, What is it that you fear most? And how could Mimi ask this when she didn't know anything about the woman? Fear needed history; it was a lifetime of misgiving and experience taking solid form, like a dough ball you wanted to stuff into your big fat mouth. Fear was more intimate than sex, even. Was it the actual moment of eradication that was the worst to imagine, when you were out by the east hill beyond the soccer field, feeling the sun on your back, and suddenly everything goes white? Or black? Or was it that you feared burning up from the core, like a potato left too long in the microwave? Or starving to death, or being mauled by feral dogs? The list was fantastically endless, an invitation to invent horror. Mimi felt thrill twist inside her and the giggling start of hysteria. She put her hand over her mouth.

Pat assessed her coolly. "Where's your son?"

The pudding, a caustic chocolate burn now, backed up in Mimi's throat. The woman clearly didn't remember Jesse's name, and still had no idea about how he had suffered at Whitehall, how he'd hated every minute of his time there. Pat's attention had always been turned to the children who mattered, the shiny ones, ones with important parents who were the donors and gift-givers. Jesse had existed well below Pat's sightline.

"Jesse," Mimi told her.

"Yes, I know. Jesse."

"Afghanistan." Mimi wouldn't have minded dying right there and then, putting her head down on the table and kissing the ancient wood goodbye. "I haven't heard from him in nine days. Not since before the announcement."

"You will," Pat said.

The woman's authority was heartening for a second. "No, I don't think so."

"You will. He'll find a way to get in touch with you. He's a smart boy, He'll figure out how. He won't let you down."

How the hell did she know anything about Jesse? How could she talk like she did? How did she dare? It seemed to Mimi an attempt at soothing, but it didn't soothe. It vandalized her heart. At Whitehall, Jesse had been an indifferent student at best, worse for him still that she worked there. He'd wanted to discuss paperback philosophies and films with kids who didn't want to talk about anything with him. He wouldn't look up for anyone, his face engulfed in pimples. He was the reason Mimi had taken the job at Whitehall—it came with Jesse's education. She'd thought the august institution would help him look people in the eye, save him from the indifferent crush of a mediocre public high school. He'd already begun to fall in middle school, to migrate towards trouble and small acts of vandalism. He'd remained melancholy during his four-year sentence at White-hall, even as she salved him with kisses and begged him to see a shrink, take some pills. He'd accused her of trying to change who he was, and how could she say that wasn't precisely true? Happiness for him was irrelevant, it seemed.

"Look there," Pat said, and pointed to a fluster of birds gathered on the grass. She took the bread outside and the birds gathered around her like she was Saint Francis, her palms open and full of crumbs. Mimi was surprised at the woman's communion with nature, but also how she stood with that particular posture of aging women—the rounding between the shoulders, the neck thrust forward, tortoise-like. When Mimi joined her outside, the birds scattered and became specks in the trees.

"Do you think they know something's about to happen?" she asked Pat.

"Birds are finely tuned, so I imagine, yes, they know something is up."

"Either that or they just want to finally liberate their poor stuffed cousins from the Bird Room." Inside Peacott House, the administration building, there was a room of old stuffed birds behind glass, the hobby of some long-past head of school. It had always intrigued and repelled her, an obvious statement of dominion over all creatures, even birds and teenagers.

"Everyone's always said you had a good sense of humor." Pat's tone suggested she'd never believed it—and still didn't.

"But I wasn't trying to be funny," Mimi said. "Let's open the windows and the glass cases and see what happens when live birds come in. All these years I've wanted to know what they've thought when they've caught a glimpse."

"Birds don't glimpse," Pat said. "Or think."

"I'm going over there." *And screw you for always correcting me.* "Come if you want."

"You don't have a key."

"Then I'll break the glass."

"No, I don't think you will."

Mimi felt powerlessly, uselessly reckless, while across Pat's face, she saw rules and propriety battle with the fact that rules and propriety were for shit now. The women crossed the quad and stopped near the chapel where some pansies, still in their black plastic flats, waited to be planted. Pat bent her thick frame down to caress them, and Mimi heard her inhale a private whimper.

Past Peacott's heavy front door and the thick smell of frayed patrician carpets, was the Bird Room, where the far wall was glassed-in and oak-framed. Stuffed birds of all varieties posed on branches. Ones that didn't belong together occupied the same perch. This was the UN of avian life; they all had to get along. Feathers lost to age had fallen to the bottom of the display. One bird clutched a mouse in its talons. The taxidermy seams were coming unglued and the mouse's tail had dropped off. Mimi lifted the windows and screens, while Pat went to her office to get the key to the case. It would be Pat, and only Pat, who unlocked the thing. They sat in the two faded armchairs and waited for the birds to arrive. The room smelled like mothballs, a touch of funeral home, old coffee. It could be ancient students instead of birds, stuffed and perched, for how the place was hooked on its own history.

Mimi shifted out of fatigue's tightening grasp. "Is this cruel, what we're doing?" she asked. "Is it like taking a child to see his grandpa dead in his chair, a corpse in his recliner, his natural habitat? Is it ghoulish?" Pat didn't respond, or show any sign she'd heard. "It's the quiet that really gets me. I can hear the blood surging in my ears all night long." There were no airplanes, lawn mowers, cars, music, cell phones—none of the constant hum. "I keep hearing gunshots."

"I haven't been sleeping," Pat finally said.

"Neither have I."

"If I had a weapon, I'd do better."

"A gun?" Mimi asked. "Do you think you'd really be able to use it? I've always wondered if I could if I had to." She pointed an imaginary gun at the doorway and pulled the trigger. "I'm not sure."

"Shush," Pat said. "This is a silly conversation."

"Really? I'm just trying to get to know you some."

Pat sighed. "I don't see the point."

"The point? Because it's just us here, in the end, we're the only ones. That's the fucking point, Pat."

"Watch your language."

"Oh, for fuck's sake. Are you serious? You're actually scolding me?"

No birds came in through the window, but the scent of newly mowed grass did. It was an unexpected, domestic smell that made Mimi wonder for a moment if the end wasn't going to happen after all, if it were just a false alarm, and the first thing someone did to get his life back in order was cut the lawn. The grass kept growing, after all, like fingernails on a dead man. But maybe what she was smelling was her own life coming in through the darkening window to make sure she remembered everything in the time she had left: a yard of fescue and Kentucky bluegrass and weeds, a cheap apartment, a baby girl, a kiddie pool, her mother asleep on the couch from the Goodwill store, Jesse briefly lit up by a Magic 8 Ball he couldn't yet read. Cruelly—or was it blessedly?—she would not be allowed to forget anything.

"You keep trying to make me laugh," Pat said, "and I don't want to laugh. Stop making a joke out of this. I don't want to be amused."

If they went in different directions after this and never saw each other again, that would be okay. Why couldn't the woman give up a single thing? They'd disagreed over the years about students and policies, and it was always Mimi who'd had to give in. How much had she hated that? She stood by the open case of birds, inhaling the ammoniac scent of decay. Soon, she'd find her way to a bed before it was too dark and she'd leave Pat forever.

"I'm most afraid that nothing matters anymore," Pat said to Mimi's back. "Not what I've done with my life, or what I was planning to do, or all those things I thought were so important. I would have made other decisions if I'd known."

What could Mimi say to something so obvious, but also

so surprisingly gentle? She wondered if the woman had ever doubted herself before, had ever wished she'd made a different decision.

"I don't know what to do with that fact of nothing in front of me. Why finish a book if you know the ending?" Pat said. "I don't know what I'm meant to do now."

"You don't have to do anything," Mimi said. "You just have to live. What choice do you have?"

Pat pointed to the clock on the mantel. "It's much later than that," she said. "I forgot to wind it yesterday."

They talked about what hour it might really be as the last of the sun backed out of the room like a sheepish party guest. Pat said she knew the precise pattern of each season's falling light on her office wall because she was so often there long after the building was empty.

"Do you know Joe?" Pat's voice was pinched. "Head of Maintenance?"

"I know who he is, of course," Mimi said, "but I wouldn't say I *know* him."

"He'd stop by and ask me how my day was, then he'd tell me it was time for me to go home, that I'd worked long enough. I appreciated that—otherwise I'd work forever."

Mimi pictured Pat at her desk making sure others' lives ran smoothly, raising money, guarding the school in her own imposing way. Joe was a squat guy, Brazilian and upbeat, with a passion for flowers, particularly orchids. He planted the pansies. To Pat, he was a dose of sympathy who'd helped her end each day with some sense of comfort. It was a shock to realize it was more than Mimi had.

Pat stood and closed the glass case. "Come back to the residence," she said, pocketing her keys. "You should sleep there."

Though the idea of another night alone in the empty dorm was terrifying, Mimi didn't know if time with Pat might be worse. Still, she said yes, and on their way to the residence, they paused at the round granite marker sunk into the ground since 1810, when the school was built. Here was the perch of Calvinist superiority looking down at the genteel and expensive town. In the evening dim, everything below was a dark, elegant mass—the obscuring trees, the renovated houses with their clapboards and historical plaques and redone kitchens, facing in to the geometry of the colonial green, the ascendant white church. Occasionally, a restrained beam of light from a candle or a flashlight appeared behind a window. Farther away, beyond the niceties of granite countertops and expensive cars, out by the pizza places and auto-body shops, a herd of sagging ranch houses and the dented trailers in the trailer park were lit up by gas-fed generators. Was it the rich or the poor who knew how to live to the very end?

As she stood next to Pat in the cool, evening air, her mouth dried up with the chilling thought that she might never be touched again. Not even have her hand held. And she would never have a chance to tell the truth about her life. Her skin flared with goose bumps, the rash of the forsaken. She bent over, hands on knees.

"What's the matter?" Pat asked.

"A cramp."

"It was that awful pudding. You shouldn't have eaten so much. You really should practice some self-restraint." She tapped Mimi on the back and began walking.

Could that have been the final touch? Disgrace bubbled in Mimi's chest. She was a little girl, a bread dumpling hoarder, a pudding-gulping piggy under her mother's stingy eye. She caught up to Pat who unlocked the residence's front door.

"Everyone thinks you're a dyke," Mimi flung back at her. "A lesbian, that is."

"Yes, I know what a dyke is." Pat stepped inside and flicked a light switch on and off out of habit. "Of course people think that—the cliché comes with the position. They say the same thing about Hillary Clinton and Madeleine Albright. Anyone who wears pantsuits and brooches."

"Are you?"

"A lesbian? No."

"It doesn't bother you that people think you are?" Mimi asked.

"Why would it?"

"Because it means that they don't know you," Mimi said.

"I don't need people to know me. Why would I?" Pat turned away; she wasn't asking for an answer.

To know you, Pat, is to not love you, Mimi thought. Mimi had been inside the residence for parties—welcoming events, most recently a memorial service for Keating, the math teacher who'd died en route to the hospital. The kids had watched him being wheeled out by the EMTs, his face the mimeograph blue-white of ancient marble. She'd been in the kitchen before to deliver a plate of cookies or cheese, or whatever she'd signed up to bring. It was always potluck, part of the notion that they were all family—a family of underpaid employees—at Whitehall. But she'd never been in the place without a crowd, or snooped around on her own, which she did now without hesitation and while there was still some mist of light left. Downstairs was like the rest of the school's public areas, impersonal and noble, heavy wood and cracked leather furniture, threadbare oriental rugs, the promise of influence lurking in the dust. There were paintings of head-masters—all men until Pat—and one of a group of boys playing soccer on the pre-turf field. This was by the artist who had graduated from Whitehall and had gone on to become a millionaire with his garish work appearing on placemats and mouse pads and T-shirts. The artist had hated his years at Whitehall—though people at the school chose to ignore this fact—and had once, in an interview, called the art teacher a fascist. Which he was, Mimi knew, from Jesse's time in old man's classroom. Horizons were not allowed to oscillate.

Upstairs, where no one had ever ventured, two bedrooms were fussy with flowery curtains, bedspreads, and fringed pillows, the smell of rose potpourri. It was all frill and pink soaps, pink towels in the bathroom, a plush pink toilet seat cover. In the room with a small television and a single armchair, there was a tableau on the shelf of a ceramic cat and her four kittens, each with a real ribbon around its neck.

"We all wondered what it was like up here," Mimi said.

Pat dogged her like an overzealous museum guard. "I don't see why anyone would be interested."

Mimi touched the ceramic kittens, changed their positions. "We were just trying to figure you out."

"That's silly," Pat said. "Don't play with those, please."

"Aren't you curious about other people?"

"Not terribly. It's none of my business. I like them to do their job."

As Mimi watched Pat rearrange her ceramic cats, she knew that it still mattered what you said, that any word—bitch, for example—still had the power to wound. She saw how Pat's back was permanently humped against attack. Mimi would not tell Pat how they all feared her condescension, her inscrutability. How they disliked her. The truth was, their speculation about Pat was fertile enough to have spawned a whole other person, one made up entirely of their conjecture. And still they would have been wrong.

They went back outside to pee, turning away from each other, squatting like shy children. Back in the residence, Pat gave her a white nightgown and an extra toothbrush. They used a bottle of water to rinse and spit together in the sink, their shoulders bumping. Mimi smelled Pat, a touch of sweat, a base of lanolin, the fustiness of an unused woman—or was she smelling herself?

In the thick dusk of the second bedroom, Mimi was electrified by sounds she couldn't identify. She wasn't tired, but she was exhausted, not hungry, but ravenous. No lights moved across the ceiling to reassure her. Soon, half in a trance of confusion, she could not even say where she was, or if she was a child or an adult. Or was she a young mother, listening for the breath of her first baby, then her second? Her life seemed like something she'd made up, none of it real, all of the details arbitrarily catalogued, not her own childhood, not the birth of her daughter, then her son, not the day the baby ate her first soft-boiled egg, and the second baby crushed the shells between his fat fingers and howled as though possessed by his dead sister.

She woke to a searing light on the ceiling. And the light in the hallway, and the noise of a television in the other room, and the sound of radios and televisions in the empty dorms which were now completely lit up, blasting across the campus, throwing a sheet of yellow over the stunned quad. The electricity was back. She fell to the floor, fumbled with her clothes, her hands shaking as she found her cell phone in her pants pockets, but the lights went off while she was still on her knees, and the noise stopped just as suddenly. Silence swift as a beheading. Her ears pounded. She'd been a breath away from her son's voice. She wasn't sure she hadn't dreamed all of it.

"Did that just happen?" Mimi asked, standing in the doorway to Pat's room.

Pat was sitting up, the white of her gown like a nightlight. "I can't get my heart to slow." Her alarm agitated the air. "I can't." She gasped. "I think I'm having a heart attack."

"Take some deep breaths," Mimi said. She sat on the edge of the bed and got close to Pat's face. "Breathe, breathe." She took the woman's wrist. Pat's pulse was a bird's heart. Her skin was cool, her terrified breath sour, her mouth rounded with the effort to live. "Better?"

"I wanted the end to catch us when we were asleep so we wouldn't have to know it was happening," Pat said after a few minutes. Her fear had turned to anger.

"I don't want it to end at all," Mimi said.

"But it's going to. There is no future. You have to face it."

"No, I don't." The future was simply the next moment, which was only in response to the one that preceded it, and you could never step out of that line of history.

Pat withdrew her wrist from Mimi's grasp "I'm okay now. You don't need to stay with me."

"You're not very comfortable with women," Mimi said.

"I don't understand women."

"No one does." Mimi kneeled on the floor, her elbows on the bed. "All these years, I never knew if you were happy or not. As if happiness didn't matter to you."

"Happiness? I don't know—should I have been happy? It isn't a useful standard to measure things by. I don't think about it much."

Mimi glimpsed the moonlight's reflection on the pool's surface and it looked like a last impression. She didn't think she'd sleep again. "Let's go for a walk. We don't even have to get dressed. I've always wanted to walk around in a nightgown anyway."

"That's a strange thing to want," Pat said, as Mimi retrieved her pink diva hoodie from the other room and went downstairs.

She wasn't sure if Pat would follow, and her nerve started to ebb. To wander alone at night was asking for it—whatever *it* was these days. But Pat descended, still in her nightgown, and armed with a flashlight. They stood for the moment on the granite front steps of the residence, then moved to the area under the elms where it was strangely lighter. The cold ground pulled greedily at Mimi's bare feet. During the days, kids hung out here, lounged on the benches. Mimi had patrolled the area a million times for kids smoking cigarettes or pot or drinking vodka they'd poured into their water bottles. She now thought that the dead men whose names were on the benches' plaques might have appreciated the drama of these intent, confused children who dug their nails and pens into the wood, leaving their marks on the world. The dead men would have enjoyed the drama of adolescence and wished they were back in it, risen from their graves.

From down below in the usually quiet and reserved town, menacing music of spoons beating pots and pans, people whooping and honking car horns reached them like a troubling odor. It was only an illusion that they were safe behind school gates—gates that seemed to weaken a little each day.

"I had an affair with the parent of a student once," Pat said.

Mimi's shock hid in the dark. A million other rumors about the woman, but never this one. She didn't think Pat had it in her. "Really? Who was it?"

"I can't tell you that," Pat said. "But that's kind of silly now, isn't it?"

"Yes, it is. Say his name. Or her name. See what happens. You could even scream it."

"His name. I've never told anyone. I should probably keep it that way."

Mimi wouldn't beg. She knew that you could think about something so often and so deeply that you wore down the outlines, dulled the colors and the sounds. The more you recalled, the less you remembered, and the memories took the shape of your sorrows and pleasures and not the other way around. Her first baby, Ava. It had been humid the day she'd died, and Mimi's own mother's face had been covered with a sheen of over-medicated sweat. *See what happens if you say it out loud*, she told herself. *If you scream it.*

"Jason Koh. He was the architect of the art center. His daughter was a senior," Pat said. "We went to museums together, and visited other art centers at other schools, site visits. When two people look at buildings together long enough, and talk about them, you begin to talk about yourselves, what you like and desire and need. I don't think I'd ever felt that way before." Pat squeezed her own thigh.

"What way?"

"Articulate, I suppose. About those things, feelings."

"Were you in love?" Mimi asked.

"Mostly I was scared we'd be found out. That eclipsed everything after a while."

"So maybe you were in love."

"Why do you keep talking about love?" Pat said, her voice clipped by irritation. "You don't understand. I can't live like everyone else. I'm under scrutiny all the time." She smoothed her nightgown over her knees. "I don't want to talk about this anymore. It's done. There's no point."

"It's never done. Look, doesn't it feel good to finally tell someone?"

"No, it just feels wrong. The whole thing was wrong. At his daughter's graduation, I shook his hand and his wife's, and I could barely breathe. Not because I felt regret or shame— because I didn't, I still don't—but because I realized I might not ever have another lover. I might die without being touched ever again. I've given up a lot in my life, and a lot for this job, but I wasn't prepared to give that up."

Was this what kept people going, the expectation of that touch?

Mimi wanted to put her hand on the woman's shoulder, but she knew it wouldn't be welcome. "I'll tell you something," she said, as the damp rose up her spine. Confession was all they had left to give. "I let some things go around here," she said.

"'Let some things go,'" Pat repeated. "I don't understand what you're saying."

"With the students. Minor infractions, small things. Kid stuff. I let it go."

"Well, yes, they are kids. But infractions are infractions. We have a code of conduct. You know that better than anyone. It's there for a reason."

Pat's tone, efficient and dismissive all over again, made Mimi shiver. "That's all," she said, her stories backing up in her throat. "Forget I said anything."

"No. Go on," Pat said. "Finish what you started."

Someone was honking and revving an engine. What did she have to lose? "I didn't think anything was going to be served by punishment," Mimi said. "Being caught was punishment and lesson enough. Humiliation is a powerful deterrent."

"You're speaking in abstractions," Pat said. "I don't know what you're talking about."

Through the trees, and down at the edge of the lake, a single light blinked on and off. It was a kid playing with a flashlight, Mimi decided, and she was for an instant, grateful that she didn't have to look at her own children—no, her son, just her son—and explain the end of the world to him. Or not explain and just let it happen, because what did she know? They were all children now. There was last month, she told Pat, when she'd stayed late for a girls' lacrosse game. Long after the team had cleared out of the locker room, leaving it steamy and slippery with their body washes and lotions, she'd found Sophie and Lacey in the shower. They were slick and shiny, the two beautiful, youthful halves making a single body, breast-to-breast, thigh-to-thigh, lips-to-lips. Hands to backs, hands to fronts. She'd been transfixed there behind the tiled doorway, and moved by their lust, their harmless, beautiful lust, she explained.

Pat sighed tightly. "And you didn't do anything. You just let it go. Is that what you're saying?"

"You would have done the same," Mimi said. "You would have let it go, too."

"Absolutely not. There are reasons for rules, and being 'moved' does not absolve you of your duty."

"Duty? Do you hear yourself, Pat? Do you fucking hear yourself?" Mimi's words rose into the trees. Somewhere, a car let out a low roar. "And what difference would it have made anyway? We'd still be here and now."

She understood that this was like telling Pat that her house had been eaten by termites—telling her too late that the foundation was rotten. Mimi didn't tell her about the two boys she'd found curled in each other's arms in the boathouse. Blowjobs she generally drew the line at because it was always the most adrift girls she found on their knees, their eyes squeezed shut. She was recorder of skipped classes and essays bought online, she was the one who counseled the kids to straighten up, to get it together, to open up, to shut up. But when she saw those seeking solace, connection, and some sense of who they were, she let it go. She'd felt too much for the kids, felt too much of her own son who had never found his consolation in someone else. She feared most that he would die without having loved.

"This is all very disappointing to hear," Pat said.

"Screw you." Mimi would not look at her. The pines heaved in a sudden gust. "All these years and you don't know me at all."

"I know more about you than you think," Pat told her. "From your son."

"From Jesse? You never even acknowledged him, Pat. Four

unhappy years at Whitehall, and did you ever have a conversation with him?" Next to her, Pat's body radiated a strange, softening heat. "Ever? Or was he beneath you?"

"Be careful with your words," Pat warned. "So you know, we met a couple of times a month in my office during his time here."

"What are you talking about?" Mimi's hands tingled. The bench seemed to levitate, her feet rising from the mossy carpet.

"I knew he was having a difficult time. I wanted to keep an eye on him, give him a place to talk if he needed it."

"I had no idea," Mimi's lungs squeezed. Soon there would be no air left in her.

"I know you didn't. And you judge too fast."

"And you didn't think you should have told me? Asked my permission? He's my son."

"It was Jesse's choice to tell you or not," Pat said. "I left it up to him."

From below, the music of car engines, horns, and metal on metal reached a crescendo and then stopped as if it had heard the women talking. What she thought she'd understood about her son slipped through her fingers, another silk scarf.

"My God," Mimi began to cry.

Mimi knew that Pat's hand hovered indecisively over her shoulder before it alighted. Her touch was uncertain, but it was a touch, an electric joining, and in it, Mimi thought the woman might understand her anguish at not being able to reach Jesse—now, and then. Pat might have helped him get through his years at Whitehall intact. She might have been his redeemer, and she might still hold his secrets, and his answers. Pat was not someone Mimi knew at all.

Pat tensed, and her hand became a heavy terror on Mimi's shoulder. The woman sucked in her breath and Mimi looked up.

About fifteen yards in front of them, under the cathedral ceiling of the elms and pines, was a darting cat and then the dog Mimi had seen earlier on the quad. The dog did not look at them, but disappeared into the dark like a devil.

Pat stood, her hand to her mouth.

"What?" Mimi asked. "What is it?"

Pat ran towards the quad, her white gown flashing as she stumbled over roots. Mimi ran after her, following the trail of high wailing. Pat went into the residence and locked the door. Mimi felt her trembling on the other side.

"Let me in," Mimi said. "Please." Something was approaching from behind, a hand at her throat. The back of her neck was exposed. "Let me in, Pat!" Pat opened the door, and Mimi flung herself inside. "Tell me what you saw out there."

Pat shook her head. Mimi hugged her, but Pat remained rigid in her arms.

"Okay, enough," Pat said, and pushed Mimi away. "I'm fine. It was nothing."

"It was not nothing," Mimi insisted, but Pat was already on her way upstairs.

In her room, Mimi kept her eye on the ceiling light, a black orb like a defunct moon, ready now with her cell phone in her hand if it went on again.

In the morning, they barely spoke, but to Mimi it seemed they had decided not to leave each other. They were like awkward lovers who'd exchanged something in the dark that embarrassed them in the light. In the dining hall, they opened a can of fruit salad and ate from it standing up, sipping the heavy syrup from stainless steel ladles. They were still in their nightgowns, Pat's now with a green school jacket over hers, her pockets bulging with keys and her flashlight. Mimi wanted to go on the trampoline, something she'd been watching the kids do for years, but had never done herself, so they went to the field house, a vast, cool space, crisscrossed with beams and basketball hoops pulled up, echoing bleachers, the smell of cracked rubber and menthol. Pat announced she wasn't going to get on the thing, and crossed her arms over her chest. Mimi climbed on with false bravery, and the taut silkiness of the trampoline reminded her of the skin over her belly when she'd been at her most pregnant, some combination of tension, elasticity, and the impossible. She took her first jump, an awkward attempt that buckled her knees and made her pitch forward.

"No, you're doing it wrong," Pat said. "Find your footing, your balance first before you jump."

"You're an expert?" Mimi asked.

"It's what I hear the gym people telling the students."

"Gym people. Is that how you think of them? Gym people? Math people? History people? I thought we were Whitehall family. You know, potlucks and codes of conduct, and personal responsibility, that sort of thing. Honesty. Openness." Her anger over Pat's collusion with Jesse stoked as she rose higher with each jump. Her gown ballooned beneath her. "All bullshit, Pat."

Pat's shoulder's pulled back. "Look. It was Jesse's choice not to tell you," she said. "I respected his decision." Her eyes followed Mimi's rise and fall. "Would you have wanted me to do otherwise? Betray him?"

"Yes. In fact, I would have."

Pat shook her head and pivoted to look at the track. On Jesse's first day at Whitehall, Mimi had parked in faculty/staff lot and turned to her boy whose knees were smashed up against the glove compartment. His face was crimson from the new acne medicine, a deeper shade as he watched the other students leap from cars, squeal, hug, call each other. The girls flitted and the boys roared, and they all radiated inherited promise and indemnity, and the easiest passage through life. Mimi wanted to tell her son that it didn't always work out that way, that many of them spent the rest of their lives stumbling away from this high point.

But she'd turned to her son and said instead, "I want you to know, that if you get in trouble here, I won't be able to help you. I can't give you any special treatment. You're on your own."

His face had become a deeper shade of humiliation, and then he'd left the car. He didn't slam the door or give her the finger. He wouldn't make that big a gesture. High up in the ether of the field house now, she knew that her first baby's death—the death of the sister Jesse didn't even know about—was always with her. What she'd said that day in the car, the way she'd thrown her son out alone into the unfriendly water, was meant to make him invincible. But why did she think that would work? He'd stayed afloat, he'd graduated, he'd enlisted. He must have understood that staying alive was just a billion moments of good timing and luck, and nothing more. Her teeth pierced her lower lip. She tasted blood and fell to her knees.

There was Pat, two feet on the earth, turning to her again as if she knew Mimi's anguish. She rested her hands on the edge of the trampoline. "Jesse had no desire to fit in here," she said. "He was hard on himself, more than any other kid I'd ever seen."

"I begged him for years to see someone, to take medication, do something." Mimi blotted her lip with her gown.

"He wasn't depressed," Pat said. "He just took everything to heart. That's a rare quality. He had to learn not to be overwhelmed by it. He wasn't there yet."

Mimi climbed off the trampoline. Through the open field house door was another beautiful day, a particular torture of lofty clouds and naïve blue sky. She left the building and crossed the quad. She lay on the pool deck's warming bluestone. The water's surface was flecked with leaves. She absorbed the heat and the sound of another gunshot, another metallic notch in her chest. In that moment, she wasn't sorry that it would all be over soon. It would be a relief now. Pat approached, the sun pouring through her white gown and revealing thick, childish legs.

"Go away," Mimi said. "Please. This is torture for me. Do you understand? He's my child, my only child."

"We talked about what he wanted to do with his life," Pat offered.

"Fight a war? Kill people? Get killed? That's what you advised him? I'm supposed to be grateful for that? Well, thank you then."

"That's a terrible oversimplification," Pat said, "and a real disservice to your son. You're too smart for that."

"No, I don't think I am. That's all I understand." Her thoughts had been decapitated—bloody and swift.

She stood and took off her clothes. She didn't understand her sudden lack of inhibition, when she'd spent her whole life trying to hide her body. But it was good to be naked, nothing left to be judged for. She looked down at herself, her breasts with their own sense of gravity, her silvery, puckered stretch marks on her flat belly, her thinning pubic hair. *Look at me, look at me, Pat,* Mimi urged silently, *this is what a mother looks like. You are not a mother. You do not know or understand.*

But Pat wouldn't look at her. Mimi dove into the water, and an icy slip fell across her back as though she was putting on something slinky. But for whom had she ever done that? Her lovers, her ex, hadn't been the types to notice a satin slip, or perfume on her wrists; they were narrow, efficient, pro-women men, but they never said she was beautiful or that she was their world. Pat suddenly moved to the gate as a man with a rifle crossed the quad towards them.

Pat's shoulders were squared, those unfortunate legs only gauzily covered asserting their foothold on the property. The man wasn't wearing a shirt, his slack, hairy belly falling over the waist of pink Bermuda shorts. He looked like the men she saw down in the town, the ones buying gin and vodka at the package store, or in the post office sending back things their wives had ordered from catalogues. They were the ones who parked wherever they wanted, who broadcast their business when they talked on their cell phones. They called the church their own. His rifle rose towards Pat as he winked at her.

"Hey there, ladies," he said. His voice was heavy with alcohol.

"Lower your gun," Pat said.

"Relax, sweetheart."

"Lower your gun," she repeated. He let the rifle fall, but he was a man for whom rules never applied. "This is private property."

"Oh, I know that," he said. "No problem. I live in town. Have for decades. Did you hear our party last night?" It occurred to Mimi that anything could have happened there, and no one would know, no one would care. The man took a step closer, but Pat moved to block his view of Mimi.

"How can we help you?" she asked.

"I'm looking for my dog." He bounced his rifle against his thigh. He struck Mimi as the kind of man who'd always wished for the opportunity to kill. The surgical invasion of fear sliced into her. "You seen him?"

"We haven't seen your dog," Pat said.

"Tan? With a purple collar?" He raised his rifle again at Pat. "You sure you haven't seen him?"

"Yes, I'm sure." Pat's voice was flat. "Put your gun down."

"Jesus, I'm not going to hurt you, lady." He looked up at the sky and took aim there. "You have enough to eat here?"

"We have no food for you," Pat said.

The man's head tilted and his gaze was distant, but alcohol was sharpening its claws. "I wasn't asking for any," he said, aiming his gun at her again. "Were you always such a bitch?"

A distant gunshot cut open the silence, and out of it poured Pat's terror as she began to piss down her leg. Her knees softened, but she kept her gaze on the man. He lifted his gun and shot arbitrarily into the trees. The sound echoed around the pool and ended with a thump at the base of Mimi's spine. He shot again as he walked away, waving backwards at them over his shoulder.

Pat fell to her knees on the grass. Soon she began crawling up the hill on all fours, her moans wafting into the air.

Mimi scrambled to get into her nightgown, but she was wet and the fabric clung and tore. She caught up to Pat who was sitting cross-legged and looking towards the lake just visible as slivers of glass between the trees.

"I need you to do something for me," Pat said, without looking at her. "Now. And I need you not to ask any questions."

"Why? What is it?"

Pat barked in frustration. She pulled at her hair, at her clothes; she was pulling herself apart. They were witnessing their own disintegration. "Will you please just do it?" she wailed. "Now?"

Pat wanted her to go to the maintenance building. Mimi nodded, though she had lost the urge to even imagine what might be so urgent. She felt oddly light—not unburdened, but without consequence. She walked, only vaguely aware of the pokes and prods at her bare feet. She went behind the library and the student center, down the path behind faculty/staff parking lot and the dumpsters which were ripe and pulsing with rot, past the varsity fields in the distance with their nets and balls scattered across the pitch like planets. Pat followed yards behind, swerving like she was made of linen sheets draped on a line, pushed by wind. When Mimi stopped for a second, Pat spoke so indistinctly that Mimi wasn't sure if she were talking to herself. It didn't matter.

"You should have gone home," Pat said. "You shouldn't be here. Why the hell are you here?"

She thought of telling Pat that she hadn't wanted to go back to her own house where Jesse wasn't, where no one was, that the solitude there was like being dead already, but she had an instant and chilling sense that the end was very close and that it was in the direction they were headed. She wanted to get there quickly, to get it done. She stopped at the single-story building's open front door.

Pat stopped inches behind her. "Joe, are you here?" she whispered, not out of secrecy, Mimi thought, but because it seemed to be the only breath she had left. "Are you here?" She looked wildly at Mimi. "Is he here?"

"I don't know." She took in Pat's thinning hair, still pressed down on one side, her piss-stained gown, her mouth with a dot of white at each corner. This was not the woman Mimi knew, even so imperfectly, and she understood that she could not trace her way back to the beginning. This was it, this was all that was left, this was all that was going to happen.

"Please, go look for him," Pat urged. Her voice was a long, painful bend. "I can't go in."

Mimi hesitated in the doorway as though a force was blowing her back, and she leaned in to the forbidding wind and stepped inside. The place was chilled, the light dappling over the cement floor. Empty soda cans and stained coffee cups were scattered on a plywood table, along with papers and clipboards, an old newspaper. The air smelled of motor oil and metal.

Unfamiliar machines leaned against the walls like spectators. There was a table saw in the next room, a dusting of sawdust, a forest of pine boards. The metal was enticing, the gleaming teeth on the blade beguiling. As though she was holding a shell to her ear, Mimi heard Pat's roaring breath mixed with her own, even though Pat was still out front. She passed into another room that held the riding lawn mowers and snow blowers. The deeper in she went, the older the building was and she saw more brick and stone, smaller-paned windows and their splintered framing, lower ceilings and less-even floors.

She opened a door on her left that led to the humid surprise of the greenhouse, bright with hundreds of seedlings and orchids and nasturtiums spilling over their pots. It was a fragrant and beautiful shock. On the right was a bathroom with a porcelain sink strained by twin lines of rust running from the faucet like a child's leaky nose, a toothbrush, a squashed tube of toothpaste. There was a last room at the end of the narrow passage, and at first, just the edge of a mattress, the puckered corner of a sheet, a sock, a book, a *Norton Anthology of Poetry*. Above it all, the air was colored violet and inviolable. She took a step back in fear—in anticipation of alarm—and kicked over a plate of cat food. There was a bowl of water too, and her urgent need to take its temperature; it was warm. When she looked up, Pat was staring into the room.

"I let Joe live here. He had nowhere else to go," Pat said, distantly. "No one knew but me."

"He isn't here." Mimi turned Pat away from the stark fact of the bereft room.

"He's here somewhere," she said and ducked out from Mimi's hands. She sat on the mattress. "Because he left the door open for the cat and he never let her out. He loved that thing to death. The cat we saw last night."

The light moved over Pat's splayed legs. Pat pressed a pillow to her nose, extracting Joe from it and holding him in her lungs. Mimi knew the gesture because it was also hers, that hoarding of a person's essence. Pat and Joe were lovers and she was filled instantly with a caustic jealousy that made her throat burn. Still, even now. Beyond the window, the green trees muttered, but she had nothing to say.

Last year, Mimi had walked by Pat's office, as the woman was being berated and bullied by a beet-faced parent in an idiotic baseball cap and a rep tie. The man's daughter, a liar, sat next to him, a smug princess who was failing calculus and blaming the teacher. The father pointed his trigger finger at Pat who had returned his spitting ire with a look so blankly cool and in control and dismissive, that Mimi had cringed at her stare, and not the berating.

"Say something," Pat said, and fanned her hand over the empty bed. "I need you to understand."

Mimi's head felt tentatively balanced. Pat was a rock, not a woman. But what a life she'd had. Pat had been saved by her secrets, while Mimi knew she was doomed by her own.

"I deserve something, don't I?" Pat said. "Don't you dare judge me." She tried to get up from the mattress, but her knees caught in her gown forced her back again. "You have no idea what I have to swallow all the time. It's the taste of shit in your mouth, and your body made out of rubber so you have to bend the wrong way. And you have to keep swallowing and at some point you've swallowed your entire self. And if you think of it too often, the shame of this life will make you want to hide under the bed. I just wanted this one thing, this one thing for myself."

Mimi sat next to her on the bed. "Let me lie down. I'm dizzy."

"You're shocked, you disapprove," Pat said. "Headmistress

and handyman. Fuck all of you."

Mimi pressed her palms against her eyes. "I had a daughter. She died." What she'd kept hidden slipped out of her like a piece of paper sliding under a door. It made a silent landing at Pat's feet.

The baby was twelve months old, Mimi said, new to walking and watched that day by Mimi's mother, while Mimi was at class—her second year of college. The plastic kiddie pool in the backyard belonged to the landlord who lived on the second floor and allowed a dark layer of leaves to cover the fetid water. The baby had wandered out the back door to the pool while Mimi's mother slept, tipped in, and drowned.

"Her name was Ava." The pair of syllables soothed her burning mouth. "I never told Jesse. He never even knew she'd existed."

"No, he knew," Pat said. She'd regained her composure, her place. "He knew there was something hidden, that you weren't really there, not ever. He carried the loss for you. That was his burden. How could you have done that to him? Selfish! Selfish!"

Mimi sat up and smashed her hands into woman's collarbone. Pat fell backwards, hit her head hit on the brick wall with a dull thud and slumped, chin to chest. *Dead*, Mimi thought; *I've killed her.* Satisfaction shivered through her body. There would be no consequences, but that also meant no atonement, and how could a person live with that? Her body twitched. She didn't know what to do next. When Pat's eyes fluttered, it was a relief to find she hadn't killed the woman after all, but she was without regret or apology. Apology was always, in some ways, about the future, and they had none of that coming.

Mimi left and walked by the shadowed side of the building, without destination. She stumbled, more tired than she'd ever been. Ahead was a chaos of a busted wheelbarrow half-hidden by weeds, discarded plastic milk crates, rakes with missing teeth, empty cans of motor oil, legless chairs, box fans, soda bottles, cracked pails, warped plywood, old TVs, a pile of rotting clothes and sneakers. No one was meant to see this, the venerable idyll's garbage heap, here behind the maintenance building, where love found its way. And then a pair of booted feet, together at the heels but angled outwards like a duck, the bottoms of blue work pants, the folded figure but the head upright as though speaking to an audience. The face was entirely gone, pulpy and raw and red, curls surrounding it like a bloody cameo. A hand that had dropped a gun onto the pine needles, and a haloed constellation of blood and bits of bone and brains on the side of the building.

Mimi's eyes vibrated; Joe seemed to move left and right, left and right.

"Stop," Pat yelled. "Stop screaming, Mimi. Stop."

Mimi heard nothing. She wasn't screaming, but her mouth was open, and the back of her throat throbbed. Pat begged her to stop. Mimi turned herself inside out and vomited. When she looked up, she saw the dog from the day before in the pines, watching her, and in its mouth was the limp cat, its bones turned to string.

"It's Joe, it's Joe, it's Joe," Pat said. "Oh, Joe! My Joe."

Beyond the trees and the dog and the cat, and above the lake, Mimi saw the force of the dead, not gone, but gathering. Gathering and watching them. The lucky dead. She did not feel Jesse or Ava there.

Pat turned over a white bucket and sat on it as if she were pulling up a chair to sit by Joe's bedside. "I waited for him, and he never came." She reached for his hand. "Oh, Joe, how is it that no one asked us to go with them? How is it that we were left here? That no one wanted us?" She smudged the spattering of his blood on his hand, then tried to clean it with her thumb.

The light changed—the shadows shifted into afternoon. It seemed to come faster every day. Mimi knew they had to do something with Joe's body, or animals would get what remained. She threw a rock at the dog, but he was watching and waiting, dead cat between his paws now. She threw another, but a ferocious crack split the air first. The earth shook and then the dog flopped over. Pat had shot him. She looked down at the gun and let it roll off her palm back to the pine needles.

She looked up at Mimi, whose ears and brain were clanging. "I want to put Joe in the lake."

She wanted to get something from the residence first, though, and she asked Mimi to sit with Joe. Mimi took her place on the bucket. She heard the flies gathering around Joe, but she wouldn't look. She recalled the arcing of his back as he kneeled for hours planting flowers around the campus. She smelled the iron in his blood soaking the ground.

Pat returned with a flowery bed sheet, a wheelbarrow, and beribboned boxes of chocolates. She covered Joe with the sheet, and then stood back as if the body was going to move itself. To move him would be to jostle a head that was likely in a thousand pieces, and to let loose a flood.

"I don't think we can do this," Mimi said. "He's too heavy."

"Help me," Pat said. She was surprisingly strong, and hoisted her dead lover from under the arms, while Mimi took his legs, and they flopped the body into the wheelbarrow, his limbs hanging off the sides. The motion of parts of his body against her—elbow, ankle, foot—made the bile rise in Mimi's throat. Pat pressed her lips together until they turned white. She took one heavy handle, Mimi the other, and they moved through the trees towards the lake, stopping every few feet to shake out their cramped hands. When they were beyond the trees and on the uneven gravel road, blood began to seep through the sheet as the spreading stain of a former face. Joe's chest rose and fell over bumps, and his fingers trilled as though he were caressing his cat. The lake was obliviously blue, the sky open and cloudless. A motorboat was out on the water, the sound of its lazy engine the sound of leisure. Pat went ahead to the boathouse for oars, while Mimi wheeled the body down the dock. They would have to roll him first out of the wheelbarrow, and then over the side and into the rowboat. She didn't see any other way. The sound of the body falling to the wooden dock was thick and wet, more so when it fell the few feet to land in the rowboat. Pat whimpered. Mimi climbed into the boat first and tried to move the body to the center, to curl it in on itself, but Joe was too heavy, the sheet sliding off, his limbs slapping against the wood. A photograph of three kids had slipped out of his breast pocket—a pudgy girl with pink glasses, and two boys—and she put the picture in her sweatshirt pocket before Pat saw it.

When Pat got into the boat, she was forced to straddle Joe's legs with her own. The boat dragged and listed, and Mimi's arms burned as she rowed. It was cold out on the water in only her nightgown and sweatshirt, and she pulled on her hood. They decided that the middle of the lake was best. Mimi wondered if a body would sink or float. Pat arranged the boxes of chocolate on the bench that was empty except for the tip of one of Joe's boots.

She threw the ribbons and box tops into the water. Gifts, she explained, from the students and their families, years and years of the stuff, and this was only a small portion of it.

"You never ate any?" Mimi asked.

"I was waiting for a special occasion," Pat said. "I think this counts."

Pat bit into a piece, and then another, tossing the uneaten parts overboard. She ate as punishment. Mimi's stomach was filled with cement; she'd never be hungry again. A small wave rocked them as the motorboat, with a man and a boy in it, came towards them. The man looked to be in his sixties, a few days of white growth on his ruddy face. He was sinewy and steered with purpose. The boy was young, black, under ten probably and shivering in a striped tee shirt.

"You okay there?" the man asked. The boy had an expressionless face.

"We're okay," Mimi said. "We're from the school."

The man looked at Pat with a chocolate pinched between two fingers, at Joe's form in the flowered sheet, the boxes of candy which had tipped and spilled onto the floor and were smeared in a scrim of water. His jaw inched left and right.

"I know what you have there," he said. "I had to stop a man from dumping his mother this morning. I don't know what you people are thinking. This may be our only drinking water soon, and you want a bunch of dead bodies floating in it? What the hell is wrong with you?"

"This doesn't seem like a conversation we should be having right now," Mimi said, and ticked her head towards the kid. But maybe it was okay, the boy would need to cram as much as he could understand about life—and death and people—into this short time. She wondered if the boy would be able to live if he were able to imagine his own death. She wanted to pull him out of the boat and put him into hers. He could be hers for now. There would be no harm in their both pretending.

The man ignored her. "So we're clear on this? You're not going to dump that thing here?"

"Not a thing, a man," Pat said, regaining her voice. "You asshole." The box of candy spilled off her knees. "Leave us alone. Go away."

"I'm just trying to save us here."

"Save us?" Pat demanded. "Don't you think that's sort of beside the point?"

"There's a child here," Mimi said. "Stop. Think about it. Think about it before either of you say another word."

They all turned to see the kid looking into the distance as the sunlight spread over his head and down his face. He was already gone. He'd risen while they were drowning, and Mimi thought maybe this was the grace she'd been looking for all these days, the moment of quiet ascension. When the man motored away, the wake rocked Joe's chilled weight against her leg. She knew they would not put Joe's body in the lake now.

At the dock, they dragged him out, inches at a time as the body seemed to get heavier and heavier. It smacked against the wood, against their shins, against the metal sides of the wheel-barrow they pushed to the boathouse. He insisted they feel his weight at every step. The sheet was soaked through with blood. Inside, Mimi dragged a nylon sail over him. It was bright yellow and white, colors of no harm. What she'd found the two kissing boys wrapped in.

She took the keys from Pat and locked the door.

"He loved me," Pat said. "I loved him. We were going to live together. I was going to retire in three years."

"You should have done it sooner," Mimi said.

"I should have done a lot of things sooner. We always think we're going to live forever. We can't ever imagine that we'll be old. The students look at us and think they'll never be like us."

"I still don't believe I'm going to die," Mimi said.

"You have to believe it."

"No, I don't."

She knew there was a reason to confess now, so she could live forever without the weight. She knew that it mattered even if no one was around to care, even if it didn't make any difference. "My daughter died," she said.

"Yes, you told me." Pat said distantly, and looked back up at the school, invisible beyond the trees.

"I didn't forgive my mother. I never talked to or saw her again after that day. I blamed her and she killed herself over it. Not right away, but within the year she was dead. She couldn't live with what had happened, and I didn't try to stop her." The two deaths had become one in her mind.

Pat's face was damp with sweat, smeared in places with blood and chocolate. A small, violent trickle ran behind her ear and onto her neck from where her head had hit the brick wall. "I don't know what to say."

"Now I've said it." Relief was a cool breeze off the water. It didn't last long enough.

"Maybe we should swim," Pat said, looking at the blood on her hands. "Clean off."

They walked back to the dock and took off their jackets and nightgowns. Pat's figure was defiantly odd in the way every woman's was, a series of pale hills, sad-eyed breasts, folds. There was nothing to hide. The heartbeat of the distant motorboat beat at the shore. They hesitated at water's edge.

"Cold," Pat announced.

"It will warm up," Mimi told her. "It's probably not even noon yet."

There was a flush of existence on Pat's face as she stirred the water with her foot, poised to plunge. "Jesse was lovely, by the way," Pat said. "A good person. He loved you."

Mimi would wait for Pat to say more, to tell her all she'd never known about her only child, but first they both dove underwater. She kept her eyes closed as though she wished to be taken away already, and too soon.

ACKNOWLEDGMENTS

Every story of mine was honed and polished by editors, readers, colleagues, and friends. For their sharpest eyes and pens, thank you to Anne Bernays, David Elliott, Justin Kaplan, Peter Kramer, Michael Lowenthal, and Nancy Rosenblum. For their untiring support, Jennifer Carlson and Deborah Joy Corey. For sun, solitude, and space, The Studios of Key West. And for giving me everything and even more, my husband, Michael, and my sons, Tobias and Alexander.